I0659545

LEGEND OF THE FOUR DRAGONS SWORD

A SWAYING HEN MARTIAL FANTASY

PHILLIP ALLEN HUMPHRIES

ISBN: 0-615-84476-6
ISBN-13: 978-0-615-84476-3
Library of Congress Control Number: 2013912720
Lucky Buzzard LLC; Fairfax, VA

Lucky Buzzard LLC

For my wife and the Buzzard Squadron, who looked after me
while I wrote this thing.

BOOK ONE

622 AD — SONGHWA MOUNTAIN NEAR THE EASTERN SEA

It lit the entire landscape in an eerie, flickering light as it streaked earthward from the heavens with a thunderous roar. It was the loudest sound most of the witnessing humans had ever heard, and many fled in panicked disarray at the sight of the flaming demon as it traversed the morning sky, west to east.

It wasn't an orb like a meteor, but rectangular in shape, its edges hazy and aglow with what appeared to be white, flickering flames. It was essentially a flaming brick falling from space.

Following the event, when witnesses had calmed down and gathered into huddled groups in the fields to discuss the celestial apparition, many reported that their jaws had felt strangely "thick," and that their cognitive functions seemed to dull or slow. It was the oddest thing they had ever seen, and, for those in closest proximity, it was also the oddest thing they had ever felt.

Whatever the "brick" was, it shook the people who experienced it to their core.

Everyone agreed that it was the work of the gods. It was also universally agreed that the object disappeared behind or into Songhwa Mountain.

On the other side of the globe, it was year one of the Islamic calendar, with Muhammad and his followers emigrating from Mecca to Medina.

Guangzhou, China, was a thriving, bustling seaport, welcoming maritime visitors from Egypt, India, Arabia, Africa, and southeast Asia.

It had been seventy years since the Korean king of Paekche sent priests to Japan to convert the population to Buddhism.

NEW MEXICO DESERT, 2049 AD — EIGHT HUNDRED FEET BELOW GROUND

"We aren't sure precisely how or why any of the events happened, Colonel. The lunar satellite dropping offline, disappearing from orbit without any sign of a problem beforehand… Yes, sir, we understand how sensitive the payload was and the seriousness of the technologies involved."

"Some of our quantum people believe it portaled and that it, uh, could be anyplace—anytime. We have the 902nd MI team deployed to the Puerta de Hayo Marka site, and our Century Horizon command staff is working twenty-four/seven to find the package."

"No, sir, outwardly it doesn't appear to be anything recognizable as US government or military equipment. It's a metallic-looking rectangle without any other features. It looks like, well, sir, a big brick."

"Colonel, as for the other events—the, uh, human temporal and physical displacement anomalies, what the science crew is calling transverse events—we have three shifts running around the clock working on the problem."

"Off the record, sir, we have increasing numbers of our senior quantum unit getting, well, scared, sir. They say we conceivably could have done some sort of, uh, dimensional damage with one of our advanced projects here. A couple of them believe there may be some comingling of timelines and potentially some reality corruption."

"Colonel, some of our folks on level five are reporting some anomalies with the walls in the facility. They say they have, uh, shifted location on a couple of occasions. One employee was caught in this 'shifting' business; his arm wound up inside the wall when it shifted its position. This is consistent with reports from some crewmen on the USS *Eldridge* during the Philadelphia incident, way back in the mid twentieth century."

"Yes, sir, our physicists believe that our current site could be blending timelines with the past structure and maybe a future structure… Yes, sir, it is a bit difficult to conceptualize."

"Our security people are also becoming nervous, saying that, with enough leaks, a reporter could possibly tie events together across a historical timeline—you know, like the incident with the US Navy destroyer in World War Two, the event in Philadelphia that I mentioned earlier, the whole Roswell thing, and the Los Angeles air defense incident, among others."

"At any rate, sir, it is the potential reality corruption that they are most concerned with—that sort of information becoming public knowledge."

"There is one other thing, sir. There has been some talk among the theoretical physics guys that, well, maybe we were not the first to do this. They say that maybe there were others before us—long before us. They have a team pouring over a pile of ancient texts from all over the world and another team dedicated to certain World War Two-era projects."

"The physicists keep referring to an SS officer named Kammler, who led some sort of advanced projects unit for the Third Reich."

"They are not certain, sir, but maybe we—our timeline and reality construct—may have been corrupted somehow. They say that transverse corruption could have occurred that would have an impact across the interconnected multiverse. No. Uh, no, sir. They aren't sure about anything. They don't know what might happen."

"No, Colonel, there is no further information as to the three, um, transversal travelers. There is also a—this relates to that corruption the physicists are worried about—but there is also a fourth human subject that likely has been impacted. We have no conclusive evidence to peg down exactly what timeline this young man belongs to or really, sir, whether our particular slice of the multiverse is where he actually belongs…where he originated."

"But, sir, a routine search of special classified holdings accessed through our counterparts in ONI indicates a possible name match with a seaman who apparently went missing off a US Navy destroyer escort back in the twentieth century…in 1943, during World War Two. The navy ship I have referred to a couple of times."

"Uh, sir, there's one other item I am supposed to relate to you—one that is extremely sensitive. We have received two reports now from the Colorado Springs surface facility that a portion of their ground combat inventory has disappeared."

"Yes, sir, an entire pod of autonomous unmanned combat vehicles—Mark Six Demons. Yessir, they are, indeed, the most advanced. Yes, we believe that is most definitely associated with the anomalies that we have been discussing, sir."

The captain listened for several minutes before talking again.

"Yessir, I am very clear on just how sensitive that loss could be. We have a field intelligence and security team en route there now, sir. Homeland Security's Unified National Police Directorate and the FBI also have teams en route."

"Sir, I was asked by Lt. Colonel Mills to remind you that the deputy director of the Texas Special Operations Executive and a national security representative from the Office of the President of the Republic of Texas are scheduled to secure teleconference with you at thirteen hundred hours today."

The air force captain listened for another minute then ended the secure communication by looking at the small, multicolored vibrating image on his right wrist.

Mere minutes after signing off, he was startled to see a shimmering haze infuse the command center.

The secure underground facility was event ground zero for what investigating officials would later call a transversal time-space reality corruption.

Those investigating officials, along with special teams from the Defense Advanced Research Projects Agency, would conclude that the personnel present in the underground center at the time of the anomaly would have been subjected to quantum transversal phasing, wherein all of their possible selves—past, present, and future, in all configurations possible in the entirety of the multiverse—would manifest at once.

The investigating officials would go on to relate that this quantum transversal multiphasing would cause all exposed personnel to become instantly brilliant—almost all-knowing—and quite mad.

Hollywood filmmakers and their teen audiences of the early twenty-first century would have loved it: brilliant zombies.

IJINASHI-TAMNA, SEVENTH CENTURY, KOREA

The stream made a lazy bend right where a small stand of trees stood on the edge of the meadow. The foliage was lush there, distinguishing it from the region's normal growth, which was decidedly less green and more scrub.

The exposed tops of semi-buried boulders could be seen here and there, some partially coated with moss, which covered most everything along the water's edge.

Bright bursts of yellow and violet flowers dotted the luxurious carpet of grass, a slight hint of wild onion detectable on occasion among the blended scent of several varieties of flowers that hung in the air. The sunlight literally sparkled as it filtered in shifting golden shafts through the canopy of leaves, themselves bright green splashes against a vibrant blue sky. The green strands of the willow tree hung nearly to the ground, gently swaying in the warm breeze. It was an idyllic setting by anyone's standard.

The wanderer stopped at this spot to revel at its beauty whenever his wide-ranging travels brought him through the area. The bend in the stream and its stand of trees were a good half-day's travel from the nearest settlement, and no roads passed near in any direction.

Derisively referred to as "The Vagabond" only by those not in the know, the wanderer was widely considered a holy mystic by grizzled shaman and learned Buddhist priest alike. Many believed he could see through time. The rural peasantry considered him nothing short of supernatural. His large stature—six feet, two inches tall and 170 pounds—made him an easily recognizable figure.

For Ijinashi-Tamna, this was a sacred place of quiet solitude, serene and unmarred by the hand of man. Ijinashi-Tamna leaned against a medium-sized tree—the same one he always leaned against—a short distance from the banks of the stream, the only sounds reaching his ears the soft bubbling of the water as it flowed past, the just perceptible rustling of leaves above, and the songs of the birds who called this their home.

It was there, leaning against that tree, that Ijinashi-Tamna had first observed the shimmering. It was here, too, that Ijinashi figured out the interactive relationship between his special sword and the shimmering.

Ijinashi-Tamna had several homes—more places of respite from the rigors of travel than real homes—where he stopped during his wanderings.

Ijinashi-Tamna was old-school Samurang, hailing from Pyongyang, capital of the Kingdom of Koguryo, but had long since left his home to roam throughout Koguryo and the neighboring kingdoms of Silla, Baekje, and the lands of the Sui Dynasty.

He spent part of the year living among a small sect of senior monks at the Shinson Temple where he spoke of the things he had seen.

The monks were the only living souls on earth who knew Ijinashi's true heritage—that he was ethnically Chinese. Well, half-Chinese, having been the product of a one-night affair in the town of Jilin involving his Chinese father and a mysterious European woman who had come to China in the company of a wandering warrior-adventurer who, frankly, should not have been in that part of the world, according to history.

Fortunately for him, Ijinashi's features were sufficiently Asian to allow him to pass as one. As far as the monks knew or cared, Ijinashi originally came from China and had been renamed and raised by Koreans. Not a big deal to the Shinson monks.

Sometimes, Ijinashi would disappear for years on end, but the one constant in his life was his continued return to the monastery and his ongoing relationship with the monks, who considered him to be family.

If you asked the temple monks, Ijinashi-Tamna was arguably among the deadliest martial artists and swordsmen in all the known world.

Had the monks been aware of another part-Chinese martial artist named Sainen Chinhung and his infamous fighting prowess, it would not have changed their opinion in the slightest.

THE ASSASSIN
SAINEN CHINHUNG, 622 AD

Few men could claim to be as bad as Sainen Chinhung. Sainen was, simply put, one of the deadliest creatures walking the planet in the seventh century AD.

Sainen wasn't just mean. He was the embodiment of wickedness. Even worse, he was also likeable with a disarming personality. He was generally the most popular guy in the room, especially if spirits happened to be flowing. Sainen was, bottom line, a blast to be around. The problem was that Sainen was damn good at killing people—the way Sainen saw it, some folks just needed killin'.

Sainen wasn't just a skilled warrior; he was big and physically powerful, weighing in somewhere around 190 pounds and standing an imposing six feet, four inches tall. Making matters worse, Sainen was also quite brilliant.

Brigand, bandit, pirate, mercenary, assassin for hire. Sainen Chinhung was so fast and agile with his sword, his cuts and maneuvering so intuitive, some said he was a demon walking the earth as a man. Some said the two large, jagged scars he bore on his left forearm were wounds he sustained when fighting a dragon.

The wicked image was made complete by Sainen's very long, dark hair, which he wore unbound, giving him the appearance of a barbarian warlock.

Sainen was not only a phenomenal swordsman; he was a great all-around fighter, his ssireum wrestling and subak empty-hand fighting skills honed while he was serving with Japanese pirates plying the waters off the Korean peninsula, where he picked up exotic fighting skills from shipmates from China, Indonesia, Malaysia, the Philippines, and Japan.

Sainen didn't know it, but he was one of the first mixed martial artists. In much later times, he would have been a UFC superstar.

But martial skills aside, Sainen was, first and foremost, a criminal.

GYEONGSANGBUK VILLAGE, 622 AD

Yeon Sadaham was a master swordsmith, edged weapons maker extraordinaire. His blades were widely reckoned to be "alive" with intrinsic energy directly linked to the ki of their wielders. The villagers considered his weapons craft to be nothing short of sorcery. His folding of iron into razor-edged gleaming demons was legendary. Had there been such a thing in seventh-century Korea, Sadaham would have been a rock star to those who bore arms for a living.

His expertise and familiarity with all things sharp notwithstanding, Yeon had never seen a weapon quite like the specimen on the bench in front of him. Wang Gi, his apprentice, had brought the blade in from a mountain meadow partway up the western slope of Songhwa Mountain. Wang said it was just lying in the grass among a growth of spring flowers. There was disturbed earth strewn about near and around where the sword had been found, as if blown outward from some great explosion. Possibly the sword had been buried and uncovered by some explosive occurrence, Wang offered—the impact of a falling star or the work of demons?

Yeon could not be sure because he had never seen anything like it before, but he did not think the thing was even made of iron. Several women from the village nearest where Wang Gi had found the sword were talking of one of their men going missing on the western slope. Some were saying that the man had disappeared into thin air. Yeon had a bad feeling about this mystery blade.

Yeon had probably made hundreds of swords in his life, and he had examined blades from China, Japan, Southeast Asia, Africa, and Arabia. He had even handled a few from Europe. To put it mildly, Yeon Sadaham was perplexed. This weapon was like nothing he had encountered in his sixty-two years. The sword…it, well, it scared him a little.

HORSEBACK, ALONG THE EDGE OF BUYONDAE CLIFF

A young General Kim Yusin of the elite Hwarang pointed his finger at his lieutenant, slowly and evenly repeating his order of a few minutes past, the heated argument that ensued from the initial utterance having subsided. "Ride to every village—e-v-e-r-y village—and speak to every man—e-v-e-r-y man. Do you understand, Gwog?"

"Wang Gi is a trusted informant, and he says the blade that came into the old swordsmith's shop was unlike any he had ever seen. More importantly, Wang says it was unlike anything that Yeon Sadaham had ever seen."

The truth was, nobody on earth had ever seen a sa-jingeom—four dragons sword—or anything remotely like the specimen currently sitting on the bench in Yeon Sadaham's shop.

Kim Yusin straightened in his saddle. "I have little patience for continued discussion. I have to meet Pak-Soo at the copse of trees by the river within a day's time. He has been in the employ of our clan for many years and enjoys a lucrative relationship, but he will not wait long."

COPSE OF TREES, BEND OF THE JANGANCHEON RIVER

Pak-Soo took money to do the clan's dark, covert bidding. He was a mercenary with close to twenty years of experience skulking in shadows, removing the clan's problems for pay. He was a decent swordsman and capable with his hands, a veteran of many a street scuffle. Pak-Soo found Yusin to be arrogant and privileged—a product of Hwarang academia. But, Pak-Soo reasoned, he did not have to like the bastard to accept his gold.

The feelings were mutual, as Kim Yusin of the secretive Grey Owl Clan and the elite Hwarang, did not like Pak-Soo much, either. His reasoning quite similar to the other man's, Kim Yusin figured that dealing with nefarious characters such as Pak-Soo was just part of defending a kingdom.

GYEONGSANGBUK VILLAGE — YEON SADAHAM'S SHOP

Yeon Sadaham stared at the gleaming weapon as it lay upon his workbench, candlelight dancing along the length of the razor-edged blade. *Who the hell made this? Where did it come from?*

Yeon Sadaham was so totally lost in pondering the weapon's origin that he failed to hear the slight creak of wood against wood caused by Pak-Soo's not-so-stealthy advance across the room's length. Pak-Soo couldn't believe his luck at finding the front door ajar and his target plainly occupied in thought, staring down at his work bench.

Pak-Soo's orders were clear and precise. He was to obtain the sword believed to be in Sadaham's shop and provision it immediately to Yusin's waiting troops, hidden a few miles from the village at the farmhouse of a loyal subject of the kingdom.

Pak-Soo found Yusin's caveat of "by any means" to be odd, given Sadaham's long weapons-making service to the Hwarang. But, odd or not, he had taken payment and planned to execute his mission precisely as it had been laid out in Yusin's riverside instructions.

Yeon Sadaham never saw the blow that killed him. Pak-Soo closed the distance completely undetected, angling in from the side so as to avoid making the work bench an obstacle. The flickering light of the single candle cast only a limited circle of light around Yeon, making Pak-Soo's surreptitious entry and approach even easier. Pak-Soo swung his blade with all his might to ensure a one-strike kill, for Sadaham was not one to be trifled with. The razor sharp metal of Pak-Soo's sword blasted through Sadaham's clavicle, cleaving him in half diagonally.

It would be six hours before a chance customer entered Sadaham's shop and discovered the body. Pak-Soo and the four dragons sword—the sajingeom—were long gone. Pak-Soo had made haste toward the nearest stretch of the Jongno Trail, which he could pick up just outside Gyeongsangbuk Village.

Kim Yusin was not surprised to hear from his troop detachment that Pak-Soo had not delivered the sword as instructed. He had planned for that possible contingency—strategy and planning being among his strong suits—and had made arrangements for a backup plan.

Pak-Soo was a mercenary, after all, and, as such, not unfamiliar with weaponry; he would likely recognize the sa-jingeom as being special—and of a value well beyond the paltry bag of gold he had received from the Hwarang men to carry out its theft.

Yusin also knew that Pak-Soo would be suspicious of the general's willingness to kill Sadaham—a long-time loyalist and servant of the Hwarang—in order to obtain the sword covertly.

Yes, it had been wise to have an alternate plan of action.

ALONG THE JONGNO TRAIL

Bitter bile rose in his throat, hot on the heels of every bit of breath as it rushed from his lungs—the blow as vicious as it was unexpected, the pain overwhelming.

Pak-Soo thought he was sneaking up on the man from behind, an easy kill. He had noticed the shadowy figure dogging his trail since he had fled Sadaham's shop in haste, hustling down the gloomy dirt path that ran behind the local drinking establishment, the quickest route out of town from Sadaham's murder scene that best avoided curious eyes along the main street through the village. Pak-Soo killed people for money, and he had made similar escapes many times in the past. He figured the man following him was some drunken hoodlum from the bar looking for an easy mugging.

The back kick was perfectly timed, the heel driving into Pak-Soo just below the breast bone, angling slightly upward. Sainen's right foot had just replanted on the ground when his hips realigned toward his target and the blade of his sword flashed at a slight diagonal, severing Pak-Soo's left wrist.

Pak-Soo's sword began to fall from his grip as the horror and shock of what had just happened began to dimly register.

Stunned, Pak-Soo barely noticed the flicker of movement as Sainen took a long slide shuffle forward and drove the tip of his blade straight into Pak-Soo's throat, the sword piercing through his neck, front to back. A moment later, Pak-Soo's frothy gurgling was cut short as Sainen's blade was deftly withdrawn, quickly raised, and subsequently arced down, hacking deep into Pak-Soo's forehead.

Sainen's extraction of his sword tip from Pak-Soo's throat, slight slide-step backward, and finishing centerline downward strike were perfection in their wickedly abbreviated economy of motion. Had it occurred centuries later, an eclectic martial arts phenom named Bruce Lee would have been proud.

Pak-Soo's lifeless body slumped to the earth.

Sometimes serendipity took an evil turn, which is how Sainen happened to glance to his left precisely at the right moment as he passed in front of Sadaham's sword shop, his eyes falling on the shop's dimly lit interior through the front window, thereby catching a fleeting glimpse of a man murdering another inside. *You just can't make this stuff up*, Sainen thought with a chuckle.

Sainen didn't vary his gait in the slightest but kept right on walking until he could easily slip into the shadows cast by the overhang of an adjacent shop, seemingly continuing on his way down the street. Instead, he stopped and watched Sadaham's shop from his vantage point in the inky darkness.

Within seconds, Sainen saw a man hurriedly depart, carrying what appeared to be two swords. The man made directly for the earthen path that ran behind the village shops, glancing furtively about as he headed into the night.

Pak-Soo had failed to notice Sainen silently observing his flight from Sadaham's shop, the first among the final three mistakes Pak-Soo would make in his life. When he finally became aware of someone following him, Pak-Soo wrongly assumed it was a thug from the bar, the second of his final mistakes. The third, and most egregious, of Pak-Soo's string of lethal errors came when he decided to double back on his pursuer.

KYUNG-SOON

Kyung-Soon's name meant "gentle and calm," which she was most of the time. Petite, fine-boned, and drop-dead gorgeous, Kyung-Soon had made the boys swoon since childhood. Absolutely nobody would have guessed, in their wildest fantasy, that she was Sulsa.

Sulsa—Korean ninja-like martialists—were tied together, like their Japanese counterparts, by tchong—blood relationship. The Sulsa were clandestine Samurang (Samurai), highly skilled warriors who owed their allegiance to their respective clans rather than any political governmental structure.

Kyung-Soon, female Samurang, was Sulsa of the Swaying Hen Clan. Actually, there was more to it than that; Kyung-Soon was Khangpae. She was a "problem mitigator" for her clan. And the Swaying Hen Clan was widely known to be Jopok, an organized and feared criminal organization much like the twenty-first-century mafia.

The Korean Jopok, like the Japanese ninkyo dantai (Yakuza), considered themselves "chivalrous organizations." Criminal enterprise was simply business. Kyung-Soon viewed her Jopok duties as a job. Along those lines, her secret contractual agreement with General Kim Yusin to eliminate Pak-Soo was simply business.

The washed-out bridge and Kyung-Soon's unfortunate delay in reaching Sadaham's shop ahead of Pak-Soo's own arrival had thrown the whole affair off kilter. When she finally did arrive on scene, Sadaham lay dead on the floor, his body cleaved in half diagonally, and there was no sign of either Pak-Soo or that damn sword that the general was so concerned about.

Odder yet, if Kyung-Soon's true skills and Jopok affiliation weren't shocking enough, her alignment with the assassin Sainen Chinhung would be flabbergasting.

Kyung-Soon, like Ijinashi-Tamna, was a native of the Kingdom of Koguryo, where, as a child, she was first exposed to the martial skills of the Samurang. Well, almost like Ijinashi-Tamna, given that Ijinashi wasn't truly Korean but a mongrel of Chinese and unknown Caucasian ancestry.

MEETING THE WARRIOR SAGE

Kyung-Soon, experienced Sulsa and Khangpae enforcer for the Swaying Hen Jopok, met Ijinashi-Tamna, mystic warrior sage, quite by happenstance.

As chance or fate would have it, Ijinashi-Tamna was making his way down a dimly lit side street in Gyeongju, a night of moderate recreational drinking under his belt, at precisely the same time as Kyung-Soon and her fellow Jopok Khangpae were traversing the same backstreet. Gyeongju was a bustling metropolis for its time and scene of considerable Jopok activity, given its population.

Kyung-Soon's partner that night, Bak, was not known for civility by any stretch of the imagination. Bak was a typical street gangster: young, brash, and not one to be trifled with. Bak did small-time work in the city for the Swaying Hen Jopok, mostly muscle stuff connected to past-due protection monies.

Kyung-Soon and Bak were to visit a particularly ill-tempered shop owner who had had the unmitigated audacity to hire his own private muscle to protect his business interests. The inconvenient fact that the shop stood on

Swaying Hen turf had led to a decision by Jopok leadership to dispatch the two Khangpae to "discuss" alternatives with the shop owner.

Kyung-Soon was uncomfortable with Bak's accompanying her, as she viewed him as crude and prone to rash action that typically involved excessive violence. Bak's temperament and his tactics were, in her opinion, neither helpful nor prudent. Kyung-Soon's experience had taught her that the threat of violence was most often enough to gain compliance.

Rounding the same sharp bend of the narrow side street in opposite directions, Ijinashi-Tamna and Bak collided nearly head on. Ijinashi merely mumbled a polite apology and made to continue on his way. Bak, on the other hand, erupted into a litany of profanity, the main theme being the questioning of Ijinashi's heritage.

Ijinashi again apologized and tried to continue on his way, wanting to avoid the profane idiot he was confronted with. Bak was not going to have it, however. He stepped threateningly into Ijinashi's path, blocking him from proceeding on his way, Bak beginning the withdrawal of his sword as he stepped in front of the other man.

Kyung-Soon was just about to order the moron Bak to cease and desist when, to her amazement, the disheveled drunk Bak was challenging seemingly materialized a sword in his hands. The drawing of the sword was so quick and effortless that Bak took note of it too late to adequately react. A glimmer in the air was all that marked the blade's sideward arc that terminated in the tip being pointed at a spot just below and about an inch away from Bak's Adam's apple.

Anger rippled through Bak, his face flushing and a guttural snarl curling his lips as he realized that the old drunk had just put a sword to his throat before his own blade had made it halfway from its scabbard. Taken by surprise, Bak momentarily halted the drawing of his weapon in mid-motion then, in a fit of blind rage, tried to jerk the sword free and bring it into action. As Bak's sword was still being drawn, Ijinashi's blade flickered and, in a controlled cut, nicked the tricep region of Bak's right upper arm—a warning cut.

Ijinashi was acutely aware of the female accompanying his protagonist and moved to position himself to both defend against the ill-tempered thug in front of him and the girl, should she become aggressive. Ijinashi took note of the way the girl moved and her calm demeanor. She was, he assessed, the more dangerous of the two he was faced with.

Kyung-Soon was captivated by the harsh schooling in swordsmanship that Bak was receiving from the old drunk, deciding to watch rather than intercede. Her reverie was quickly interrupted, however, by the howling shriek that emanated from the now-wounded and psychotically enraged Bak.

Bak, marginally intelligent street thug that he was, failed to comprehend the lethal danger intimated by the old man's skillful display of fencing. Consumed in the throes of a blind temper tantrum, Bak jumped backward in an attempt to afford himself the distance he needed to complete the drawing of his weapon, envisioning hacking the old man to pieces, his rushed movements punctuated by anger rather than skill. A most unfortunate choice.

Ijinashi judged that he was simply not going to be able to extricate himself from this needless altercation without maiming or killing—most likely killing—the idiot bellowing in front of him.

At the same moment that Kyung-Soon realized her Jopok partner intended to kill the old man, she also realized that it was going to be the other way around.

Ijinashi followed Bak's backward movement skillfully, parrying Bak's now-drawn sword and, as he stepped past on Bak's left, executed a brutal waist cut as his kihap shook the night. Deftly placing Bak's body between himself and the girl, Ijinashi cut through the soft flesh just above Bak's left hip, slicing through the spine and sweeping his blade out Bak's back as he stepped through. Bak died instantly, his body above the cut falling backward, and the now mostly detached lower portion falling slightly forward, the whole grotesque mess smacking the street surface with a sickening splash, a pile of gore and entrails.

Kyung-Soon looked from the hideous gut pile that seconds before had been Bak and saw that the old man—having flicked the blood from his blade—was now facing her, his sword raised and ready, eyes steady, his breathing even.

She had just made the acquaintance of one of seventh-century Korea's greatest warrior sages and bladesmen.

IJINASHI AND KYUNG-SOON

Ijinashi observed that the female, Kyung-Soon, had drawn her sword and was in the ready position, her sword pointed at his throat, as his was at hers. Ijinashi further observed that the girl he was squared off against was calm—almost serene—and that her gaze was steady and unwavering.

Ijinashi spoke first. "I am Ijinashi-Tamna, and I desire no further senseless loss of life."

A week later, Ijinashi-Tamna and Kyung-Soon met again, this time over rice and wine in a more peaceful setting. Ijinashi surprised Kyung-Soon by proposing a business arrangement between the two of them. He asked if he could hire her to assist him, given her talents and the resources of her criminal clan. He wanted her to help him track someone and recover an item.

Kyung-Soon nearly spilled her wine when Ijinashi told her that it was a bandit known as Sainen and that the bandit had stolen a priceless sword from a shop in Gyeongsangbuk Village, Yeon Sadaham's shop, that weapon being the sa-jingeom.

Kyung-Soon quickly realized that someone of Ijinashi's talents could be of great assistance to her in retrieving the sword she had previously failed to obtain. And, she reasoned, by recovering the weapon for Yusin, she could remedy the break in relations between her clan and the Hwarang that had resulted from her failure.

Ijinashi must not know that the sword had been stolen by a mercenary employee of the military, and that Sainen must have subsequently relieved the original thief of the sword, Kyung-Soon thought as she sipped her wine.

Kyung-Soon also pondered the other options she might entertain, such as keeping the weapon for her clan...or for herself. She did not wish to betray her acquaintance Sainen, and possibly she could conjure a way to allow them both to benefit. If not, well, it was business, after all.

This blade must be a powerful talisman for so many to be seeking it, she thought.

With a dazzling smile, Kyung-Soon agreed to help Ijinashi.

GONE

Sainen put several yards between him and his opponents before halting and staring over the extended length of his sword, its tip hovering steadily in his vision at throat level, Sainen's posture erect, rear heel raised.

His clothes were soiled an earthen brown with streaks of beige and green from being grounded on several occasions during the fierce altercation, his tattered garments picking up dirt, mud, and grass stains from hard contact with the moist earth adjacent to the stream.

Sainen grinned wickedly before wheeling about and, in a smooth symphony of silky motion, sheathed his sword and seemingly stepped into thin air, instantly popping from Ijinashi Tamna and Kyung-Soon's sight in midstride. Gone. Just like that, in the blink of an eye.

Ijinashi-Tamna and Kyung-Soon's efforts to recover the stolen sword had failed miserably.

The green strands of the willow waved gently back and forth in the light breeze.

Ijinashi gave no indication of being surprised and simply sheathed his weapon. Kyung-Soon stood frozen in shock, her heart pounding and breath rasping.

For Ijinashi, the only thing troubling him was how, when, and under what circumstances Sainen had become aware of the shimmering. More specifically, how had he so quickly discerned the sword's secret and learned to exploit it?

HWAEOMBEOMNYUSA, SEVENTH-CENTURY KOREA

Ijinashi-Tamna and Kyung-Soon sat inside the small wooden Buddhist temple known as Hwaeombeomnyusa, located in what would someday be known as the North Gyeongsang province of South Korea. They had met there for lessons many times since meeting so many months ago. It seemed like a lifetime to Kyung-Soon.

The two had been sitting for hours, Ijinashi teaching Kyung-Soon her final lessons before she began her journey. Kyung-Soon had learned many things from the warrior sage Ijinashi-Tamna.

Knowledge of the shimmering gateway was, by far, the most esoteric of his teachings. Had Kyung-Soon not seen with her own eyes the mercenary killer, and her sometime partner, Sainen Chinhung step into the shimmering and disappear into thin air, she likely would not have subscribed to Ijinashi's tales of walking in time. Kyung-Soon had heard village shamans speak of similar things but never really considered their wild tales truly factual.

Ijinashi had warned of the dangers inherent to entering the shimmering, not the least of which was never being able to return to where you started.

Ijinashi had told tales of entering the shimmering gate and returning before he left, in a different location, many days' travel away. He told of once finding himself suddenly standing in the middle of an icy mountain stream.

Kyung-Soon sipped her lukewarm tea as Ijinashi-Tamna told of visiting what he believed was Japan in a time long before their own. He spoke of flying dragons—mechanisms, he believed—and of great aerial battles, fantastic weapons, images and voices of distant people visible on the magic surfaces of special boxes, underwater cities and structures, and of strange suits of "armor" worn by those who flew through the heavens in those dragons.

Ijinashi spoke of a people called the Jomon, who lived in Japan, and of another special group known as the Dogon. The Dogon lived in Africa, Ijinashi told Kyung-Soon, but the Dogon and Jomon shared knowledge of flying apparitions and of people from the stars.

Ijinashi also told her of how the Jomon of Japan and the distant Dogon of Africa even shared some words of their respective languages.

Ijinashi spoke of figures who flew around in "shells" and who taught the Jomon many advanced and wonderful things.

He described the special "living" sword that he had brought back with him from the ancient Japan of the Jomon and described the miraculous powers his sword seemingly possessed.

Ijinashi spoke of a seemingly supernatural young man he met during his special travels to Japan across time. Wild birds—songbirds and hawks alike—would sometimes fly up and land on him. He described the man as having an incredible command of qi and its use in martial art. The man, Ijinashi told Kyung-Soon, taught him many sword techniques using a Chinese sword—called a jian—and taught him Chuanfa, an ancient version of Kung Fu. He was a warlord, Ijinashi thought.

He tried to describe the special "sword light" that resided within the katana, and he related his belief that somehow the Jomon katana protected him and allowed him to repeatedly transit through the shimmering portal into time, just as the learned teachers to the Jomon and Dogon had done many thousands of years ago.

Ijinashi pointed out to Kyung-Soon the special design woven into the tsukamaki (grip wrap) of his sword, a design believed holy by the Dogon people of Mali.

Ijinashi would relate to Kyung-Soon that he believed Sainen Chinhung possessed a similar sword.

He explained to her that his Jomon sword and the sa-jingeom carried by Sainen were much more than mere edged weapons designed to slice through flesh and bone. They were, he told her, in addition to being excellent defensive tools, advanced implements able to activate the lines of dragons' breath.

The lines of electromagnetic force known as dragon lines were called ley lines in Western civilization, Ijinashi told Kyung-Soon. She wondered how in the world the old man could know such things. Very odd. Maybe he had been a seafarer in the past.

Mostly she suspected that Ijinashi was a shaman himself, a male witch. Wild birds would fly up and land on his shoulders sometimes, just like they did with the warlord he talked of knowing in ancient Japan. And, that not being odd enough, he told her that she would one day adopt a strange name that would sound like "Jay Jew" in a foreign tongue. He also told her that someday she would escape danger in a boat, a very fast boat, in a place with trees like those that grew in Southern China. How could he see the future were he not a shaman? Kyung-Soon had never been to Southern China and consequently knew nothing of the palm trees that grew in the warm climate there.

Kyung-Soon also wondered how Ijinashi supported himself—obtained food and drink and clothing—as he never had held a job, to her knowledge. He just seemed to have what he needed when he needed it. Kyung-Soon suspected that maybe Ijinashi was not the benign soul many believed him to be. *Maybe he is a shaman with criminal tendencies?* She was amused by her own thoughts.

It was said by some of the shamans who followed the ancient ways, and by the more esoterically leaning Buddhists, that one who had mastery of the dragon lines (ley) could transit the universe-to-universe dimensional portals that were scattered around the globe.

Although Ijinashi Tamna was not specifically aware of it, he was describing to Kyung-Soon figures that would someday be known as Kappa in Japanese mythology. In the twenty-first century, fourteen-thousand-year-old clay pottery figures known as Dogu would be on display in Japanese museums, depicting people wearing the strange "armor" that Ijinashi described in his tales.

Many years in the future, ancient Shinto legends would tell stories very similar to those Ijinashi related to Kyung-Soon during their sessions in the old wooden temple. History would record that certain peoples in Japan would believe themselves descendants of beings from the stars.

History would also record the spectacular fact that the Dogon people of Mali in Western Africa possessed star maps of uncanny accuracy—star maps that conventional logic said they couldn't possibly possess.

Ijinashi surmised that Sainen likely knew the true nature of the four dragons sword—or would soon figure it out—and that Sainen's having taken the weapon with him through the shimmering gate was potentially catastrophic.

SA-JINGEOM

The four dragons sword—sa-jingeom—was unearthly.

Upon hefting the weapon, it was immediately apparent to the wielder that the weapon was unnaturally light. The blade was thin yet, for all intents and purposes, impervious to damage; it held its edge regardless of any abuse it was subjected to. Literally, one could hack at a stone wall or iron bar with it and not find any perceptible damage on the blade afterward, the edge as sharp as ever, not even the tiniest of scratches. It was eerily resistant to everything, it seemed. The sa-jingeom's sturdiness and resilience were not its most fantastic qualities, however.

The weapon was superbly balanced—all the time. It seemed impossible to put the weapon into such a position that it did not appear to its holder to be perfectly in balance.

The blade directed itself along the most suitable path to optimally impact its intended target, regardless of any imperfections in its user's fencing skills. A mediocre swordsman became a master with the sa-jingeom. Some would consider it to be a demon blade.

A twenty-first-century laser could not cut any cleaner than the cutting edge of the sa-jingeom. In fact, should a comparison be made, the cut of the sword would appear cleaner than that of the most advanced medical laser scalpel.

The tightly wound fabric grip wrap of the weapon bore a strange design woven meticulously into it that depicted the sacred tertiary star system of the Dogon people of sub-Saharan Africa—a star system today known as Sirius.

That very same design adorned the grips of Ijinashi Tamna's Jomon katana swords.

JOURNEY

Kyung-Soon, Khangpae of the Swaying Hen Jopok, bid her farewells to her boss, explaining that personal business required her to travel abroad for an extended period. She cleared out her living spaces in town and deposited her possessions with Ijinashi Tamna for safekeeping during her absence with instructions to donate the entire lot to the monks at Hwaeombeomnyusa Temple should she not return.

Ijinashi Tamna accompanied her to the bend in the stream among the copse of trees on the meadow's edge. He walked her to the tree where he often took refuge from the world and handed her a Jomon katana very similar to his own, complete with a Dogon weaved handle. He explained that she should safeguard it at all times, protecting it with her life if she must.

Kyung-Soon was the second human being that Ijinashi had watched blink from this world under the swaying green strands of the willow tree that stood near the bend in the stream. Sunlight sparkled as it filtered in glimmering shafts through the canopy of leaves, bright green splashes against a vibrant azure sky.

Of course, Ijinashi had done it many times himself.

LONDON, ENGLAND, WHITECHAPEL DISTRICT, OCTOBER 1888

S ainen took a couple minutes to comprehend that he was standing in what he reasoned was a stone passageway of sorts, open to the night sky, and that it was chilly. He had nearly fallen when, in midstride, his foot touched down on the uneven and trash-strewn cobbled surface. Sainen had never seen a "modern" city alleyway before or brick buildings like the ones that formed the metropolitan London alley that he had just stepped into. Of course, Sainen had every right to be disoriented and shaken, given he had just arrived in nineteenth-century London from seventh-century Korea in the blink of an eye.

Sainen heard a short gasp from behind, and, upon swinging around, drawing and bringing up his sword, he saw what he supposed was a woman—dressed rather oddly, he thought—standing in a partially open doorway, the dim light spilling out into the darkness, forming a thin, elongated triangle of yellow across the narrow alley. Upon getting a good look at Sainen and, more significantly, Sainen's raised sword, she turned her gasp into a scream, reverberating up and down the confines of the brick canyon.

Sainen didn't really panic; it was more of a quick assessment that he needed to stop the woman's inconvenient screeching before others arrived to see what the disturbance was about.

SCOTLAND YARD AND LONDON METROPOLITAN POLICE CID TEAM

Constable McGuire handed the handkerchief to Chief Inspector Ian Randolph so he could dab the remnants of vomit from his lips. The detective inspector straightened from his stooped posture in the alley and looked back at the crime scene. This was a bad one—a bad one indeed.

The woman's body appeared to have been sliced almost in two with something very large and very sharp. The torso hadn't just been hideously slashed, like most of the other victims turning up in Whitechapel; it had been bisected, head to navel, its contents grotesquely strewn on the threshold planking.

Chief Inspector Randolph once again fought for control of his stomach as he walked back to the gaggle of Metropolitan Police CID, Scotland Yard detectives, and uniformed bobbies arrayed around the carnage that lay sprawled in the prostitute's dingy apartment doorway, stepping cautiously to avoid the ugly puddle of congealed blood at the foot of the door.

Ian Randolph imagined the horror of the woman's last moments, his mind conjuring up vivid images of the unspeakable terror she must have experienced.

The chief inspector of Scotland Yard turned to wretch yet again.

LONDON METROPOLITAN
POLICE ARCHIVES

The infamous Whitechapel murders of the period ended on Friday, November 9, 1888, with Mary Jane Kelly. The prostitute who died by Sainen's sword was never officially counted among the five to eight victims attributed to one of the world's best-known serial killers, her manner of death being inconsistent with the grisly modus operandi of Jack the Ripper.

Investigating officials chalked up the murder of Sainen Chinhung's singular victim in the Whitechapel District of 1888 London to the work of a copycat killer, likely armed with some sort of razor-sharp saber.

THE MARTIAL ART OF GENTLEMEN

When it came to martial arts training, Sainen had not been idle during his stay in London, England. His natural gravitation toward, and eventual affiliation with, the underground criminal world of late nineteenth-century London had advantages besides money. Sainen was able to live well and, as a man of means, was able to study several fighting arts during his time in the United Kingdom.

Sainen, already adept at the Korean martial arts of ssireum, subak, and haidong gumdo, immersed himself in the study of bartitsu, the hybrid art of nineteenth-century England that combined boxing, jujitsu, cane fighting, and French savate.

Taking to fighting like a fish to water, Sainen soon became very proficient in a short amount of time, blending the bartitsu techniques with his own hybrid fighting style, itself actually an eclectic blend of traditional Korean systems with the Japanese and Chinese martial styles he was exposed to during his pirating days. Sainen used what he liked, and he liked what worked.

Most of Sainen's training partners were true gentlemen and never had occasion to utilize the techniques of bartitsu outside the training hall.

Sainen, on the other hand, was able to hone his skills in real-world altercations, sometimes a daily event in the dark underworld that had become Sainen's home.

The Asian community—Chinatown—that Sainen inhabited could be a treacherous place, with Tong and Triad thugs running the street crime as well as the upper-tier criminal enterprises. Besides vicious street altercations, challenge matches were commonplace—death matches.

Of course, Sainen only resorted to empty-hand combatives when it was not all that serious an affair. For serious business, Sainen was all about weaponry. Like any savvy street fighter, he cheated whenever possible. Sainen was not, after all, a sportsman.

THE ALLEY

S ainen couldn't complain about his lot as he had done okay, all things considered, during his time in the United Kingdom. Sainen had learned English easily. His struggle over many months to simply fit into a different century had taxed him more than anything else. He had money and could therefore do pretty much whatever he liked. His relatively comfortable lifestyle notwithstanding, Sainen had made it a habit to periodically check that alley where he had first stepped into 1888 London, just in case the shimmering might be there.

Sainen couldn't describe the shimmering in scientific terms, but he understood that it was a portal—a window—into time. Because Sainen knew that Ijinashi Tamna was aware of it, he reasoned that the old warrior sage had used it. In logical progression, Sainen figured that the wandering sage's presence in Korea was evidence the man had been able to travel through the shimmering and then somehow return back to the timeline he started in: seventh-century Korea. Or was the warrior sage actually from another timeline? *A very interesting concept*, Sainen mused.

Sainen became obsessed with the shimmering—the time gate. Regardless of whether passage through it would return him to the Korea of his original times or permit him travel to another time and place, he was intrigued by the possibilities the gate represented, and he relentlessly sought evidence of its reappearance.

Over time, Sainen had figured out where in the alley it should be—the precise portion of the brick wall on the west side of the alley where the shimmering should appear, if it were to manifest again. He even made it a habit to touch the brick wall in that spot, just to see if there was something different about it that he could feel, something he couldn't see.

Sainen always took the blade—the sa-jingeom—with him when he visited that place in Whitechapel, unwilling to chance leaving it behind should he ever detect the shimmering. He had made up his mind that, should he ever again see the shimmering, he would pass through it without a second thought.

Sainen viewed the shimmering—the time window—as a mechanism for achieving immortality. There was no way in hell he was going to let that slip through his grasp.

Sainen also carried both his pistols with him and extra ammunition whenever he visited that spot. He reckoned that if he was able to travel back to his original time in Korea, those weapons would allow him considerable advantage indeed.

Months later, his obsession with the time window unabated, Sainen Chi-nhung, ever the realist, had resigned himself to spending the remainder of his days in this time, in this alien place. While he never stopped checking the wall in that alley, over time, he had stopped believing that the shimmering would reappear. He almost couldn't believe it when, one cold winter morning, it was there, just barely perceptible in the shadowy depths of the alleyway.

TWENTY FIRST CENTURY AMERICAN MIDWEST, THE ABANDONED PROPERTY AT 709 NORTH HARRISON STREET, ALEXANDRIA, INDIANA

The backyard was heavily shaded with blotches of yellow sunlight illuminating the lawn here and there. A narrow spit of grass formed the side yard along the southern side of the house, affording access from the small square of a front lawn to the more expansive backyard. Fragrant lilac bushes graced nearly the entire length of one side of the lush green lawn; across the yard to the north, slightly unruly hedges marked the opposite boundary.

Along the northern edge of the property, an old-fashioned driveway made of two parallel strips of concrete, just wide enough to accommodate the tires of the average sedan, stretched from the street eastward to a detached two-car garage that filled the northeastern corner at the rear of the yard. The structure was old and sagging, ready to collapse at any given moment.

A white-painted wood picket fence adorned the rear boundary, leaning at its south end in disrepair. Weather-worn remnants of a crudely built tree house were still visible in the single large tree that stood among the dense tangle of foliage at the rear of the yard, its rotting floor planking precariously hanging where the main branches spread upward from the trunk, rusted nails poking out here and there.

At one time, the now-dilapidated house at 709 North Harrison had been a warm, happy family home. It wasn't a large house, but it had been a comfortable home. The front bedroom was a spacious room with plenty of natural light from the expansive windows that dominated the west and north walls. The living room had four side-by-side, full-sized windows that allowed plenty of light in and provided a view of the small town's tree-lined main street out front.

Just off center about halfway back in the home's rear yard stood a maple tree, its soaring branches casting shade across the bulk of the lawn's expanse. The tree had been planted by a young boy whose family once lived there. A cracked and crumbling walkway was also there, its cement sections unevenly strewn along a path leading from the back porch to a spot a couple of yards past the maple tree, where it abruptly ended at a shallow depression in the lawn.

It was here, in that shallow depression in the grass, that the shimmering could be noticed, almost indistinguishable among the dancing rays of sunlight filtering through the canopy of maple leaves.

THE SHIMMERING

The shimmering—as anyone who had occasion to notice the anomaly would likely call it—had simply appeared one day. To the rational mind of anyone who happened to see it, it could be described as eerie—profoundly surreal, for sure.

If those who lived nearby ever did notice it, nobody ever admitted it. It was one of those things that the human mind creates a special little niche for so as not to alarm or frighten. It was far enough removed from the mundane that it would boggle the intellect. Hazily defined, it most likely would evade most common folks' reasoned attempts to fathom its mystery, to rationalize its existence.

The shimmering was akin to a dreamscape, where some of the rules were slightly bent. The faint of heart might describe coming into close proximity of the anomaly as nightmarish. There was a bit of a foreboding aura to it. It was mind-bending and, for those unfortunate enough to stumble into it, man and animal alike, a total upheaval of reality.

Truth be known, few living beings actually had occasion to even notice the anomalous aberration in the backyard of 709 North Harrison Street in sleepy Alexandria, Indiana, United States of America. For those whom happenstance allowed to view it, virtually no one would recognize it as an enigma of incredible significance.

Alexandria could be described as the quintessential American small town, very Norman Rockwell in character. Kids who grew up in that neighborhood enjoyed as normal a youth as one could conjure in as normal a setting as ever existed in the tapestry of American small-town life.

Unbeknownst to a soul, including the parents, there was once a child who lived in the house that once stood at 709 North Harrison Street who did, in fact, glimpse the shimmering. That child boldly approached the anomaly, curiosity overriding his fear of the strange and unknown.

As the golden rays of the morning sun splashed across his eyes, sparkling against the green backdrop of the trees and the brilliant blue of the sky, a brave young human soul had indeed made the acquaintance of the strange shimmering.

After coming into proximity of it, the child found that, thereafter, sunlight made him sneeze. Sometimes, following the strange backyard encounter, that child would wonder if maybe he wasn't totally normal—maybe suffering from a slight neurological aberration—that caused the sneeze response to direct sunlight (or any bright lights, for that matter).

Most profound among the effects following that fateful morning discovery were the periodic manifestations of what could only be described as a miasma of undulating light that would unexpectedly invade the boy's vision. The lights started in his peripheral vision and worked their way inward to the center of his sight, growing in size and intensity as they did, and partially obscuring his forward vision. Thankfully, it didn't occur often, and he never let on to anyone about those things.

Scarier than the visual abnormalities, the child was also bedeviled by a dream—was it a dream?—throughout his childhood wherein there was what he thought of as a "brick" that sort of floated up by the ceiling in the corner of the living room. He couldn't remember if it was a nighttime dream or more of a daydream of sorts. It was one of those things you segmented off in the mind in a special compartment of its own and told no one about.

It was always in the southeast corner of the living room, an amorphous object without sharp definition but more or less a brick shape. The boy recalled that his face—his jaw specifically—felt "thick" and his consciousness "dull" during these "brick" episodes. He sometimes mused that maybe others had similar experiences and that those experiences were the origin of the term "thick as a brick." Thereafter, the boy always thought of himself as a bit odd—not crazy or deranged in any way—but somewhat different. He did not dwell upon it, really. He figured everyone's reality was a bit different. For some, maybe a lot different.

That same boy oftentimes wondered why he dreamt repeatedly of the navy, a base with two buildings set among trees, and vivid dreams of a building interior, hallways and multiple rooms that seemed to be classrooms. He had, of course, never been in the military. His dad had been in the army during WWII, and his older brother would serve in the air force; nobody in his family had been in the navy. It was an odd thing to dream about, he thought.

History would never record any of this because the boy never uttered a single word about it to anyone. The boy would, in fact, pass from the scene before he ever told anyone at all. His childhood friends, years later, would still talk about their neighborhood pal whenever they reminisced about their days of youth.

The young Indiana native who lived on North Harrison Street had never actually entered the shimmering or placed any portion of his body into it, not even a finger. He had been right next to the "disturbance" and had experienced the peculiar effects when standing adjacent to it. He had never conjured up the courage to actually enter the space occupied by the shimmering. He just stood and watched.

The boy did not know, nor could he understand, what caused the shimmering. Someday, though, he would come into possession of its source. And, proving that reality is indeed stranger than fiction, after decades of absence, he would return to this very spot through a very odd set of circumstances.

SOMETHING WICKED THIS WAY COMES

The shocking thing about the shimmering was not the odd sensory phenomena associated with close proximity. What was mind-warping was what had instantaneously materialized at the shimmering spot in the back yard of 709 North Harrison, right out of thin air.

Decades after the original young resident's family moved away, another family lived in the house. It had been remodeled and updated several times since the first family lived there, but the basic structure remained the same.

The latest young resident, a thirteen-year-old boy, was staring out the bathroom window into the backyard at around seven-thirty one warm, sunny morning in late May, contemplating the leisurely Saturday that lie ahead, when a figure just popped into view as if walking through an invisible door right onto the rear lawn in midstride. He remembered that it occurred, quite literally, in the blink of an eye.

Both fascinated and stunned, the youngster watched slack-jawed as the oddly clad figure, appearing to be a male, strode from the slight depression at the end of the walkway, quickly disappearing to the south outside the limited field of view afforded by the small bathroom window.

The man's clothes—waistcoat, trousers, and top hat—were the attire of a wealthy gentleman of the nineteenth century and were like nothing he had seen outside of a theater or TV screen. The clothes were somewhat like the ones he had seen on some of the characters in Disney cartoons and animated movies.

Three things stood out in his recollection: the man's long and unkempt hair, what looked to be a long leather case, and the man's Asian face. The boy did not see many Asians in his neighborhood.

The case or sheath was affixed diagonally across the figure's back, but, due to the inconvenient viewing angle from the bathroom window, the boy did not have an unobstructed view. The man was moving at rather a quick pace, so total viewing time was measured in seconds.

The boy recalled bolting from the bathroom and through to the south window of the kitchen that the figure's last seen path should have taken him past, but he was nowhere to be seen when the youngster arrived at the window. His traversing of the kitchen had taken mere seconds, so he reasoned that the man had either reversed course outside of his view and exited the yard out the east (rear) side or possibly shot through the break in the lilac bushes to the south.

Regardless, the figure had vanished, leaving the boy shaken and grasping for a rational explanation of what he had just observed on an otherwise unremarkable weekend morning.

THREE ADAM SIX FOUR

O fficer John Hendrickson had been with the small suburban police force for nineteen years, and he was pretty sure he had seen just about everything the jurisdiction could cough up in the way of crime and depravity.

Until now. This one was different. It topped all the other violent crimes Hendrickson had encountered as a uniformed cop.

It was 1837 hours—6:37 p.m.—when the onboard computer mounted in John's squad car directed him to 2125 West Madison Avenue and the small mom-and-pop retro clothing shop that occupied that commercial address. The 911 central dispatch center put the call out as a welfare check for the proprietor. John was still trying to get used to the onboard dispatch computers in the squad cars. It was now summer, and John's small agency had just finished installing the systems in their patrol fleet in October of last year, the device being in John's unit for only a few months.

A passerby had noticed that the lights were on in the shop, the door was locked, and the open sign was still facing the sidewalk on the glass of the front door. The passerby, it turned out, walked by the shop every evening on his way home and knew that it closed at 6:00 p.m. He also knew that the proprietor always turned the sign in the door to its "closed" side and turned out the primary overhead lights before leaving, the only illumination left on after closing being a small nightlight left on in the rear office area.

John digitally acknowledged the call—finding the computer use awkward, as always—and proceeded to the address, arriving on scene within five minutes of dispatch.

Front and rear doors were both locked, and nobody responded to John's knocking on first the front and then the rear service doors. Nothing inside looked out of order, and there was no sign of the shop's proprietor.

John keyed the small mic clipped to his left uniform epaulet and had the dispatcher phone the afterhours contact number for the business. Within a few minutes, the dispatch center advised John that there was negative contact at that number and no alternate number on file. Damn. A simple welfare check was now turning into a pain in the ass.

2125 WEST MADISON AVENUE

Officer Hendrickson stuffed a Marlboro Light between his lips, lighting it with a Zippo bearing the famous USMC emblem as he strode back around to the rear of the building, wanting to check again that the shop was locked and that, given the lack of a keyholder, he had no way to enter.

John wanted to simply advise dispatch that all appeared secure with no indication of foul play and then go back "ten-eight" (in service). However, he knew that his responsibility on scene was not yet satisfied; he needed to make sure the proprietor was not lying dead on the backroom floor from a heart attack or stroke before "unassing."

Master Patrolman Hendrickson heard it as he was rounding the corner to recheck the rear service door. It was barely noticeable, almost lost in the background noise of the traffic out front. Hendrickson stopped, pulled the cigarette from his mouth, and listened. Out of many years of habit, John unconsciously transferred the cigarette from his right hand to his left, freeing his gun hand, should he need it. He stood for a good two minutes—nothing.

It had been just a light "tink," the sort of sound that would occur if one bumped two coffee mugs together. Nearly two decades of graveyard shifts had attuned Hendrickson's ears to the sound, having been repeatedly exposed to it in coffee shops and restaurants around the jurisdiction. John looked around for a possible source, a bit more alert now, years of street experience telling him it was time to be more cautious, to more carefully scrutinize his surroundings.

John looked up—something every tactical instructor he ever knew had told him to do—and saw for the first time the swing-out window about two feet above his head. It was open—swung outward about two inches.

John reasoned that the sound he had heard may well have emanated from within the shop, just audible to him through the slightly open window above his head. Not good. If there had been foul play, potentially the perp was still on scene.

John was just turning to walk a short distance from the window, so he could key his shoulder mike without risking alerting a bad guy inside the shop when he heard it again. Shit.

The commemorative Civil Air Patrol and Boy Scouts of America coffee mugs rested on the dilapidated metal shelving that stood as crude, but probably effective, camouflage in front of the shop's wall safe. The shelves bore an assortment of framed photographs, manuals, marketing books, figurines, and a couple of bowling and soft ball trophies. A casual observer likely would not notice the small wall safe, line of sight mostly obscured by the shelving and their contents.

The proprietor had probably been planning on closing and securing the safe prior to leaving for the day and was rearranging the shelf contents to better conceal the safe's presence. The small rectangular door stood open several inches, revealing the two shelves inside the safe.

The mugs had lightly clinked together when pushed further to the side to allow the safe door to be fully swung open, bringing into view the neatly stacked cash packed inside. That little clinking sound was the only inadvertent noise the intruder had made.

Hearing the sound of gravel on pavement being lightly crunched under the weight of a man's shoes, the intruder had frozen in place to listen. A moment later, the barely perceptible static of a portable radio and a man's hushed voice reached the intruder's ears. The intruder was not particularly familiar with such things as police walkie-talkies, but he knew it meant trouble and that he had to act immediately to make good his escape.

Twenty-five minutes later, John Hendrickson and the two uniforms who had arrived to assist him were inside the shop.

The local locksmith contracted by the police department had arrived, and entry had been gained. The two backup officers, both members of the department's small SWAT unit, had geared up with the appropriate armor and assault weaponry from their squad car trunks before going through the door and beginning their systematic tactical search of the interior.

No intruder was found. Whoever had been inside had managed to flee out the front door while Officer Hendrickson was still out back and before the responding backup units arrived. What had been found, however, was the proprietor.

CORONER'S SCENE

Mike Connelly had been the county coroner for five years, a mortician for fifteen, and a volunteer firefighter and EMT for more than two decades. Mike had never seen anything like what he was trying hard not to avert his eyes from as he stood in the store's rear office. It was his job to look at such things, but it took all of Connelly's professionalism to push himself through the routine of the investigation. What lay on the backroom floor of the little retro clothing store was like something from a horror movie. Even the police officers, including Master Patrolman John Hendrickson, were not keen on spending any more time than absolutely necessary working the scene. The fire department's rescue squad paramedics stood out front of the store, talking among themselves in hushed tones. Everyone, to a man, had been shaken by what they had witnessed this night.

Meg Nelson had worked as a paramedic in the ghetto district of a large eastern metropolitan jurisdiction prior to joining the local fire department. Before that, she had served a tour in Afghanistan with the army as an MP. She had never encountered anything comparable to what lay on the shop floor.

Mike Connelly had summoned Dr. Cynthia Richardson, MD, to the scene from the county hospital's ER. Mike needed a medical doctor's perspective as to the likely weapon involved, which he surmised was a sword or saber of some sort, given the nature of the wound.

Subsequent to her examination, Doctor Richardson had offered that it was, more than likely, a long-bladed, razor-edged sword such as a Japanese katana that had caused the horrendous wound. Cynthia also went on to relate that whoever wielded the weapon had considerable skill with it, as strength of blow alone probably would not have resulted in the singular precision cut that had felled the victim.

After a lengthy scene investigation, police detectives, the coroner's office, and medical authorities—in this case, Doctor Richardson—agreed that the victim had died instantaneously from a single blow from an edged weapon or sharp instrument to the right occipital lobe from a right-handed assailant.

The victim had apparently been approached from behind by the assailant and was most likely unaware of his attacker's presence, having not turned to look behind before the blow had landed. The proprietor had apparently been either opening or closing the wall safe or possibly retrieving something from the metal shelving that stood in front of it.

What made this case a standout was not the circumstances of the crime nor the fact that an edged weapon had been used in a robbery-murder. It was that the victim's head had been cut completely through diagonally, the murder weapon entering just above the right ear and continuing at a slight downward angle through the skull and out the left side under the left earlobe, the top of the skull subsequently falling to the floor next to the body. The head had been lopped in two with one stroke.

The brain had been cut through as cleanly as if by a surgeon's scalpel. The image would haunt Master Patrolman John Hendrickson for the remainder of his life.

The exact amount of money and valuables potentially missing was yet to be determined. The wall safe was devoid of content, with one notable exception. A box of nine-millimeter cartridges was discovered at the back of the lower shelf of the safe, minus sixteen rounds. Inventory of the victim's wallet revealed that the shop's proprietor possessed a valid concealed carry permit.

Given that no firearm had been recovered on scene, investigators surmised that the perpetrator may have gained possession of the victim's personal firearm. Follow-on investigative actions would indicate that the proprietor owned a Glock-19 nine-millimeter semiautomatic pistol.

The police detectives assigned the case opined that the shop's proprietor had loaded one fifteen-round magazine into the weapon, chambered a round, and then inserted another round into the magazine to bring the weapon's load to sixteen rounds, one chambered, which explained the partial box of shells they found at the scene.

WINNABEGO FIFTH WHEEL, KOA CAMPSITE, SUMMIT LAKE

The long-haired figure in blue jeans and t-shirt stepped over the body of the camper's owner and sat down at the kitchenette table to examine his recent acquisition.

The lightweight handgun with the strange configuration was quite different from the 1884 Harrington & Richardson "Young America" double-action .32-standard-caliber revolver with the two-and-a-half-inch barrel the intruder was accustomed to.

This piece would bear further investigation and some field testing to determine if it was, as he hoped, a major upgrade from the underpowered H&R .32 and the much bulkier 1879 .450 military revolver he had characteristically concealed under his garments when the seasons warranted the wearing of heavier clothing. This new weapon, being flatter with no cylinder bulge, would be easier to hide than the big .450 wheel gun but still would not be easily hidden on his person during the warmer months. Even the H&R .32 was difficult to hide under the light t-shirt and jeans that had become his favorite apparel.

Sainen had learned many things besides the speaking of English during his several years in nineteenth-century England. English had come so easy to him. That was strange, Sainen thought.

Sainen had become a firearms aficionado, particularly fond of handguns. He had, in fact, become a rather good marksman.

Two years there—in what Sainen Chinhung understood to be the United States of America—had brought him up to speed with many aspects of twenty-first-century culture. He had not had time nor inclination to procure new firearms—he had so much else to learn—but had recognized that he needed to eventually upgrade from the antiques he had been carting around since arriving there.

Sainen had a strange understanding of this period in time, which was difficult to explain. None of the things he encountered in twenty-first-century America surprised him.

This pistol that the shop owner had been trying to surreptitiously remove from the shelf in front of the safe was an unexpected perk. Its angular shape was somehow familiar to him—why, he wasn't exactly sure.

He was not, however, willing to give up the silent effectiveness of edged weapons just yet. Especially not the sa-jingeom.

BOOK TWO

KOBE, JAPAN, 2013

The tires on the Acura NSX squealed briefly as the sleek red car wheeled through a U-turn and came to a stop, double parked, in front of the nightclub. As the driver-side door opened, the high volume strains of the K-pop band Baby V.O.X. spilled into the evening air—at eight years old, vintage music, by popular standards. A paper-thin hand phone glued to his ear, resplendent in a black Alexander Amosu suit, Sainen Chinhung glided from the low-slung, 480-horse power concept car and strode toward the gleaming glass and metal front of the trendy club, widely known as the favorite haunt of the Yamaguchi-gumi wakagashiro's right-hand man.

THE YAKS

Yamaguchi-gumi was the largest and most infamous of the Yakuza organizations. Based in Kobe, it was also operating in Tokyo, the United States, and multiple places around the globe. Yamaguchi-gumi was estimated to count fifty-five thousand among its membership—45 percent of the total Yakuza underworld—making it one of the largest criminal organizations in the world.

Yamaguchi-gumi is also among the world's wealthiest criminal outfits, bringing in billions of dollars each year through extortion, gambling, the sex industry, guns, drugs, real estate, construction kickbacks, stock market manipulation, and Internet porn. Yamaguchi-gumi provided significant relief in the wake of the 2011 earthquake and tsunami that devastated a considerable portion of the Japanese economy. Winning hearts and minds was not a concept exclusive to the US Special Forces.

Known to the Japanese police as boryokudan—violence group—the Yakuza as a whole was estimated to comprise upward of 102,000 members.

Koreans made up only about 0.5 percent of the Japanese population but figured rather prominently in the Yakuza. None figured more prominently than Sainen Chinhung, feared henchman and confidant of the powerful Yakuza boss of the Yamaguchi-gumi.

SUMIYOSHI-KAI, "KS," AND JE-JU "J" LEE

With twenty thousand estimated members, Sumiyoshi-Kai ranked as Japan's second-largest Yakuza group, itself a confederation of smaller groups.

What made the Sumiyoshi-Kai a standout among Yakuza organizations was that its sosai, or president, permitted a female to rise to a position of prominence. In such a harsh, male-dominated world, it was totally unprecedented for a female to achieve any formal position within the Yakuza, let alone one of leadership.

Because Sumiyoshi-Kai was a confederation of smaller Yakuza groups, the standout female ascended to power because she had worked her way into a subordinate and informal leadership position with one of those smaller groups—one that was heavily ethnic Korean and known on the street simply as "KS."

The group KS was, in actuality, a street gang whose members tended to be connoisseurs of trendy clothing, pop music, hot bikes, fast cars, and the form of street racing known as drifting. Besides their various criminal enterprises, KS members could be found in parkour gyms, extreme martial arts studios, and pop culture clubs. When an odd twist of fate left the group's male boss behind bars, the charismatic female Yak wannabe had assumed a de facto position of authority, given her expertise in business administration and her truly exemplary street skills.

The fact that she was hugely popular among the younger gangsters, particularly the Zainichi Koreans, fueled her rapid elevation to prominence. She was a pop star, of sorts.

Whether the Kai's sosai liked it or not, it was easier to permit her ascension to power than to create upheaval among the mostly Korean membership of her group. Besides, her group was quite productive, bringing in an inordinate amount of revenue, given the group's small size.

Sumiyoshi-Kai had profited considerably from the phenom organized crime upstart who, just a couple of years previously, had apparently been a student trolling the trendy shops of the Sinchon, Hongdae, and Edae neighborhoods of Seoul. At least that was what a due diligence of her background would indicate.

Hapkido black belt, music lover, and fan of the Guinness-sponsored Hong Kong dodgeball tournaments, Je-Ju "J" Lee appeared like any other female Zainichi within her age demographic.

ISLANDS OF THE MOON

The small East African country of Comoros, officially the Union des Comores, is tiny as nation states go. The poor island nation's capital city of Moroni, with a modest sixty thousand residents, was on Grande Comore, one of three islands that made up the country. The tropical marine climate was, as far as Doctor Priscilla Patton was concerned, a welcomed change from the arid conditions of her last World Health Organization (WHO) assignment.

Today Dr. Patton was trying to decide how to explain her findings in the WHO communiqué she had been constantly editing over the last two days. Before she punched the button on her laptop and sent the report, she wanted to be sure it was as clear and as coherent as she could make it, given the somewhat incoherent content.

Priscilla chuckled to herself as she considered the historical name of the three islands that made up the country of Comoros: Djazair Al Qamar, Islands of the Moon. The lunar reference was, she mused, damned appropriate, given the lunacy she had had to contend with this last week.

Of the three official languages spoken in Comoros—Arabic, French, and Shikomoro—Priscilla's patient spoke Shikomoro, a blend of Swahili and

Arabic. This unfortunate circumstance made the doctor's job that much harder, necessitating the hire of a local merchant to interpret. Given the odd subject matter being discussed, the three-way conversation had quickly devolved into a real circus.

Priscilla's friend and fellow doctor, Jean-Paul Cartier, who was posted to Tsimbeo over on the island of Anjouan with the French Medecins Sans Frontieres—better known as Doctors Without Borders—had been visiting her in the WHO offices when the patient first arrived. Jean-Paul had been visibly disturbed upon hearing her patient's strange story. He had been oddly withdrawn ever since the local priest had brought the villager to the WHO offices in Moroni, and he had heard the man's odd ramblings. Priscilla had to admit that the story was indeed an odd one.

With only 2 percent of the country's population being Catholic (98 percent Sunni Muslim), the Vatican's presence was rather sparse, and young Father Joseph Piero Folli had a lot on his plate. Normally, Father Folli, being a busy man, would have simply referred an ambulatory patient seeking routine medical assistance to the closest local doctor. In this case, the bits and pieces of the villager's fantastic story that Father Folli could make out prompted him to opt for the WHO presence in the capital city.

Father Folli, not particularly conversant in Shikomoro, understood enough of the man's story to be concerned that the excited villager was trying to describe something that could be medically significant. It sounded to Father Folli that the man had suffered from a form of delirium, making the priest fear that some sort of tropical fever might have been involved. You didn't take chances with contagions in that part of the world.

As best as Priscilla could tell, the villager, whose first name she had established as being Idriss, was describing what appeared to be a swirling light that he had seen emanate from the ground on the outskirts of his small village southeast of Moroni. Given the vagaries of the imperfect translation the local merchant was struggling to provide, "swirling" and "light" might not quite have been the right descriptive terms for what Idriss was trying to describe.

What Idriss had seen, based on Priscilla's interpretation of the story, was a visible disturbance in the air that floated near the surface of the ground. The air was luminescent and moving. The light from the sun, according to Idriss, was bent and twisted in the air above the spot in question. The sunlight, he said, bounced around in that strange spot and was confined to a space approximately twice the size of the refrigerator that stood in the lab area where she had initially spoken to him.

Finally, after an hour of back and forth among Idriss, the translator, and Dr. Patton, the description that Priscilla went with for her report was a "wavering or flickering image," which Idriss likened on several occasions to being like a "reflection on water." Idriss went on to relate that he could look through the "moving air" and see the trees behind the disturbance, which he described as looking like they would if viewed through heat waves rising from the street on a hot day.

The best translation, Priscilla later learned, for the Shikomoro words that Idriss repeatedly used to describe what he saw would be "shimmering." "Shimmering" was one of the descriptors Priscilla decided to use in her official communiqué back to WHO headquarters when describing the patient's visual symptoms.

The problem of describing the strange visual aberration the patient experienced was the least-troubling aspect of the case Priscilla was saddled with. What was truly disturbing was the rest of Idriss's story.

Idriss said that he noticed the shimmering in the air while walking between homes in his small village. He related that he had been walking with his head canted downward, looking at the ground, and he suddenly felt a strange tingling on his skin and looked up, just in time to see the shimmering, wavering air pocket directly in his path. Idriss said that he was upon the disturbance by the time he looked up and saw it, too late to stop, and he subsequently walked directly into the shimmering. He felt disoriented, had a strong tingling sensation on his skin, and was nauseated. Once he passed through the shimmering, Idriss related that the aforementioned symptoms had quickly dissipated.

Idriss said what was most disturbing about the whole thing was the reaction of his neighbors and even his relatives, who began crying and wailing upon laying eyes on him. He said that the color of two of the houses in his village, including his own, had somehow changed in the few seconds' time that it took for him to walk through the shimmering. And, he said, his family and neighbors had changed—their clothing, their hair, their faces were not the same. The cars in the village, Idriss stammered, were all different from the vehicles he remembered and unlike any he had ever seen.

The oddest aspect of Dr. Patton's strange case was the patient's insistence that it was 1998. Priscilla had no explanation for the fact that Idriss had an apparently mint-condition driver's license in his pocket, issued in May of 1997, and for the fact that a records query indicated that Idriss had not renewed his license when it had expired in 2001. In fact, subsequent questioning of Idriss's astonished and visibly shaken relatives and neighbors seemed to indicate that, until just recently, nobody had heard from or seen Idriss since that day in 1998 when he says he inadvertently walked into the patch of wavering air.

Idriss was trying very hard to deal with a discrepancy in time that, to his relatives and neighbors, amounted to fifteen years; to Idriss, it was only a matter of a second or two.

Idriss beseeched Dr. Patton to cure him of whatever evil disease he was afflicted with.

LAKE ARTHUR, NEW MEXICO — POPULATION 439

Chaves County Deputy Sheriff Randy Dunham calmly entered the complainant's statement into the departmental issue smart tablet that was assigned to his patrol vehicle. Randy's reports and call log would be downloaded at shift's end back at the county jail.

This particular complaint was one of six that Randy had responded to during his shift so far. He kept expecting to look up and see the complainant wearing a tin-foil hat. This was one of the more flamboyant tales he had heard in some time.

Randy and the complainant, Mr. Ryan Jenkins, stood in the driveway of Jenkins's house next to Randy's patrol car. The Jenkins' residence was just off North 1st Street and was a modest two-bedroom ranch home with a well-kept yard. Ryan Jenkins appeared every bit the stable family man, employed as a loan officer with a bank on West Main Street in nearby Artesia, New Mexico.

Unfortunately, the image of the stable family man quickly degenerated in Deputy Dunham's mind as Mr. Jenkins began relating an account of how he had witnessed a "light tornado" in his backyard. Jenkins insisted that it was a swirling, sparkling funnel of subdued, multicolored flickering light, like a small tornado made up of twisting and spinning rainbows.

Since his town was in the same county as Roswell, Randy was used to folks going on about strange things in the sky, aliens, and so on. So Randy calmly listened as Mr. Jenkins articulated his account of the strange light apparition he alleged to have witnessed spontaneously materialize in broad daylight in the middle of his backyard.

"It was a crackling sound, sort of like static, and I felt the hairs on my arms stand up and tingle. I looked up, and there it was, not ten feet away.

There wasn't a cloud in the sky, just clear blue as far as you could see. No rain, no lightning, nothing weird about the weather conditions."

Randy typed the whole affair into the pad as Jenkins excitedly described, for the second or third time, sitting on his patio reading the paper and drinking an iced tea when, from nowhere, this flickering tornado-like disturbance popped into the middle of his yard, shimmered and spun for a few seconds, and then disappeared as quickly as it had popped into view. There and gone.

"My birdbath had been right where the light tornado had materialized, and when that thing, that, uh, luminescent twister, disappeared, my birdbath had disappeared with it. In a blink…it was just gone."

Jenkins took Deputy Dunham around to the backyard and pointed excitedly at the small circle of exposed dirt where the birdbath had once stood. The small circle of dirt was surrounded by a larger ring of decorative stone; it was readily apparent that a lawn fixture—probably a birdbath—had recently sat in that spot.

Randy finished taking Mr. Jenkins's statement, took a photo or two to humor the complainant, and reentered his squad car. He turned the air up a notch and sat for a second, thinking about the call he had just finished. Jenkins didn't look like the kind of guy who would fabricate such a wild story—and risk the false reporting penalty—just to cover the cost of a stolen lawn ornament. Oh, well. He had taken stranger calls.

Randy picked up the mic and went ten-eight. *Brother, never a dull moment.*

SERIUSCRUX INC., MCLEAN, VIRGINIA

"**D**o you think anyone has pieced it together? I mean is there any likelihood that elements of the scientific community, whether government or private sector, have taken serious notice?" Dr. James Randolph was quite concerned, as his small defense technology company's future currently rested squarely on the success of a single, highly classified government contract.

Dr. Randoph, the company's CEO, and Dr. Michael Nelson, theoretical physicist and SeriusCrux's chief technology officer, sat in a small sensitive compartmented information facility (SCIF) inside the corporate headquarters building.

"Jim, I know this is potentially serious stuff, but we have seen no concrete evidence of anyone, private or government, asking questions. I fully realize that, should this DARPA project be compromised, it could spell the end for you, me, SeriusCrux Incorporated, and its thirty employees. That said, I am just not inclined to worry just yet. Uh, it bears watching, but I would not go into panic mode at this point."

"Mike, all we need is for some major news network to get wind of these… anomalies and jump on it, smelling a good popular-interest story."

"I know…I know. Look, let's sit this out for a bit before we pick up a secure line and start setting off bells that we maybe don't want to set off. That is my advice…my two cents' worth."

"Okay, good enough. We will cool our heels for now. But if this draws the attention of the military or scientific community or winds up a story on CNN, we need to have a prepared statement to provide to those guys over in Arlington."

"Don't get me wrong, Mike. I accept your input and won't reach outside the company to anyone as of yet. But if the crowd over at DARPA—especially Don or someone in the Security and Intelligence Directorate—gets nervous and starts wringing their hands over the potential political fallout, we need to have our shit together when we address the issue."

"Right, Jim, I agree, and I will have a plausible risk-mitigation statement ready, no worries."

Within a few minutes of finishing the conversation, Jim walked to his car and, using an encrypted Samsung smart phone, dialed a number at another corporation—one not many people knew existed. He had a brief conversation and hung up, walking back into the building.

The man on the other end of the conversation, an employee of a company called AVI, hit a button on his desk console and asked his secretary to call a number in Japan and let him know when he could pick up the line.

WASHINGTON, DC

The meeting was short and to the point. Present were representatives of three Department of Defense intelligence components. There were officers present from the US Air Force, Army, Navy, and a couple of civilian DoD elements. A navy captain chaired the meeting.

"The briefing materials in front of you are self-explanatory, so I won't get down in the weeds verbalizing what you can read for yourselves. We need to run down what is causing these anomalous electromagnetic events and come to a consensus on whether they represent significant matters of interest to the director.

"That is your mission, in a nutshell. Socialize this material among your staffs. Find out what these events mean, if anything, and do so quickly. We don't want other elements of the IC getting ahead of us on this, should these events be of any national security consequence. Make it happen, gentlemen."

The meeting had lasted barely ten minutes and broke up with each officer heading back to his respective component carrying his individual briefing packet in a locked security bag.

One of the officers assigned to a Pentagon office made a slight detour, continuing to the elevators and making a quick visit to his car in the parking lot.

Major Richard Dombroski opened the center console in his personal vehicle and removed the prepaid Samsung SGH t301G cellular phone he kept specifically for occasions like this. He dialed a number that activated a pager on the belt of an army intelligence officer in a US Army Intelligence and Security Command office that few at Fort Meade knew existed. Upon the pager's activation, its owner walked out to his personal vehicle and removed an inexpensive prepaid cell phone from the glove box.

The INSCOM officer dialed the number of Dombroski's prepaid cell and listened while the Pentagon major recounted the gist of the meeting he had just attended. Major Dombroski finished his brief report with: "The director's office is aware of the…uh, anomalies and a preliminary investigative tasking has been issued." Both officers hung up without further conversation.

Neither Major Dombroski nor his INSCOM contact was away from his office for more than twenty minutes, both officers returning to their normal duties immediately after concluding their brief cellular conversation.

Nobody else on earth, save for a small cadre in Austin, knew the significance of both Major Dombroski and his INSCOM contact being members of the Texas National Guard on active duty with federal forces.

Later in the day, both would dispose of their respective prepaid phones and purchase new ones on their way home.

KOREATOWN, MID-WILSHIRE DISTRICT, LOS ANGELES, CALIFORNIA

The two Koreans walked out the front door of Ji's Garden Korean BBQ restaurant and stopped under the awning to light cigarettes, eyes scanning the busy side street, a colorful jungle of signage, power lines, and shop fronts. Their eyes and those of the Chinese driver of the dark-colored SUV met as the driver gunned it, and the SUV rocketed ahead.

Both Koreans dropped their smokes and flung their open sport jackets back in rushed efforts to draw their pistols while diving for cover. The SUV was now even with the restaurant awning, and the rear passenger-side window was coming down, revealing the protruding muzzle of the Chinese AKS-47 assault rifle.

The controlled full-auto bursts of 7.62x39 rounds chewed through car doors, restaurant windows, and the empty metal newspaper box the unluckiest of the two Koreans dove behind, two of the .30-caliber AK slugs catching the gangster just off center of his sternum, sprawling him on the sidewalk.

The second, and luckier, of the two Ssang-Yong-Pa gunmen, using the engine block of a parked car as cover, racked off five rounds from his Springfield Armory XD nine-millimeter, one of the special 135-grain barricade-penetrating Hornady rounds finding the jaw of the Triad shooter, painting the vehicle's interior and its driver with blood and shattered dental work as the SUV sped away.

And so began the street war between Chinese Triads expanding their turf and Korean "Pa" protecting theirs in the City of Angel's Koreatown.

LAPD GANG AND NARCOTICS DIVISION

Detective Lee Han-Jae had seen it all too many times before—crime scenes in Koreatown adeptly tampered with to cover local muscle. In this case, the body of a drive-by shooting victim and suspected organized crime gunman "disappeared" before the first responding units arrived on scene. Although vehemently denied, Det. Lee suspected that the restaurant owners likely aided in spiriting the dead "iljin" away.

The awesome culture of LA's Koreatown had many facets, the Wilshire District neighborhood populated by a proud and hardworking people. The vast majority were solid citizens, contributing daily to the great city's economy. Unfortunately, among those facets was Korean gang culture, sometimes referred to as "Korean Pride."

You could pretty readily spot the "gangsta" crowd: baggy clothes, ghetto talk, lowered Hondas with high "skyscraper" spoilers, super-powered stereos, and oversized mufflers.

In Los Angeles, the predominant Korean mob had been Korean Killers, "KK," now thought by some to be inactive, for the most part. Detective Lee wasn't quite so sure. Nowadays, it was crews like Koreatown Gangsters (KTG) and Last Generation Korean Killers (LGKK) that ran the streets. In total, there were something along the lines of seven Korean gangs in Koreatown, Central-side, and the San Fernando Valley.

Detective Lee's trained eye knew what to look for amid the colorful and rich tapestry that gave LA's Koreatown its unique flavor, and Lee could easily translate the story told by the streets—the cigarette burn marks, the dragon and tiger tattoos, the scratch and slash marks. Lee's ears expertly tuned into telltale signs such as the music of Miami-based rapper Flo-Rida blaring from a slow-cruising street racer.

The detective also knew the signs of the more serious and sophisticated organized criminal elements: the twin dragons of Ssang-Yong-Pa curling over each other on the upper arm and the seven-star pattern on the chest signifying Chil Sung Pa.

Lee was even familiar with the covert killings and behind-the-scenes intimidation that Hwan-Song-Sung-Pa occasionally carried out for major South Korean corporations.

Detective Lee had noticed the changes among the denizens of the criminal underworld as newer generations inherited leadership from the previous—the disappearing gakdoogi hair with the sides shaved, the replacement of all dark attire and black luxury cars with a much wider range of coloration and style, and the evolution of huge tattoos to smaller, more readily concealed ink.

Detective Lee Han-Jae had also noticed the increasing incursion by Chinese Triad gangsters into Korean neighborhoods. He knew that the Triads were making similar incursions into Japanese Yakuza territories.

The growing power and holdings of the Chinese had not gone unnoticed by the leadership of the Yakuza. Upper management in Yamaguchi-gumi, Sumiyoshi-Kai, and Inagawa-Kai had all taken notice. Also among those taking notice was Je-Ju "J" Lee.

Likewise, senior elements of Ssang-Yong-Pa and Chil Sung Pa were becoming increasingly alarmed and were passing their concern on to the leadership within LA's Korean criminal underground.

Something needed to be done.

TOKYO

"This trend must be halted. Send Je-Ju Lee to coordinate with our people in Los Angeles. Her ethnicity will permit her to assist in liaison efforts with the Koreans there, as well."

"Hai, sosai."

KOBE, JAPAN

"This is serious, and we must not sit idly while the scales tilt further in favor of the Chinese. I want this dealt with decisively."

"Of course, sir. I will see to it personally." With that, Sainen Chinhung strode confidently from the wakagashiro's private office.

WHITTIER BOULEVARD

Warren Gun-woo was the class clown in high school—a smart ass if you asked most of the teachers and school staff. Warren suffered through a couple semesters of college before walking off campus one morning and never returning, devastating his mother and infuriating his father. After several unsuccessful tryouts at local improv comedy clubs and a few months working at a pharmacy, Warren was thinking there had to be something better out there.

A chance encounter at a local street racer's hangout changed all that for good.

Warren and Mike Ji-hun hit if off straight away. They were the same age, grew up in similar households, had compatible senses of humor, and were both adrift in a sea of boredom, zealously seeking life's adventures. The difference was Mike Ji-hun was rolling in dough, a perk of membership in Koreatown Gangsters, the KTG.

CHINATOWN, SAN FRANCISCO

Je-Ju "J" Lee and a local cohort with the street moniker "Animal Mother," a name taken from the character played by actor Adam Baldwin in the Vietnam War film *Full Metal Jacket*, walked from the alleyway into the Chinese restaurant at 150 Waverly Place at 1:53 p.m. on a rainy Tuesday afternoon.

Triad muscle Ronnie Chan, Dave Hsin, and Harold "Guns" Li looked up from their late lunch just in time to see the CZW9 and Spectre M4 submachine guns swing up from behind the thighs of "J" Lee and "Mother," their upward arcs bringing the weapons to bear directly on the back wall table. There was no time to react, barely time to register the fact that they were likely going to die in the next instant.

The CZW and Spectre subguns, with 780 and 850 rounds-per-minute cyclic rates of fire respectively, belched nine-millimeter rounds in short, staccato bursts, the bodies of the three Triad gunmen twitching and jerking like marionettes on a puppeteer's strings.

Before the last brass casing had bounced off the dining room floor, Je-Ju and Mother had pivoted on their heels and walked back out the front door of the restaurant, dark figures melting into the rain.

The lifeless bodies of Chan, Hsin, and Li slumped from their chairs and onto the blood-splattered floor amid the screams of terrified patrons and restaurant employees.

BACK ROOM, STOCKTON STREET PRODUCE MARKET

Triad boss Jason Mark Wen glared at the messenger who had just brought word of the triple shooting over on Waverly Place, his brow furrowed deeply. After a second or two of silent thought, Wen instructed the messenger, a low-level Triad player, to have Bobby Shing report to him immediately.

Within two hours, Triad lieutenant and professional shooter Robert "Bobby" Shing had assembled a small crew of armed men, and was en route to Los Angeles.

LOS ANGELES, 6TH STREET AND ALEXANDRIA, KOREATOWN

Warren Gun-woo and Mike Ji-hun stood in front of the brightly lit strip mall with the green awnings that housed, among a number of other Koreatown businesses, a Korean BBQ and a cleaners. The towering hulk of the Center Bank building rose from behind, silhouetted against a darkening sky.

Warren and Mike were boasting of the girls they had met at the Korean Festival, each boisterously trying to out-posture the other. The two young men had become fast friends, almost from the moment they had met at the street racer gathering on Whittier.

A widening smirk spread across Warren's face as he saw the aging Pontiac sedan, its rusting form standing out in the stream of newer-model vehicles flowing past in the early evening traffic. It was the kind of heap he would have been condemned to drive were it not for his KTG affiliation and the resulting fire hose of cash his friendship with Mike had afforded him.

For whatever reason, Warren's eye did not detect the business end of the machine pistol rising up in the vehicle's backseat. Warren was just about to make a smart-ass comment to Mike maligning the decrepit vehicle when the night exploded.

Detective Lee Han-Jae had been to a number of similar scenes during his tenure with the Gang and Narcotics Division: young bodies grotesquely twisted in death, lying face down on the pavement in the aftermath of gang-land violence. Young lives cut short. Lead poisoning, the division detectives called it.

Lee looked on as the crime scene processing and medical examiner's people did their thing. He stared numbly at the lifeless eyes in the young face that stared back up at him from the sidewalk, the perforated body of one Michael Ji-hun having been turned over during the course of the scene investigation. A ragged line of holes stitched the previously white shirt of the DOA.

A marked LAPD unit sat a few yards away, the surviving victim in the caged backseat of the cruiser. A crime suppression unit that had arrived with the first responding uniforms had IDed the stiff as a KTG gang member, and the surviving victim had been put, following a pat-down, in the cage car with the assumption that he, too, was likely a KTGer, one whose mug wasn't in their book.

Two passersby had identified the survivor as having been standing with the deceased, engaged in casual banter, just prior to the shooting. A customer exiting the cleaners had looked up at the sound of gunfire to catch a glimpse of an older-model sedan, possibly a Pontiac, speeding from the scene. Unfortunately, no plate information was obtained, and the witness wasn't even sure there was a plate on the suspect vehicle. Most of the folks going about their business at the little mall that evening had never witnessed a drive-by shooting before, shock and confusion preventing any accurate recounting of the incident that would be useful to investigators. The usual drill.

Handcuffed and seat belted in, Warren leaned slightly forward, canting his head and chin down in an attempt to use his shirt to wipe the tears from his cheeks. His mouth was dry, and bile was threatening to rise in his throat. He couldn't get the burned-in image of Mike's last moments out of his head. The look on Mike's face—it was… surreal, awful, out of context with everything he had known in his young life. The sickening wet plop of the bullets smacking Mike's chest, the way his body just dropped straight down like he had been just…switched off. The stomach-turning thud Mike's head made as it hit the sidewalk. Funny, the stuff you remember.

Warren didn't know Bobby Shing, but Shing's grinning face was seared into his memory, staring back at him over the muzzle of the full-auto-converted TEC9 from the back window of the rusty old Pontiac.

Warren glared defiantly at the plainclothesman as the policeman opened the squad car's rear passenger side door. He sputtered through the tears and the shock and the rising bile, "Those fucking bastard, sons of bitches are gonna fucking pay. That Chinese motherfucker grinned and winked at me. He…Mike…was my…my friend." Warren struggled to contain the vomit and to maintain his rapidly degenerating composure, anger and terror twisting in his gut.

In an uncharacteristic burst of emotion, crimson storm clouds of rage contorting his face, Detective Lee Han-Jae grabbed Warren's right sleeve and bellowed, "You fucking idiot!" Pointing back at the police officers and technicians working the crime scene, Lee Han-Jae shook Warren violently. "Those…those are the good guys! Those men and women go out, day in and day out, and tread into darkness, slosh through the blood and death caused by assholes like your dead buddy, venture into situations and places that would make most citizens piss their panties! Shit-for-brains assholes like that Koreatown gangster shot to hell over there—those…those aren't your fuckin' friends." Twisting Warren's face toward the scene, Detective Lee Han-Jae growled, "Take a good fucking look…that's gonna be your dumb ass one of these days!"

After a couple of moments, Han-Jae had regained his professional cop composure. "What makes you say he was Chinese?"

CHINATOWN

Je-Ju spoke quietly into the cellular phone, a specially encrypted custom device, the entire communication taking only twenty-seven seconds.

"The old man, a traditional Chinese medicine practitioner here in Chinatown, knows the reality of things. Most people locally believe him to be an eccentric proponent of ancient mystic beliefs, but my investigation reflects that he has direct knowledge. He worked for the American OSS during the last year of World War Two and later, in the nineteen fifties, for their air force at Wright Field in Ohio, then Wright-Patterson AFB. He knows.

"No, no...there is no need for alarm. I will take care of it. It will, as our other efforts have, appear to be the doing of organized criminal elements. Our manipulations have created a veritable gang war. Excellent cover for action."

The old man's little herbal medicine and acupuncture shop was off one of the narrow alleyways that, crammed with shops and restaurants, gave the section of Chinatown its Hong Kong-like flavor. Perfect.

Je-Ju decided to use Ijinashi's special katana to do the old man, hoping to mimic the well-known MO of the Yakuza as part of her cover for action. The entire street war that was boiling among the Koreans, Japanese, and

Chinese had been an orchestration to cover their activities and to avoid alerting the wrong people.

Neutralizing the small cadre who knew the truth was proving to be a more complex task than originally envisioned by those within the small cabal of AVI employees and a handful of upper-echelon members of international crime.

SPECIAL
OPERATIONS
EXECUTIVE

ALIKA HAYATO AKEE AND BRADLEY JACOB WALKER

Alika Hayato Akee was like a character from an Avengers comic book or, as most thought, a Bruce Lee movie. Even the name was like something that would be conjured in Hollywood. "Alika" was of Hawaiian origin and meant "defender of mankind." "Hayato" was Japanese for "falcon." "Akee" was a Chinese-Hawaiian surname.

Alika Akee was nothing short of a phenom when it came to martial arts, having trained consistently since childhood. He boxed in high school and went on to study muay Thai kickboxing, Brazilian jiu-jitsu, wing chun kungfu, kajunkenbo, and finally jeet kune do, the famed martial art created by Bruce Lee. At age forty-five, Alika was more capable than most half his age, working out daily.

Alika was a transplant to Texas, his family settling in Crystal Beach near Galveston when his dad's company transferred him from Los Angeles to the Houston-Galveston area.

Alika's family origins traced to Hawaii and included Polynesian, Japanese, and Chinese ethnic ties. He spoke conversational Cantonese but never progressed beyond a casual level of proficiency.

Shortly after his resettling in Crystal Beach, Alika's new Texan friends quickly nicknamed him Al, shortening the somewhat out-of-place "Alika." The name stuck, and he was known to most as Al Akee.

Al Akee met Brad Walker in Houston, and, for the decade they had known each other, they had been both close friends and professional colleagues. They shared many traits and interests, among them honesty, integrity, and a fascination with martial arts, so it was natural that they would take an immediate liking to each other.

Bradley Jacob Walker, eleven years Al's senior, hailed from Virginia, moving to Plano, Texas, from the Washington, DC, area. Brad later relocated from Plano to Austin.

Brad's family originated in Indiana, Michigan, and Wisconsin, with Brad spending his childhood in north-central Indiana, growing up in Alexandria, a little town of roughly fifty-five hundred residents about an hour north of Indianapolis.

Military service took him to Virginia, and a succession of jobs following honorable discharge from the military kept him in the Washington, DC, metropolitan area for a number of years, first as a cop in Fairfax and later as a member of the federal intelligence community.

After serving in a number of capacities within the national security arena, Brad decided to leave government service, subsequently relocating to Texas, where he went to work as a private investigator. Eventually tiring of the convoluted hours, Brad quit the private security and investigative firm he was working for and took a job with Texas Military Services as a civilian employee, working as a subject matter expert for the Texas State Guard as part of their Defense Support to Civil Authorities (DSCA) mission. It was through the guard and the hand-to-hand combatives program within the Special Operations Executive that Brad met Al Akee at a DSCA conference in Houston.

TEXAS STATE GUARD HEADQUARTERS, CAMP MABRY, TEXAS

Tucked in among operations, logistics, administration, commo, and a number of other state military functions at the Camp Mabry headquarters of the Texas State Guard was an almost unknown little unit that provided specialized direction and support to subordinate units throughout the guard, to the governor, and to the adjutant general. This was the State Guard's intelligence and security element, unofficially known as SOE for Special Operations Executive. It was unofficially known as SOE because SOE would not be found on any org chart anywhere within the Texas State Guard. There were no references of any sort on any table of organization and equipment that would point to its existence. But it did, in fact, exist, and it had covert ties throughout the twelve regiments, divisions, and brigades that comprised the Texas State Guard.

One of the collateral duties that Brad had with the State Guard was serving as a combatives instructor. Brad had a lengthy background in martial arts that included tang soo do, chun kuk do, krav maga, and jeet kune do. His direct, no-nonsense approach to fighting was similar in many ways to the martial philosophy espoused by Bruce Lee. His easygoing nature made him a favorite among those he trained, although every one of his students knew he had the ability to kill a man with his bare hands.

PHILADELPHIA NAVY YARD, OCTOBER 1943

"Yes, Captain, we are certain that we can contain the Eldridge incident sufficiently. We have already begun working on removing the, uh, anomalous evidence from the affected sections of DE-173's bulkheads."

"No, sir, we have no clear idea of why it happened, but the scientific support team has some, uh, theories they are tossing around."

"That is correct, Captain—you can relay to the admiral that our scientists are confident that they can eventually reproduce the effect."

"No, sir, none of our people has any answer whatsoever as to the, uh, status or whereabouts of those who were…lost off the ship. Yes, we have a list of names of the missing crewmen: Carter, Maloney, Jenkins, Forry, Janski, McNeal, Morrison, and several others. I don't have the list with me at the moment, sir. Yessir, I will have it sent down to you immediately."

LOWER SILESIA, POLAND, 1945

The nervous scientist, a member of a highly classified team of physi-cists working on a super-secret Nazi project hidden in a special underground bunker, again assured the SS general that the incident with "The Bell" had been of no consequence from a security standpoint. The strange effects reported among the local population would not compro-mise the work.

The physicist, in answer to the general's pointedly direct question, said that he had, in fact, witnessed the odd incident; he also told the general, again in answer to a direct query, that he was pretty sure he had a good idea as to the nature of the new physics he had inadvertently witnessed.

Hans Kammler, four-star SS general, took his service pistol from its holster and shot the scientist point blank in the forehead. The general turned and, as he headed to the main lab, looked back over his shoulder and ordered his aide to summon the Junkers 390 and to have a security squad meet him in the lab.

SEOUL METROPOLITAN POLICE AGENCY HEADQUARTERS, TWENTY-FIRST CENTURY

I n an unmarked access controlled office suite in the bowels of the Seoul Metropolitan Police Agency's Headquarters—within a nondescript vault within a warren of nondescript offices—sat an impeccably groomed gentleman in a flawlessly tailored business suit. Gray streaked the man's longish, expensively styled hair—hair that set the senior inspector apart from his peers, whose close-cropped institutional haircuts were, for the most part, interchangeable.

The room the senior inspector occupied was strictly controlled by a secretive, little-known intelligence element that answered directly to the intelligence chief of the Republic of Korea's National Police Agency. Only a handful of police officials knew of the vault's existence, and only one had unfettered access.

Even senior members of Korea's National Intelligence Service (NIS) were unaware of the special police unit's existence, let alone its activities and global relationships.

One of those relationships was with the Tokyo Metropolitan Police Department, the Keishicho. In actuality, it was two relationships, to be precise: one with the Organized Crime Control Bureau and another with the Public Security Bureau.

These special relationships with the Japanese police authorities, like the Korean police unit itself, were unbeknownst to even the upper echelons of the Republic of Korea government, except to a very special select few. The same was true of the covert relationships that existed with special offices within the intelligence apparatus of the Los Angeles Police Department, New York Police Department, New Scotland Yard, and the Royal Canadian Mounted Police.

Most within the Korean government were also completely unaware of the special National Police Agency science and technology division that the senior inspector's intelligence unit was part of. The S/T Division, as it was known, was one of the most closely held secrets within the Republic of Korea. It was easily on a par with the American DARPA, Defense Advanced Research Projects Agency. As with DARPA, very spooky things happened in the S/T Division.

The senior inspector was partially reclined in the office chair, staring passively at the screen of the laptop computer that sat on the desk in front of him, slowly twirling a departmental ink pen in the fingers of his right hand. The hardest part of handling a deep-cover officer was waiting for the covert communications to come through.

The familiar feline icon popped onto the screen, followed by a single line of text, the "parole" used to both authenticate the sender's identity and as proof positive that the undercover was not under any sort of duress or hostile control.

White Tiger was the most successful deep-cover operative in the history of the Seoul Metropolitan Police Agency. Intelligence she had provided had been disseminated to the special international group of cooperating intelligence units and had resulted in the saving of untold lives and a veritable windfall of global—and very closely held—law enforcement successes. Her operations had also permitted political landscapes to be shaped by those select few government officials who populated the secretive global police and security web.

White Tiger's face was well known among the Japanese criminal underground and the detectives of the Tokyo Police Organized Crime Control Bureau, as was her pseudo of Je-Ju "J" Lee. The same would be true for the detectives of LAPD's Gang and Narcotics Division, particularly those working Koreatown in Wilshire District. They would all recognize the pretty little banger.

The senior inspector paused—briefly focused in thought—then responded to the undercover detective's special email communication with his half of the parole sequence, followed by a routine directive to temporarily stand down for a cautionary "cool-off" period.

It wouldn't do to have what could arguably be described as one of the world's most critical undercover police operations unraveled by the unmasking or death of its key investigator. The inconvenient political whining that would result if the Korean detective's operational activity on US soil were to be publicly revealed was also a matter of concern.

The senior inspector sighed with relief as he mentally elected to dismiss the tiny inconsistency in the undercover's parole that had made him pause moments before. White Tiger always left off the period at the end of her parole text. This time, she had inexplicable included the proper punctuation. After another unnerving moment of uncertainty, the senior inspector stood from the desk, stretched his limbs, and headed for the door to set up the alarm panel, secure the vault door, and call it a night. Nobody is perfect. Likely just fatigue.

Senior Inspector Ijinashi Tamna walked down the hallway to the elevator bank deep within the confines of Seoul's police headquarters and reflected on how proud he was of the brave undercover that was his protégé, Detective Inspector Kyung-Soon.

Deep down, however, he knew that the heinous acts that Kyung-Soon had committed—in the course of doing his bidding under color of law in her undercover role—were totally inconsistent with morally proper law enforcement tactics. He knew that those acts had forever removed them from the roles of the good guys. Pity. Wouldn't be the first time.

AUSTIN, TEXAS, HEADQUARTERS OF THE TEXAS DEPARTMENT OF PUBLIC SAFETY, 2014

I n an innocuous back office at the headquarters of the storied 144-member Ranger force, Texas Rangers Bob Wall and Bill Sanchez were wrapping up a secure video tele-conference (VTC) with counterparts at the Dallas Police Department, the Fairfax County, Virginia, Sheriff's Office, the Milwaukee Police Department and half a dozen other agencies.

This was an extraordinary alliance of law enforcement entities, especially given the semiautonomous political status that Texas had, as a state, recently obtained. By popular vote among the Texas population, and with the concurrence of newly elected Tea Party elements within the US government, the State of Texas had become, for the second time in history, the Republic of Texas.

The state political organs had taken on the duties of national governance, and the Texas Rangers had suddenly become the "FBI" of the new Republic of Texas. The Texas Department of Public Safety went from being a state police organization with predominantly highway-patrol duties to a national police force overnight.

The Texas National Guard had overnight become the "national" army and air force of the new, semi-autonomous republic.

It was a nascent evolution, this new "republic," still connected in myriad ways (power grid, water, telecommunications, roadways, porous political borders, supply lines) to the United States, and there was a long way to go before it was truly independent in any meaningful way from the infrastructure of the United States of America.

The relationship between government bodies in Texas and the US government was similar in some ways to that of Puerto Rico's National Guard, legislative bodies, economy, and police forces and the United States. That would, of course, change over time.

The ticklish political issue of the nukes in the possession of the Texas military forces was of particular prominence in the relationship between the United States of America and the Republic of Texas. The new Texas government had so far steadfastly refused to discuss turning its small nuclear arsenal over to the United States.

Elements of the Texas National Guard and of the DPS had joined to create a new border security force, most of the new force being deployed along the Texas/Mexico international border. That said, more and more personnel were being moved to the line between the United States and Texas.

Texas Military Forces—the state administrative organ that owned the Texas Army and Air National Guard forces—was scrambling to create a full-time naval force to cover coast guard duties, building upon the existing Texas State Guard's Texas Maritime Regiment (TMR).

The assistant adjutants general for Air, Army, and Domestic Operations were working to put together a naval command structure to oversee the new nautical force. A real navy would have to wait until later. For now, counterterrorism, counter-narcotics tactics, illegal immigration mitigation, maintaining commercial sea lanes servicing the new republic, and port and border security were the most urgent concerns.

Civilian and military elements of the Texas Military Forces, as well as selected personnel from DPS and various Texas police departments, were being quickly assembled to create a new Republic of Texas intelligence and security apparatus to serve as the spy service of the new republic. It was a work in progress, being loosely modeled after the Office of Strategic Services (OSS) of WWII fame, which wed military and civilian elements to quickly form one of the most successful intelligence agencies in history.

For the time being, the assistant adjutant general for Domestic Operations was spearheading day-to-day intelligence and security operations while helping form the bureaucratic architecture that would eventually become the Texas Special Operations Executive (SOE), a name swiped from the famous British intelligence commando group of the Second World War. The new SOE would be an organ of the Texas State Guard, and its director would answer to the major general, who served as adjutant general of the Texas Military Forces. The AG/TMF answered to the secretary of defense and to the president of the Republic of Texas.

It wouldn't be long before the nascent Republic would be a full fledged, independent nation state, answering only to itself.

Probably the most curious aspect of standing up the government of the new Republic of Texas—strangely reminiscent of the elections of Hollywood's Ronald Reagan and Sonny Bono previously in history—had been the appointment of actor and martial arts celebrity Chuck (Carlos) Norris as secretary of defense and the popular election of his friend, former Texas governor and US president, George W. Bush as the republic's new president.

"We should consider initiating the arrests soon. I don't see any further intelligence value in letting these people continue on."

"Roger that. They are an ugly, virulent blight and something free societies can certainly live without. It is time the good guys won one."

"I second that; it is time this was ended. Now that we are aware of the identities of those running this…this cabal, we should move ahead decisively."

"If we all concur then I offer that we should likely get started, as this will require coordination to ensure that all the collars go down simultaneously so nobody gets a chance to warn the others. We have some serious time zone issues to deal with, not to mention the fact that many of our targets are senior people in their respective organizations, both government and private sectors."

Many strange anomalies were occurring all over the globe, which the intelligence units of various government and police entities believed were tied to the machinations of some sort of international criminal network. Consequently, many of the peace officers involved with the Texas Ranger-SOE joint task force saw themselves as white horse crusaders, helping to render the world a better place by stopping those who might be destroying it.

News of these weird occurrences was seeping into the mainstream media, and the general population of earth was waking up, the people beginning to grasp, to some degree, what was happening.

"Okay, let's get to it then." With that, Texas Ranger Bob Wall, the ranger captain in charge of his agency's contingent to the still-forming Texas Special Operations Executive, clicked off the VTC link, and dozens of special police units around the globe began a very discreet roundup.

SEOUL METROPOLITAN POLICE AGENCY HEADQUARTERS

The doors to the elevator opened, and Senior Inspector Ijinashi Tamna found himself staring down the bores of a twelve-gauge riot gun and three raised pistols.

The arrests had begun. So had the betrayals.

AIRBUS A380-800

Kyung-Soon smiled and accepted the drink from the stewardess then returned to gazing out the window of the Singapore Airlines flight, comfortable in her first-class seat. The young Asian woman's appearance—the nose stud, tiny eyebrow ring, and brightly colored streak in her otherwise jet-black hair—gave away none of her true character. It would be highly unlikely for anyone outside of a select few international law enforcement officers to peg her as Je-Ju "J" Lee, Yak enforcer.

Kyung-Soon had been informed of Ijinashi's arrest by South Korean authorities. She felt sorry that it had been necessary for her and her colleagues to throw Ijinashi under the bus, so to speak. But, as happens often in the harsh climate of business, it had unfortunately been a necessary sacrifice.

Kyung-Soon watched the clouds drift by below her as she sipped her drink and reflected back on her unusual relationship with Ijinashi. To call it bizarre would be a clear understatement.

Ijinashi had always been more good than bad, but Kyung-Soon had noticed the gradual slide toward wickedness manifesting in her old mentor.

He was, she observed, becoming more like her. And she was, after all, a gangster.

Kyung-Soon felt a momentary rush of regret and shame wash over her at the thought of her cold and calculated betrayal of Ijinashi. She thought of how she embedded herself into his special police intelligence unit, at first thinking that she was turning over a new leaf, taking her life down a different path. But soon her attraction to the gangster lifestyle with the Yaks overshadowed her thoughts of a life change. She couldn't peg the exact point—the precise moment in time—when, in her clandestine role within the Yakuza, she shifted from being a police agent playing a cover role as a gangster to a gangster playing a cover role as a police agent.

As Kyung-Soon thought of how she had cultivated the secret relationship with Sainen, another brief rush of guilt poured over her. She and Sainen—both possessing the otherworldly swords and both harboring the secret knowledge of the time portals—had conspired to turn those circumstances into a wildly profitable and totally mercenary entrepreneurial endeavor.

Carefully orchestrating their moves and feeding edited versions of who they were and what they were capable of, Kyung-Soon and Sainen gained the support of their respective syndicate bosses in approaching AVI, a clandestine multinational private corporation that operated, for profit, in the shadowy realm that lay between the governments of the world and global organized crime.

Applied Violence International, Inc. (AVI) had established a unique niche in that netherworld of black government operations and syndicated criminal enterprise, a below-the-radar company that provided services for a fee—violent services to those who could pay.

AVI, because of its covert dealings with various national governments, had established contacts within the highest tiers of more than a few intelligence, police, and security organizations around the globe. It had deep connections within the highest echelons of world politics, and it wielded considerable power and influence as a result.

Sainen and Kyung Soon saw the benefit of contouring a special relationship that would allow them, their Yakuza bosses, and AVI leaders to realize enormous profit from the manipulation and marketing of the time portal technology to those select entities who could afford the immense cost of developing it.

Kyung-Soon genuinely felt bad about all the people who had been adversely affected as a result of the profit-driven science experiments that AVI, segments of Asian organized crime, elements of the US government, various government contractors, and other national-level government bodies were all complicit in.

Once she and Sainen, smelling big money and power, had leveraged their knowledge of the time portals, along with the ancient and exotic technologies embodied in their special swords, things had quickly spiraled out of control. Greed and power are like that. They had gotten what they had both conspired to achieve: unimaginable personal wealth while maintaining the ultimate escape mechanism. They had boatloads of money and the world's greatest get-out-of-jail cards.

The unholy alliance among the Yakuza, AVI, and global governments had spawned some truly unfortunate events. But, Kyung-Soon rationalized, she could not control human nature; however, she could certainly capitalize on its vagaries.

Kyung-Soon smiled politely as she accepted another drink and the lunch menu.

NEAR DAEGU, REPUBLIC OF KOREA POHANG CORRECTIONAL INSTITUTION, 36° 4'20" N, 129° 19'26" E

Prisoner number 004—a special detainee—was sitting in the institutional psychologist's cramped cubicle in the administrative area just outside the cell blocks.

Pohang was a very progressive facility, its blocks patrolled by robot guards and its inmates provided routine psychological counseling. Pohang was state of the art.

Today, however, a serious mistake had been made.

Normally, 004 would have been in a secluded single-inmate cell away from the main population, only going into the yard for exercise when the others were inside, eating alone, and never, ever leaving the secured blocks for any reason, including psychological counseling sessions.

This morning, incidental to a mistake made by a temporarily assigned correctional administrator in the front office, 004 was in the admin area for an overdue interview with the prison shrink, which the temporary admin guy thought had been an egregious oversight on the part of the prison staff that he was proud to have discovered and dutifully corrected.

The psychologist, a large but somewhat overweight middle-aged man, entered the room, his clip-on identification card indicating that he was the prison psychologist.

Normally, the prisoner's administrative file jacket would be on the desk waiting for the doctor. However, this morning there was no file there.

The doctor glanced at the desk as he entered the cubicle, noticed the discrepancy, and was turning to dial the phone to notify the records people when 004's left elbow slammed down into the side of his neck in a short, powerful arc. The arm immediately extended out and encircled the stunned doctor's throat as a knee was thrust up into the man's crotch. 004's right elbow crashed into the doctor's right temple, retracted, and smashed down on the exposed face as the left arm brutally wrenched the head rearward toward 004's chest as the prisoner short-stepped backward to keep the doctor off balance. This rain of elbows and knees was in rapid succession, splattering the cubicle with blood from the doctor's crushed nose and dropping the unconscious man into a crumpled heap on the floor in less than two seconds.

Number 004 reached down and unclipped the laminated ID badge, removed it from the doctor's shirt, and focused momentarily on the body he was standing over, briefly assessing the utility of using the psychologist's clothing.

Nobody responded, 004 thought, *so the brief struggle must have gone unheard. I have, potentially, about fifty-five minutes before the session would be over. I have time to think.*

Shock and awe, as the Americans call it, might be the best course: simple, direct action. I can't dawdle…someone might—would—notice that the wrong prisoner is up in the front, outside the secure area. It is absolutely extraordinary that nobody in the control room has noticed, that nobody on the cameras has noticed. It must truly be an unfortunate series of errors on the part of the staff for this to happen. No time to waste.

Prisoner 004 quickly went around to the desk and began opening drawers, the first one being the shallow center drawer designed for pens, paper clips, and such. He found what he hoped would be there: a thin-profile plastic stun gun the doctor must have kept on hand in event an inmate went off during a session. He grabbed the device, placed it on the desk blotter, and continued opening the desk's remaining drawers.

Next, 004 removed a 3M Scotch tape dispenser and put that on top of the desk with the electric stun gun. In the deep-well bottom right drawer, 004 found another prize, a canister of professional- grade pepper spray, which he removed and placed with the other items. The doc must have been fearful of an altercation.

Scanning the rest of the cubicle—a prefab, fully enclosed office, actually—004 looked more closely at his surroundings now that his heart rate and adrenaline dump were subsiding.

To his astonishment, the doc had a blue sports blazer hanging on a hook on the wall next to the door.

The twenty-something correctional officer manning the front desk, the only uniformed officer among the front office staff of civilian administrative workers, was startled by the sharp metallic clang. The officer twisted in his chair to see what had been dropped in the open bay admin area behind him and was momentarily frozen by the incongruity of what he saw. *Is that a pepper spray canister?* The young officer did not register the blur of motion in time to defend himself.

Several of the screaming and panicked office staff fell over each other in their blind rush to distance themselves from the rolling canister that was hissing a choking cloud of toxic mist, its trigger tab taped down.

Shifting the stun gun to his left hand, 004 reached around the slumped form of the uniformed officer with his right hand and began feeling the underside of the front desk surface, finding the button that released the electric lock on the door leading outside.

Unaccustomed to the bright sunlight, Ijinashi squinted as he turned toward the sound of the horn and walked toward the blue Lexus in the front row of the staff parking lot, having used the electronic key fob to identify the prison psychologist's car.

Sainen held the phone to his ear as he strolled down the quiet, shaded side street. He was discussing recent events of mutual interest with Je-Ju. Mainly, he was just listening.

"We don't know what Ijinashi's intentions are or what his overall agenda may encompass. Revenge would certainly be among his motivations, I would think. He has to know he wound up in the slammer because he was dimed out. Only a few people would have had the wherewithal to pull that off. He knows, of course." Je-Ju paused to let that sink in before continuing.

"Even as he drifted further onto the dark side, it was evident that he was troubled by what he viewed as a divergence from the honorable path. He was fearful—and ashamed—of his downward slide towards greed and manipulation. It rubbed against the grain of his soul." Sainen listened without comment.

"This escape from the South Korean correctional facility resulted, I think, from a comedy of errors on the part of an inept staff. I don't think he had any way to access his sword. I also do not believe he had outside help. The escape was simply Ijinashi taking full advantage of his jailers' mistakes. I believe that he likely has the sword—his original katana with the Dogon grip—somewhere he can get to it but where it would be relatively safe from discovery. It is, after all, how he got here—to this time. He would protect it at all costs, as we do ours.

"We should take all prudent precautions. He is a patient man. We may not hear from him for months or years. But someday we will."

TAIWAN

An observer of global organized crime's trend toward multinational, multiethnic composition would not have been surprised to find a Yak in Taipei doing business as a partner of Zhulianbang—The United Bamboo Gang, Taiwan's largest triad. Nor would that same observer be at all surprised to find that Yak with a man with the street moniker Panji, an Indonesian preman, as members of Indonesian organized criminal gangs are known. The fact that the Yak was thought to be ethnically Korean would, likewise, not have raised an eyebrow.

The luxury apartment was located in the center of Taipei City, at most a ten- to twelve-minute walk to the Songjiang Nanjing subway station, and only one subway stop from some of Taipei's finest restaurants, department stores, and select shops.

There was even a secure parking spot for Sainen's 545-horse power Nissan GT-R. In his estimation, it just didn't get much better than that.

MANILA

The historic and elegant Manila Hotel was among the most exclusive of metro Manila's luxury hotels. Most of the travelers who lodged at the Manila were oblivious to the fact that within the hotel was a segregated luxury suite that was recently—and covertly—converted to an apartment residence. Only the most well-heeled and influential could coerce the management of the famous Manila Bay landmark to create such a residence. Of course, being on a first-name basis with the upper echelons of Kuratong Baleleng and several other underground criminal organizations out of Tondo, Manila, went a long way toward getting one what one wanted in the Philippines.

Most Filipinos, including government officials, were not keen on irritating the upper tier of Kuratong Baleleng, nor were they anxious to piss off the ruling members of Sigue Sigue Comando (SSC) or the Watch Dogg Committee (WDC). The fact that Je-Ju "J" Lee maintained friendly relationships with all of those entities made her someone you simply did not wish to aggravate or disappoint. The Manila's owners were more than happy to accommodate Ms. Lee's request for permanent residential status at their hotel. In fact, it was their distinct honor to do so.

DAAN DISTRICT, TAIPEI CITY

Twice a week at seven in the morning, Sainen ventured into a progressive martial arts gym located in Section 4 on Ren-ai Road in Taipei City. Having found the place by accident, Sainen had been surprised to discover a wonderful blend of effective and practical fighting arts offered by a friendly and professional staff that didn't ask too many questions of its clients. Quickly deciding to train there, Sainen was now a regular at the MMA gym.

One of the staff, a certified instructor of jeet kune do and an MMA practitioner, took Sainen on as a student, teaching him the freestyle eclectic martial philosophy that thoroughly permeated the world of twenty first century mixed martial arts.

Sainen was a natural fit, already possessing a majority of the skillsets utilized in the contemporary martial arts genre generally covered by the popular term MMA. The skilled eye of a trained martial artist would quickly pick up that Sainen cared little for ring sport.

This gravitation toward the non-sportive "reality" side of things led Sainen to the small, exclusive backroom group whose training leaned in that direction. They practiced behind closed doors a blend of Dog Brothers kali-eskrima coupled with modern empty-hand methods that proponents of Tony Blauer's SPEAR System or Israeli krav maga would find recognizable. Sainen was brilliant at it, quickly proving himself adept with both empty-hand and weapons skills.

It was a great place to hone and maintain one's essential survival skills.

Sainen also practiced the traditional martial arts that had been a part of him since he was young. He tended to favor the powerful Nanquan—Southern Fist—of South China and Korean Taekwondo for their directness. What nobody who knew Sainen would have guessed, in their wildest dreams, was that he was a dedicated practitioner of Taijiquan and had been for years. Such a soft, graceful and refined practice did not fit Sainen's persona. He attributed his robust health and physical prowess to Taiji. He also attributed his superior mental skills to the ancient martial art.

MANILA METROPOLITAN AREA, QUEZON CITY

O n the fifth floor of the Karen Building on Annapolis Street in Quezon City was located a hybrid martial arts studio where one could find progressive martial arts instruction. Je-Ju's instructor was somewhat of a hybrid himself, being of Filipino-Chinese-Malay ethnic heritage. The fighting methodologies he taught were not particularly adaptable to the ring, being predominantly street-oriented in their focus and quite brutal in their implementation.

There was no formal name given the blended system, a concoction of kuntao, kali, and qin na that was tailored to, and optimized for, the individual practitioner based on his or her unique physical and psychological makeup. There were no belts or sashes involved, just a simple progression of certifications that attested to the practitioner's competency.

Even the individual component arts were, themselves, compilations and street simplifications of an assorted mishmash of traditional styles of kuntao and Filipino martial art (FMA) married with Chinese qin na techniques cobbled from a variety of gungfu and taiji systems.

Very much in the same spirit of pragmatic street effectiveness that spawned the urban systems of sanuces ryu jujitsu and vee arnis jitsu, the end result of Je-Ju's training was a very workable system of street viable martial art that was—relatively speaking—easily absorbed and executed.

Most importantly, from a "real-world" point of view, the hybrid system afforded the student usable competencies in blunt impact weapons, edged weapons, and bare hand technique. It was perfect, in Je-ju's estimation, for her street needs.

GURO

Remy Ernesto Caballero Sanchez walked from the little-used side door of the historical Barasoain church, Our Lady of Mt. Carmel Parish, and disappeared into the humid night, darkness shielding his path as he blended into and was lost among the pedestrian traffic on Broadway Avenue, New Manila, Quezon City, Philippines. Also unobserved was the exit from the same church by Osvaldo Prio Torrado, who likewise melded into the foot traffic along Broadway Avenue.

THE CHURCH

The first Catholic mass held in the Philippines having occurred in 1521, Catholicism eventually became the nation's predominant religion. With over seventy-five million members, the Philippines, as a country, boasts the third-largest number of Catholics in the world.

Of the original strategic goals harbored by Spain for the occupation of the Philippine Islands—participation in the spice trade, influencing the great societies of China and Japan, and spreading Catholicism among the peoples of the archipelago—the conversion to Catholicism was firmly entrenched and still held strong today.

Early Spanish missionaries did not have an easy task given the endless varieties of languages and dialects in the Philippines. Native Filipinos, who worshiped nature and prayed to their ancestors, considered the main value of the Spanish—and of conversion to their Catholic religion—to be the protection the Spanish afforded them from the predations of Japanese, Chinese, and Muslim pirates. Otherwise, they had limited to no use for the European invaders.

Today, the Philippines still have need of protection from the Chinese, whose growing military prowess and accompanying belligerence once again threatens the sovereignty of the archipelago. Consequently, the Philippine military leadership are aligning themselves with the Japanese, their former oppressors, along with the United States and Vietnam.

There were other players in the game. Among patriotic Filipinos, a clandestine faction existed, hidden from view and unknown to most of the population. This shadowy group practiced many of the old ways but possessed a very progressive worldview. This small, heavily compartmentalized underground element was also quite unknown to the authorities. A few astute police and intelligence officials might have suspected their existence, but none had any substantive proof.

Remy Ernesto Caballero Sanchez—Arnis master and Filipino patriot— was a leader of the New Katipunan. Although loosely aligned with Partido Komunista ng Pilipinas or PKP, the New Katipunan maintained its own agenda. The New Katipunan also maintained close ties to the Vatican—ties that were hidden and well protected from public disclosure.

Also hidden and well protected from unwanted observation was the close tie that Remy Sanchez—and consequently the New Katipunan— maintained with Osvaldo Prio Torrado, a senior officer of the Direccion de Inteligencia, or DI, of the Republic of Cuba.

Osvaldo Prio Torrado was a personal friend of Miguel Diaz-Canel, first vice president of the Republic of Cuba, heir to Raul Castro. This direct relationship with the highest echelon of Cuba's ruling elite—and a long-standing membership in the Cuban Communist Party—made Osvaldo Torrado one of the most powerful and influential men in the Cuban Intelligence Directorate. This alignment with power, combined with a shared philosophy, was why Ijinashi Tamna of the New Weathermen sought out Mr. Torrado as an ally.

The New Katipunan's relationship with the Cuban Intelligence Directorate was one of both necessity and convenience. Remy Sanchez, on the other hand, maintained an alliance with the Cuban DI because Osvaldo was his friend—and a likeminded friend, at that.

BARANGAY SIMUAY, MAAGUINDANAO PROVINCE, PHILIPPINES

Remy Sanchez addressed the small group of insurgents and political activists in the smoky back room of the bar; among the group were several members of the Central Committee of the Moro Islamic Liberation Front. Nobody, they reasoned, would suspect Muslims to be present in an establishment that served alcohol or employed scantily clad women.

Quoting from an interview Che Guevara gave to two Chinese journalists—K'ung Mai and Ping An—on April 18, 1959, Remy Sanchez energized his audience. The specific part of the interview he would like to quote, Remy explained, pertained to the killing of a Cuban revolutionary and contained a valuable lesson regarding winning the hearts and minds of the working class that could be applied to today's struggle.

"'…a tragedy occurred in Santiago de Cuba; our Comrade Frank País was killed. This produced a turning point in our revolutionary movement. The enraged people of Santiago on their own poured into the streets and called for the first politically oriented general strike. Even though the strike did not have a leader, it paralyzed the whole of Oriente Province. The dictatorial government suppressed the incident. This movement, however, caused us to understand that working class participation in the struggle to achieve freedom was absolutely essential! We then began to carry out secret work among the workers, in preparation for another general strike, to help the Rebel Army seize the government.'"

Remy finished his quote and let the message sink in for a moment before continuing.

"It was true in 1959, and it remains true today, gentlemen. We must—must—have the buy-in of the workers, the middle class, in order to gain any traction, any headway whatsoever. Otherwise, we will be but a small cadre easily steamrollered by imperialist forces, insignificant in the grand configuration of global society, of history. We cannot allow this to be the case. We cannot. It is imperative—paramount—that we engage and gain the participation of unionized workers if this struggle is to succeed."

CORRUPTION

Je-Ju and Sainen's alliance eventually came to be known among international criminal elements as the Cloud Dragons, a loosely allied confederation of criminal underground players that spanned the globe. Broken into semiautonomous cells, much like terrorist groups, the network's security precautions proved more than a match for the international police and government forces arrayed against it.

Je-Ju and Sainen ran the criminal enterprise from their respective bases in Taiwan and the Philippines. Maintaining judiciously solicited ties within the national security, police, and corporate establishments in Taipei and Manila, the two kingpins managed their empire essentially without interruption or interference from anyone in or out of government. By greasing the palms of select local criminal outfits in Manila and Taipei, Je-Ju and Sainen were more or less untouchable. More or less.

Although considerable amounts of money were made via the well-established mechanisms of money laundering, protection, intimidation, grand theft, smuggling, assassination, and various other common underworld revenue-generating endeavors, the Cloud Dragons had moved well beyond those ordinary methods.

Multiple blog sites and Internet forum boards addressing various international political causes, social issues, and business agendas had been linked to the reelection-campaign social media platforms of select US Congress members. This ultimately led to a flow of campaign contributions that the American public would find ill advised, at best, and would in all likelihood view as outright criminal. Through some very creative engineering, the Cloud Dragons had manipulated those monetary contributions into substantial leverage of the politicians involved. Because of the complex and intricate interconnectedness of the American political machine in Washington, DC, Sainen and Je-Ju were able to push their leverage upstream to the highest levels of US national power.

As a money-making and power-brokering enterprise, it was without peer. It was a sweet system, and it worked like a charm.

Beyond the control—and even the comprehension—of Sainen, Je-Ju, and their profit-focused mob cronies, the tentacles reached well beyond the realm of an organized criminal business scheme, reaching into the highest echelons of government and military power on an unprecedented international scale. The greed and power-mongering possibilities were beyond the scope of anything that had ever existed in the course of human history.

It was both the grand ultimate weapon and preeminent global political power-leveraging implement—one of unparalleled reach that permitted the manipulation of the peoples and resources of the earth in ways hitherto impossible. It was a narcotic with unspeakable addictive powers, and it infected the management architecture of nearly every government and corporate structure on the planet.

Those who wielded its evil power were able to shape governments, co-opt multinational corporations, subvert nonprofits, guide public opinion through global media exploitation, and manipulate the world's workers. For corrupt and obscenely powerful American politicians, it was an irresistible aphrodisiac.

A savior was needed.

TAIPEI

S ainen could charm dew off of honeysuckle, being equally adept as a conman as he was as a thug, subtle psychological manipulative skills being an important competency for the professional criminal and martial artist alike.

Today, however, as he negotiated the maddeningly heavy morning traffic, Sainen's mood was not conducive to good manners or skillful verbal interaction.

The carload of brash punks rocketed up on Sainen's bumper, coming to within an inch or two of achieving bumper lock, then hung there in an attempt to intimidate Sainen into relinquishing his lane to them. Sainen glanced at the idiots in his rearview and side mirrors, guestimating the offending vehicle to contain four males, including the driver. It could be three males and a female but four occupants total.

Sainen maintained his speed and kept to his lane, temporarily ignoring the car riding his ass through the morning congestion. Once Sainen was closer to where he planned to turn, he let off the gas just a little to make the punk driver behind him have to apply his brakes. After another block,

Sainen tapped his brakes, causing the car on his bumper to quickly brake. Now the bozo was pissed, just like Sainen wanted him to be.

A small white-panel truck on Sainen's right turned into a business, leaving a momentary space in the right lane. The driver riding Sainen's bumper, now clearly enraged, aggressively shot over to the right lane into the gap in traffic created by the panel truck's departure. The punk driver then accelerated to come up directly alongside Sainen's car.

In unison, the heads of the driver and passengers in the punk mobile swiveled to glare at Sainen as they rode next to him. Knowing what would piss them off the most, Sainen glanced over and smiled, giving them a little wave with his right hand.

The expression on the driver's face hardening, he swung his BMW over to within an inch of the right side of Sainen's Nissan GT-R, all four punks glaring maliciously.

Sainen, again baiting the morons, looked over and grinned, this time blowing the driver a little kiss. The look of astonishment on the punks' faces was priceless, Sainen thinking that this would make a great Mastercard commercial. He chuckled at the thought and this, of course, further enraged the car load of nuclear physicists next to him.

Anger clouds judgment and inhibits fluid movement, Sainen knew—something he had counted on more than once.

The BMW accelerated sharply forward and then abruptly careened to the left, bullying into the space directly in front of Sainen, barely avoiding a multicar collision in the heavy congestion. Then the driver slammed on his brakes, causing Sainen to have to do the same to avoid rear-ending them.

Sainen knew this drill: the punks would decrease speed and force him to follow behind them in traffic at a snail's pace while the backseat passengers glared menacingly out the rear window. Sainen grinned once again and, with his right hand, simulated a pistol with his first finger extended and his thumb up. They should just about be ready now.

Sainen saw where he would turn about three-quarters of a block up on the right and began preparing for a sudden right turn across the right lane and into the supermarket lot.

He jerked his wheel to the right and shot into the far right lane of traffic, spurring a cacophony of horns as he caused morning commuters to slam on their brakes, drop their cell phones, and dump their coffees. Immediately after entering the right lane, Sainen again made a hard, sudden right turn into the entrance to the supermarket parking lot he had chosen as his exit point. He then raced through the lot and disappeared behind the grocery store, pulling to a stop by the market's loading docks and adjacent to two large commercial refuse containers.

The driver of the BMW, now almost apoplectic, blasted into the right lane, sideswiping a Mini Cooper and causing chain-reaction rear-end collisions among the cars behind the Mini. Amid blaring horns and the angry shouts of drivers, the BMW scorched into the apartment complex lot adjacent to the supermarket and doughnutted around in a cloud of smoke and road dust. The Beemer shot across the apartment parking area toward the supermarket, jumping the curb and cutting across the grass divider that separated the residential complex from the supermarket property.

Sliding into the parking area on the side of the supermarket, the BMW driver spotted Sainen's parked GT-R out of his left peripheral vision. The Beemer swung into a skidding, smoking, wide arc left turn that would have made any drifting enthusiast proud. The Beemer then raced behind the store and screeched to a halt fifteen feet from where Sainen's Nissan was parked.

The four punks, arrogantly expecting to throw Sainen a beat-down, were still releasing their seatbelts when Sainen shot them.

As soon as the BMW had slid to a stop, Sainen had stepped out from between the two metal trash bins, pistol raised, and covered the short distance to their car in several quick strides, firing as he did so. He approached their vehicle from the front and angled to the left, coming close alongside the passenger windows.

Sainen initially put four rounds through the windshield, two each into the driver and front passenger respectively. Gliding down the side of the vehicle, Sainen then pumped four rounds into the rear passenger area, hitting the two rear passengers. Sainen's gait and maneuvering around the car, front to side, was smooth as silk. Smooth is fast.

After the initial string of eight rounds, Sainen stopped briefly, fired four more rounds into the Beemer's interior, one per occupant, and calmly walked back to his GT-R, changing out the mostly spent magazine in his Beretta PX4 Storm Compact for a fresh one.

Sainen drove back out into the morning traffic flow and continued on his way. It was three males and a female, he reflected, the left rear passenger's decidedly feminine facial features now partially splattered onto the Beemer's rear deck and interior door panel.

RADICAL

The clandestine meeting took place in a coffee shop near the editorial offices of *People's World* on South Halsted Street in Chicago, Illinois. A senior member of the staff from *People's World*, a publication affiliated with the Communist Party USA, along with a ranking official of the powerful AFL-CIO labor union were present. Ijinashi used the meeting to introduce and map out his concept and to solicit the buy-in of the organizations represented.

A similar meeting had taken place in Santa Cruz, California, with representatives of the Committees of Correspondence for Democracy and Socialism, an organization put on the map by Angela Davis of leftist political activism fame.

Yet another meeting had been orchestrated in Quebec, Canada, with ranking members of the Socialist Party of Canada and Parti Quebecois (PQ), the secessionist party of Quebec Province. Senior representatives of the American Federation of Government Employees and the American Federation of State, County and Municipal Employees secretly attended, as did officials of the Fraternal Order of Police National Lodge.

Other meetings with grassroots labor rights groups and citizen movements took place clandestinely in various locations throughout the United States and Canada.

Ijinashi mobilized animal rights groups such as ALF, ecological activist groups, Green Party activists, libertarian groups, Latino and American Indian rights groups, along with the contemporary remnants of the Black Panther Party, and a little-known current rendition of Students for a Democratic Society (SDS-Weathermen) of 1960s and '70s fame.

It was that little-known, modern-day version of the infamous Weathermen that Ijinashi had made his own.

Ijinashi solicited the compliance of centrist and constitutionalist militia groups in the Midwest (avoiding the virulent right-wing racist militias), and he sought and cultivated the backing of local politicians sympathetic to the cause.

Ijinashi even managed to recruit key players within the US executive branch of government, where the law prohibited organized union representation, and employee abuses were rampant.

It was a loosely affiliated network of groups, oftentimes with divergent agendas, who were now united against what was universally perceived as the greater evil.

Regardless of which US group one happened to be aligned with, all shared a deep hatred of what the elected government in the United States (and elsewhere) had become.

Seated in a rear booth in the trendy Chicago coffee shop, Ijinashi cleared his throat and addressed his small audience of activist luminaries. Sitting next to Ijinashi was a middle-aged Cuban gentleman, full name Osvaldo Prio Torrado, who was introduced by Ijinashi as simply Osvaldo.

"My name is Ijinashi, and I represent the outreach element of the New Weathermen. For simplicity's sake, you can just refer to them—us—as the Weathermen. You can look at us as political meteorologists, forecasters of which way the winds blow, to steal from the original group and Bob Dylan.

"Scumbag politicians in the Senate and House are raking in the money from insider trading while pounding their fists on the pulpit and preaching cutting the government's spending, all while cavalierly throwing the American worker—particularly the government and public safety worker—under the bus in the process.

"These same elected idiots were the ones who readily approved giving the government more and more power to intrude into the privacy of its citizenry, putting more drones into the air and more hidden surveillance on the Internet, all while voting down efforts to afford more oversight of Congress and its members' nefarious activities.

"Politicians want to regulate the size of soda you can buy but care little about whether you have a job, a roof over your head, or gas in your car. Somber-faced officials rattle on about the evils of firearms in the hands of the honest public, citing the gun crimes that plague the innocent and downtrodden in American cities, but suppress media coverage of the horrendous financial criminal acts that are being perpetrated behind the scenes by these very same elected officials, under color of law and hidden behind a wall of officialdom.

"These pontificating morons want the citizens to walk the line in an orderly fashion, all while these Washington vomit sacks are running amok behind the scenes, making money hand over fist.

"These are the insane officials who supported the arrest of ten-year-old kids for pointing their fingers like guns during recess at school but couldn't be troubled to prevent the destruction of the Arctic, America's domestic infrastructure, the family farm, the manufacturing sector, or the middle-class economy.

"We need to realize that these strutting, arrogant bozos are the fuel for the revolutionary fires and recognize that most decent citizens would not cross the street to piss on a congressman if he were on fire.

"At some point, the people have to decide to take action, to stand up for themselves. Let me quote from a nineteen sixty-five speech of Che Guevara that he made in Havana that beautifully addresses this point.

"'Then came the stage of guerrilla struggle. It developed in two distinct elements: the people, the still sleeping mass which it was necessary to mobilize; and its vanguard, the guerrillas, the motor force of the movement, the generator of revolutionary consciousness and militant enthusiasm. It was this vanguard, this catalyzing agent, which created the subjective conditions necessary for victory.'"

Ijinashi made a similar speech at countless meetings all over North America, motivating those who would mobilize a workers' army. An enraged populace was rising.

Select individuals within the Chinese People's Liberation Army and the People's Armed Police were recruited, as were decent and morally driven folk within the police and military apparatuses of Canada, the United Kingdom, Germany, and a slew of other countries.

Like-minded people within the Cuban government and those of multiple Latin American countries united in a common front. Ijinashi's burgeoning network spread to Africa, Japan, Southeast Asia, the Pacific, and the Middle East in a tsunami of political activism.

More and more people, previously not disposed toward radical politics or activism of any kind, were now taking up the cause. The more radically inclined were popularizing the chant, "All governments are pigs. All pigs must die."

From humble beginnings, the resistance was born. Its architect and de facto leader, Ijinashi Tamna, had transitioned from soldier to policeman to international criminal to, now, people's revolutionary.

As the Chicago meeting broke up, and the attendees were saying their goodbyes and leaving, Osvaldo leaned close to Ijinashi and said, "I have someone you need to meet. His name is Remy."

As Ijinashi walked down the city sidewalk following the meeting, his thoughts centered around his hope that a new day had dawned, for the people themselves were the only ones who could save the world from what awaited it at the hands of the greedy.

Hours later, Ijinashi sat alone in his Chicago hotel room, sipping on a soda from the room's fridge. He was bone-tired but knew that he must drive this global people's movement, as it was the only mechanism he could think of that might stand a chance of preventing the worldwide disaster he knew was coming. With enough energy and indignant rage driving them, the people could potentially stop the government and corporate conglomerates from pushing the world toward destruction. It was, he reasoned, very much a long shot but also very much worth trying. He needed to do it. He needed to atone.

If the world—the general populations—only knew of the great danger posed by the unholy technology that had been unveiled. If they only knew the consequences of the greed and power-driven quest to exploit that technology—a technology he himself had helped bring to light. The guilt was paralyzing, gut-wrenching. He was at fault. Some things, he thought, should just be beyond mankind's ability to know. Better—and much safer—that way.

If this people's movement did not show signs of having the desired effects, he would have to actually go to more extreme efforts. He might just have to take the damn sword and go public. He could, of course, always use the sword to run where nobody could follow. Well, almost nobody, anyway.

Ijinashi finished the soda pop and fell into bed, exhausted from the day's activities.

Although Ijinashi, along with Sainen Chinhung and Je-Ju Lee, had a hand in the proliferation of the technology and knowhow that would lead to truly horrendous events, they were not the first to be exposed to, or tamper with, such technologies. Not only had an elite cadre in Nazi Germany dabbled in the unholy science in the 1940s; others had done so thousands of years before them.

THE EVENT:
TO HELL IN A
HANDCART

SECURE CONFERENCE CALL, EIGHT HUNDRED FEET UNDERGROUND, AMERICAN SOUTHWEST, 2014

The shrill cry of the alarm and the spinning red lights mounted to the ceiling in the secure vaulted area of the subterranean command and control complex made it difficult to talk or concentrate one's thoughts. The US Air Force staff sergeant had to nearly shout to make herself heard above the din, the sophisticated electronic communications array at her disposal notwithstanding.

The flickering imagery field that the sergeant was looking at was dominated by the projected holographic images of a US Air Force general and an American civilian national security official, both grave-faced and haggard-looking. Standing to the rear and slightly off to the side were three other men, one a general in the uniform of the Chinese People's Liberation Army, one a representative of the Russian Federation's Federal Security Service, and the other a Canadian general assigned to the North American Aerospace Command. The seal of the Pentagon hung behind them.

The conversation was stilted and tense.

"General, our science staff is beside themselves, and the situation here in the center is just short of total panic. "

The sergeant paused to clear her throat.

"We—they believe we are on the cusp of some sort of time corruption event horizon, from what I can elicit from the panicked technologists. The chief scientist is ranting about how the—I apologize, sir, these are his words—idiots in Washington and the seats of world power did not take this seriously. He is nearly incoherent but says that the event is imminent and will be potentially catastrophic in nature on a global scale."

"Sergeant, what is that man behind you saying?"

"Sir, that is our chief scientist. Our chief scientist says that this could have been avoided had the establishment in Washington not been so power-hungry and greedy. He says you should pray and start doing so right now, sir. Like I said, he is, uh, a bit rattled and has been acting very odd, saying some things that are difficult for me to interpret. He has also been quoting that Asian leader of the New Weathermen leftist group."

A ponytailed, wildly gesticulating graying man in blue jeans behind the sergeant could be heard screaming, "Pigs, you are all fucking pigs! It is a government of the pig, by the pig, and for the pig. You should all burn in hell for your crimes! This shit is your fault, you...you fucking pigs!"

"General, sir, our science and technology division has been working on, uh, a special eyes-only reporting package. It is quite strange, sir, the contents, I mean."

"Apparently they are concerned over some, uh, inventory from another timeline, midcentury or so, that they speculate may have portalled through some temporal fluke associated with some of the current technological projects being worked on."

"What exactly are you—they—referring to, Sergeant?"

"Advanced ground combat vehicles, sir. Very advanced. I don't know...I am not technically savvy enough to provide a down-in-the-weeds explanation of how they would know this, General. But they, and our chief scientist, say that that is the case, sir."

"That isn't all, sir. There is more…more stuff that may have come, uh, over in this temporal anomaly."

"Go ahead, Sergeant."

"Well, they say that they have acquired, an advanced piece of military hardware that was a component of the ground combat vehicles I mentioned earlier. They called the combat vehicles AUCVs, sir—autonomous unmanned combat vehicle, I believe it is, General. And there was a bipedal robotic platform that is integral to the AUCV's equipment suite."

"Go on."

"The robotic, uh, thing, sir, was described to me as an artificially engineered bipedal biological entity fused with cybernetic technology. The, uh, main computer—the brain—is based on a reptilian brain, bioengineered and matrixed with a nano super computer. The machine's visual sensors are based on a spider's eyes and similarly arrayed on a triangular head. They called the thing… they said the model was called Araneus.

"General, our science guys know this because, well, they say that they acquired—temporarily acquired—this piece of inventory due to the temporal transversing that has been occurring around the globe, sir."

"The thing is armed, General. The science team that examined it say it was equipped with embedded nano cannons in both forearms. They fire a fleshette round, high velocity."

"Worse than that, General, are the people who have been displaced. They are very, very dangerous, sir."

As the general began to respond, the image flickered wildly as a faint shimmer filled the command and control center, obscuring the video image, which subsequently went dark.

On the surface, the hiker who had stopped to drink from his camelback was startled to see what he could only describe as the brief but vivid image of a giant bird flicker across the blue canvas of the sky. Had the hiker been knowledgeable in ornithology, he might have likened the apparition to the

Haast's eagle, or harpagornis, a six-foot-tall, thirty-pound bird of prey that lived during the Pleistocene historical epoch and should have perished from the skies of its native New Zealand—and from the planet—over five hundred years ago.

PENTAGON

The general and his Russian and Canadian colleagues were excitedly talking among themselves when the video teleconferencing unit began to flicker back to life, the link to the underground site reviving. When the screen returned to a functional state and image clarity was restored, the general and the others saw that the sergeant was still there and that she appeared to be wiping something from her mouth. That wasn't all, though.

Of much more concern to those viewing from the Pentagon was that her hair was a different color, a different length and style, and she had a visible birthmark—not there before—evident on the side of her neck just above her uniform collar. Oddly, her voice was different, too, as was her accent. How could that be?

The general stared uncomprehendingly at the image of the sergeant, swearing that her image was wavering and appearing like an old-fashioned photograph that had been "double exposed."

The men watching from the Pentagon were still wrestling with the incongruity of her appearance being different when the sergeant projectile vomited, a pinkish spray of vomitus rocketing from her mouth, vivid on the large-screen image at the Pentagon.

"B'lyad!" exclaimed the Russian. Staring at the chunky puke that was dripping down the front of the sergeant's uniform blouse, he asked, "Is that…is that a *fingertip*? A fucking *fingernail*?"

A half grin curled one side of the sergeant's mouth, bearing red-stained teeth.

Although some of the staff managed to escape from the underground site before it could be secured, the US military successfully sealed all accesses to the subterranean installation. They covered the entrances with concrete and established a mile-deep security buffer zone, its perimeter equipped with electrified fencing, razor wire, and multiple sensors.

Special teams were deployed to the desert to round up and "neutralize" those who had gotten out.

NEW YORK CITY

The upper three floors of the gleaming glass corporate tower simply evaporated, disappearing in a shimmering haze that lasted but a blink of an eye. Multiple elevators began their free falls, the screams of scores of passengers unheard as they plummeted to their deaths thirty stories below, the cables severed.

Panic and raw fear gripped those within FDNY and NYPD's emergency command centers and among the throngs of pedestrians out on the streets as word spread. Particularly horrified were those in adjacent skyscrapers who happened to bear witness to the event.

All hell had just broken loose.

SAUDI ARABIA

An entire portion of the oil refinery vanished. It was there one moment and gone the next. Terrified locals fell to their knees, believing it must be the will of Allah. Equally terrified Western oil workers at the refinery stared in disbelief at the empty space that had moments before been filled by an acre or more of structure. Momentarily frozen in horror, most of them perished seconds later in the chain of fiery explosions that raked through what was left of the stricken facility.

DEMOCRATIC PEOPLE'S REPUBLIC OF KOREA

The upper tier of the North Korean mobile midrange missile TEL (transporter-erector-launcher) dissolved into nothing.

The young military officer and his noncommissioned assistant stood paralyzed in abject fear, having witnessed something that their rational minds told them could not occur.

One moment they were doing a function test of the TEL, running it up and down to ensure it was operating properly, and the next moment they were looking at only half a TEL assembly, the rest having dematerialized in front of them—the part with the nuclear warhead.

The cigarette fell from the noncom's mouth as the midrange nuclear-tipped missile of their companion mobile launch vehicle, situated a few meters away, leapt from its rails into the morning sky.

His attention then drawn to the skies west of him, the sergeant stood petrified as he watched the trails of midrange missiles from his unit's other mobile batteries arc upward and disappear into the cloudbank.

This all occurred as his lieutenant frantically attempted to punch in the numbers to call his superiors on their field phone, hoping to relate what had just occurred without sounding like a raving lunatic.

Beginning with terrified soldiers and their commanders in the field, the alarm quickly spread to Kim Jong-un's national command echelons, panic and fear ultimately gripping the young Korean dictator, who—believing the DPRK to be under attack by some unknown American technology—gave the fire order to his strategic rocket forces.

Equally terrified and appalled soldiers, sailors, and airmen in Japan, South Korea, Australia, and the United States—beads of sweat on their brows—reluctantly reacted as their respective training had conditioned them to do. Simultaneously, flabbergasted elements of the Chinese People's Liberation Army struggled with what their equipment was telling them as they, too, in a haze of adrenalin and terror, began reacting as they had been trained.

MOSCOW, RUSSIA

His pulse quickened as the Russian president saw the stricken expression on the face of his top national security advisor as the wheezing, flush-faced man burst into the room, unceremoniously interrupting Mr. Putin's conference call.

WASHINGTON, DC

The president of the United States stood speechless as the national security advisor tried to encapsulate the totality of the situation in a breathless, rushed dialogue.

RIDGEWAY, WISCONSIN

The dairy farmer had never heard his cows sound so terrified, their bawling bringing him outside at a run to see what the hell was scaring them so thoroughly. Winded after running full tilt across the large expanse of the rear yard, he stumbled in midstride, unable to believe what his eyes told him was crouched a few yards from the northwest corner of the dairy barn.

Had Mr. Groenke been a trained paleontologist, he would have recognized the creature as velociraptor, not that that recognition would have in any way changed the equation in his favor.

The flashlight slipped from his sweaty hand as the agile and speedy prehistoric beast shot across the distance in a blur, followed by several others who had initially been out of sight around the corner of the barn. The oversized talons—three to a limb and designed to rip flesh—ended the mental confusion that had stricken the ill-fated Mr. Groenke, the beginnings of his terrified shriek ending in a subdued gurgling as the razor claws of the lead reptile tore into his torso like hot knives through butter.

BUENOS AIRES, ARGENTINA

Ninety-five-year-old Hans Kammler put the phone back down on the nightstand next to his bed, having listened as his old friend in the Argentine national intelligence service—the Secretaria de Inteligencia—brought him up to speed on some disturbing current events.

Kammler, who more than half a century ago had been SS Obergruppen-fuhrer Kammler, was a doctor of engineering who had held a position of incredible power within Nazi Germany's Schutzstaffel, directly underneath Himmler in the SS hierarchy.

Having disappeared without a trace in April 1945, Dr. Hans Friedrich Karl Franz Kammler had been a resident of Argentina for decades, living in secrecy.

Hans leaned back against the headboard and thought for a moment about what his friend had related to him. He reached over to the nightstand and pulled a cigarette from the top drawer and lit it up, slowly drawing the smoke into his lungs as he mulled over his recent phone conversation.

He always suspected that "The Bell" and the associated technology would come back to haunt mankind at some point, the unexpected appearance of the device in Kecksburg, Pennsylvania, on December 9, 1965, being the least of the ramifications.

The global instances of time-space corruption and random time storm anomalies that his Argentine intelligence friend had described were no surprise to Dr. Kammler. Having been in charge of the Third Reich's most exotic military special projects, he found that not much surprised him, especially when it came to science and technology.

Idiots, he thought, as he stubbed out the Parliament Light, fluffed his pillow, and turned out the light.

PORT AU PRINCE, HAITI

The voodoo priest—Houngan—was staggered by what he saw, unable to reconcile what his physical senses were telling him with what his mind said was possible. Jean-Paul Manon stopped dead in the middle of the ceremony, the rhythmically gyrating circle of white-clad women stopping in their tracks, all staring disbelievingly at the impossible image before them.

The shimmering orb floating in the air in front of them was a fuzzy purple color with a pink tinge, its shape fluctuating and its edges ill-defined.

That wasn't what shocked those who were present, however. It was the trembling, wide-eyed figure clenching a vintage flintlock rifle who had popped into existence in the midst of the flickering orb, simultaneously with the orb's appearance.

The figure, a clearly frightened white man, was wearing what appeared to be a French military uniform from the 1700s.

Head swiveling from side to side in rapid, jerky movements, vomit spewing from his mouth and down his chest, the sweat-drenched French-man cocked the rifle and, in one fluid movement, brought it to bear and fired. The huge lead ball slammed into the chest of the woman closest to the figure, the round blowing out a chunk of her back in a spray of blood as it exited, dropping her lifeless body straight down to the ground as if she had been switched off.

The French soldier began swinging the spent, smoking rifle side to side, trying to sweep the remaining voodoo women from his path, screaming something unintelligible in French before he suddenly dropped the long gun and grabbed for the flintlock pistol in his belt. In an instant, before he could reach the ancient pistol, and just as he had appeared, he "blinked" out. Gone.

The stunned crowd of worshippers, some praying, some crying, stared at the slumped figure of their colleague on the ground, an ugly crimson blotch staining her white blouse.

SUMMITVILLE, INDIANA

The sleepy hamlet of Summitville, Indiana, was as serene a Midwestern town as one could ever hope to find, nestled among the cornfields of central Indiana. The most talented of Hollywood movie directors could not have conjured up the horror that visited Summitville early one morning, just as people were getting out and about, beginning their days.

In fact, few people outside of DARPA and the select scientific research and development elements of the armed forces whose job was to design the war machines of the future would have dreamt of such horrific things.

The low-slung, smooth-surfaced, slope-sided vehicles were nearly featureless topside, except for some flush, geometric panels of slightly different shade from the otherwise drab-colored machines. And, of course, for the wicked-looking apparatus mounted on top that sort of looked like a cannon.

The machines were completely autonomous, intelligent ground combat vehicles that should not have rolled over the earth for decades to come. While the concept of autonomous unmanned combat vehicles—AUCVs— was certainly around in the early twenty-first century, super-intelligent, independently operating, multi-mission versions would not become routine components of military arsenals until midcentury and later.

Nobody saw the shimmering disturbance in the night out in the fields north of town. The super-intelligent robotic fighting machines, designed to move quickly and efficiently over almost any terrain, popped into existence among the shimmer of the time storm that briefly visited Madison County, Indiana, in the early morning darkness. They quickly assembled and shot off across the agricultural fields as effortlessly as water bugs across the surface of a pond.

Snatched out of time and separated from their big data sources and satellite support, the machines went immediately into doomsday self-defense mode, switching all of their onboard supercomputing power to the mission of self-protection.

The machines moved in a pod, working in unison similar to how wolves hunt in the wild, connected electronically and using their combined sensory and computing power to interactively survey and analyze their environment for threats. Unfortunately, the effects of the time storm had caused issues with the artificial intelligence.

Officer Bill Hill of the Summitville Police Department, actually a town marshal's office consisting of three full-time and five reserve officers, was winding down the last hour or so of his graveyard shift.

With no reserve officer riding with him this night, Officer Hill was the sole Summitville PD unit on duty, patrolling the still-vacant streets of the small town that was just beginning to awaken to a new day. Other than an occasional county sheriff's unit or state trooper randomly passing through town on the main drag, one regular officer was all that was out in the little town at any given time. Summitville wasn't a dangerous place.

As the pod of machines neared the town limits and sensed the signatures of living beings and other machines, they moved immediately into an assault posture, weapons hot. The little squadron swept to the east and then back west, approaching the target environment from out of the rising sun.

Officer Hill rounded the corner of Main and 5th Street, and the rays of the brightly shining morning sun assaulted his vision, causing Bill to reach to the console and retrieve his sunglasses.

When Bill looked back up, he thought he saw an undefined shape disappear behind the houses on the outskirts of town, briefly visible in the distance ahead of him down 5th Street, which ran east and west in the town's grid system. Officer Hill couldn't be sure, but he thought that the object might have been in the farm field that lay on the east side of Monroe Street, the town's easternmost street within the corporate limits before the county began.

Believing what he saw was possibly a car driving through the farmer's field, Bill sped up to check; maybe it was a drunk left over from the night before or a marauding teenager joy riding.

Arriving at the T-intersection of 5th and Monroe, Officer Hill swung a right onto Monroe and headed southbound toward where he had lost sight of the object. Nothing. Monroe Street was vacant for as far as he could see ahead, and there was nothing in the field along the eastern city limit.

Whatever it had been, it had to have gone into the residential neighborhood along the west side of Monroe. It was then that Bill saw the section of barbed wire fencing that was crushed down into the grass where a vehicle had obviously crashed through.

Bill sped up again, determined to catch the vehicle, especially if it was a drunk trying to make it home. Bill turned immediately right down 4th Street, slowing for each subsequent intersection he came to, looking both directions down the intersecting streets, hoping to catch sight of what he now believed was likely a fleeing drunk.

Had Bill continued south along Monroe, he would have seen that there were other sections of the fence line similarly damaged.

Bill grabbed his mic and called county dispatch, the central 911 emergency communications center located fifteen miles away in the county seat of Anderson, advising the dispatcher that he was attempting to catch up to a suspicious vehicle, providing his coordinates and direction of travel.

When he unkeyed the mic, he was surprised that there was no response from dispatch. It was then that Officer Hill noticed that there was no traffic on any of the police and fire channels his scanning radio monitored. It was all dead air.

Bill had no way of knowing that all communications in Summitville, including cellular, were now being jammed by the sophisticated electronic warfare suites onboard the AUCVs.

As Hill slowed for the Jackson Street intersection, his peripheral vision caught movement to his left. It was a fleeting shadow that was gone in an instant. Now somewhat alarmed but unaware of the true danger he was in, Officer Hill stomped the brakes and swung the squad car hard to the left, careening onto Jackson and accelerating hard to the next intersection, where he thought he had seen whatever the hell it was he saw…a car, he surmised.

Braking hard and then quickly releasing as he rocketed through the right turn to go back westbound, now on Washington Street, Bill only briefly registered a fleeting blur of movement a block ahead. Now Bill was starting to sweat, wondering what in the hell he was chasing; whatever it was, it was damn fast and, oddly, he had yet to hear any engine noise or the sound of tires screeching on the pavement.

Bill tried the radio again, to no avail, then dropped the mic on the seat and put his right hand back up on the wheel as he accelerated west down Washington toward where he thought he had seen the elusive shadow shoot across the roadway.

It was just about as gorgeous a morning as you could ask for, Roy Hudlin thought as he rode his John Deere lawn tractor out of the garage, off the driveway, and onto the grass of his side yard, still glistening from the night's dew. He loved this time of day, the sky turning a brilliant blue and the rays of the morning sun warming his face. He loved the smell of mown grass; there was nothing better.

Roy had just reached down to engage the mower blades when he saw the ominous shape stop in the street in front of his ranch-style home in the quiet residential neighborhood on the northeast side of Summitville. For a second Roy thought it must be an army vehicle—that the National Guard was passing through town or something. That was Roy's last thought, for in that instant the automatic cannon on top of the AUCV swung sharply in his direction and let loose a short burst of "smart" hypersonic explosive rounds. Roy and his John Deere were immediately converted into a spray of flying parts. Pieces of Roy, the lawn tractor, and chunks of turf pelted the side of the Hudlin residence, painting the yellow siding with splotches of red where body parts struck and slid down the wall.

Roy's wife of forty years came to the front window to see what had happened, fearing that there had been some sort of accident with the mower. She arrived in time to see the mower blade helicoptering through the air just before her vision focused on the red splatter that coated the outside surface of the windowpane. Her scream never made it out of her throat, as the second burst from the AUCV's electric cannon chewed her in half, spreading her body parts across the living room carpet and up the far wall.

The high-tech rounds that punched through the far interior living room wall also found Roy's thirty-six-year-old daughter just as she was replacing the soap in the dish, in the middle of her morning shower on the second day of her visit with her parents. Her head and torso exploded, briefly coloring the shower wall red and spackling it with bits of bone and flesh before the shower spray washed it away and down the drain, the bigger pieces catching and bunching on the grate.

Roger Foudray had just turned the corner next to the Hudlin residence, barely having time to hit his brakes in alarm before the hulking form blocking the road in front of him swung its weapon system to him and fired, completely obliterating Roger's tow truck, killing him instantly. Roger's black lab, Elroy, sitting on the passenger side of the bench seat, died with his master.

To the electronic brain of the AUCVs, the slab-sided garbage truck looked like another ground combat vehicle, complete with multiple biological heat sources outside the hull, which the AUCV interpreted as infantry.

The church bus with Girl Scout Troop 16 on board, which was behind the refuse truck, manifested a heat signature that the AUCV read as a troop carrier.

Three of the AUCVs skittered across the small neighborhood park's expanse of lawn, smashing through the playground equipment as they arrayed themselves to engage the garbage truck and the church bus, which were now just pulling up to the intersection of Hermosa and Nutley, adjacent to the park.

Although huge monsters of machines, the AUCVs were agile and their advanced propulsion technology gave them an almost water-bug-like mobility across most surfaces.

Danny Day and Mike Brewer were hanging off the rear of the truck, serving as the can handlers, dumping the residential garbage cans into the rear of the vehicle, where the contents were then hydraulically compressed. Joey Donahue was riding in the cab's passenger seat, and Mark Mason was driving the truck.

Joey and Mike saw the AUCVs first, staring blankly, not registering what they were looking at but initially thinking that some sort of industrial containers had been deposited on the park property. Then they saw the wrecked playground equipment and realized something was very wrong.

Several of the Girl Scouts were pointing excitedly at the AUCVs, which drew the attention of Jenny O'Neil, the church bus driver and assistant scout leader for Troop 16. Jenny had served in the Army National Guard but did not recognize the vehicles as anything she had encountered during her military service.

The vehicles appeared to Jenny to definitely be military, and the apparatus mounted on top she was pretty sure was a weapons system—likely an automatic cannon. Their presence this morning in Summitville, Indiana, sitting in Mitchell Park, was incongruous. Jenny's gut told her that this was not good. When she saw the twisted and mangled playground equipment strewn behind the strange, squat vehicles, her stomach turned.

Officer Hill heard the screams and the tearing of metal through his open driver-side window. He thought he heard an explosion too. Fifteen years of small-town law enforcement would not prepare him for the carnage he would shortly lay eyes upon.

Madison County Sheriff's Department Patrol Deputy Chuck Bell and Indiana State Police Trooper Jason Kennedy were parked in a manner known in police jargon as "sixty-nine," their squad cars pulled adjacent to each other, facing opposite directions so that their drivers' windows were aligned. They were sitting in the gravel driveway of an old abandoned farm property, its grain elevator the only remaining structure.

The two cops often met there to shoot the shit when they were working this area on night shift. Both had recently noticed that their radios and cell phones had gone dead, causing them concern, as this complete interruption of both radio and cellular comms had not occurred before. It was strange—damn strange.

Being only about a mile from Summitville, they elected to head over there to see if they could run down the on-duty SPD patrolman; he could let them in the police station to call their respective dispatch centers on the land line to see what the hell was up with communications. A solar flare, maybe. Some sort of cyber attack?

Now that the sun was up, both officers would be finishing their tours soon and were anxious to resolve the commo problems so they could go home.

One behind the other, the officers headed toward Summitville at a high rate of speed along County Road 200 East.

AUCVs utilized small, "brilliant" unmanned aerial vehicles—known to most as UAVs—that incorporated the best nano technologies available in the midtwenty-first century.

These little birds were launched from portals in the hulls of the AUCVs and established what amounted to a combat air patrol umbrella over the AUCV's area of operations. The advanced and stealthy UAVs provided aerial surveillance and early warning, some electronic warfare features, and over-the-horizon fire control for the AUCV's weapons suite.

The rapid approach of MCSD Deputy Bell and ISP Trooper Kennedy was detected and analyzed before the police units had gone thirty feet. Their direction of travel toward the AUCVs' AO made them a threat.

As Bill rolled behind the huge hedge that bordered the rear yard of a residence and stopped his squad car in the narrow alleyway, he could hear what sounded like flames, detecting little pops here and there, as if something was on fire. Exiting his car and moving to where he could see better, Glock nine-millimeter in hand, the officer saw the three plumes of black smoke billowing into the blue of the morning sky.

Moving carefully through the backyards of the residences so he could get a view of Mitchell Park and the public streets, Officer Hill stopped in his tracks as his view fell upon a scene from hell. Scattered before him in the street were the burning hulks of three vehicles.

What remained of a small bus was surrounded by the smoking, dismembered remains of what Hill soon realized had been Girl Scout Troop 16, likely on their way to camp. Fighting back the vomit that was rising in his throat, Hill fought through the paralysis of shock and moved closer to the nearest house for cover, creeping forward to allow himself to peek around the corner for a better view. That was a mistake.

In the yard of the yellow-sided house he was pressed against, Bill saw what he could only describe as a gut pile, mixed with what appeared to be the mangled remains of a green John Deere lawn tractor.

In a macabre stripe across the lawn, a trail consisting of red chunks of human flesh and lawn mower parts led to and then up the front side of the house, which looked like it had been sprayed with a red slurry of blood and diced meat from a garden hose. Flies were buzzing around the gut pile and along the entire expanse of the grotesque swath.

Leaning further out, Bill could see that one window appeared to have been blow out, and the siding was pockmarked around the window frame with closely spaced holes—bullet holes, it appeared.

Still fighting back the vomit, Bill began to more closely survey what lay in front of him. On the street, he recognized the shattered hulk of the B&M Refuse Company garbage truck, its side and cab literally honeycombed with ragged holes, tires blown out, flames flickering from the engine compartment and ruptured gas tanks.

He couldn't tell about the occupants of the truck's cab, as it had been melted down and twisted by the fire, but he could see the broken bodies of two men spread in what he could only describe as broad brushstrokes of gore on the side of the truck near the rear footing areas, where they would have likely been standing.

One of the men—whoever had been standing on the far side of the truck's rear—was piled in a fly-covered heap about a yard from the rear bumper. Tattered parts of the overalls they had been wearing were still smoking.

Temporarily distracted by a brief buzzing sound—like electricity—and a slight tingling of the hairs on his arms, Officer Hill glanced around and behind, checking his "six" for threats. Seeing nothing, he stood frozen for a second, listening to his environment. Nothing. Reluctantly, he returned his eyes to the sickening mess by the park.

He fought doing so but, knowing he had to, he turned his gaze to the church bus—the bus from the First United Methodist Church that he knew had been taking Girl Scout Troop 16 to their spring lake adventure, the first of several camps the girls would do during the spring and summer seasons.

He knew this because the girls had been talking of nothing else during their visit to the police department last evening, excitedly chattering about today's adventure. Tears running down his face, Bill forced himself to survey the scene; it was his duty to understand what had happened as best he could.

His mind resisting what it had to focus on, his first impression was that all of the tires were flat, ragged holes visible here and there in what remained of the side-by-side tires, with shreds of rubber dangling to the road surface. The two metal steps at the bus passenger door were twisted and dented inward. The drive shaft was drooping to the pavement, apparently partially blown in half.

All of the side windows were blow out with much of the metal between them twisted and bent. The side of the bus—the entire side—appeared to have been hit with a giant shotgun blast. There were holes everywhere, covering most of the metal surfaces.

Flames were barely visible, licking upward from the engine compartment and ignited fuel, the hood twisted and buckled from the heat of the fire that had consumed most of the front end of the vehicle. A portion of the bus roof was raggedly flayed back as if opened by a giant manual can opener. A trickle of smoke continued to drift upward, joining the larger plume emanating from the garbage truck.

Hill's eyes now descended to the pavement just aft of the rear emergency door of the little bus. There, on the street, was strewn what he could only guess were eight bodies, but it was hard to tell. The pavement was dug up, as if a chorus line of giant jackhammers had dredged ragged ruts through the road surface. The street's surface glistened with what appeared to be oil stains, but Bill knew that wasn't what it was, the clouds of flies swirling about offering grim testimony to what lay there.

Smoking bits of green and white cloth mixed with a horrific jumble of hair, limbs at obscene angles, eviscerated torsos, distorted faces, shoes, even bits of cloth Scouting badges were discernable to Hill's eye. Unable to resist it any longer, Bill turned and wretched onto the grass at his feet.

Jenny, the assistant troop leader, must have tried to usher them out the emergency exit, Bill surmised, a last-ditch attempt to escape the horror that visited them that morning.

Bill thought of how Jenny's hair had smelled the night before while he was talking to her at the scouts' career day event.

Funny how the mind works under stress, when presented with unspeakable horror.

It was then that it struck him, as his eyes scanned the array of death that lay on the pavement at the rear of the bus. The bodies—they were all small. Jenny's larger frame was not evident among the mutilated corpses that were strewn across the blacktop. Not wanting to create any sense of false hope within himself, Bill looked harder, moving his eyes slowly back and forth horizontally across the scene. No, he did not see anything that he could identify as an adult's body. Maybe she did not make it out of the bus.

He knew he had to check. The last thing he wanted to do was to approach any closer to the carnage, but he knew it would be an error not to be sure. He had to go look.

Bill noticed that his hand holding his service weapon was trembling and that his knees were wobbly as well. He steeled himself, took a deep breath or two, wiped the spittle and remnants of puke from his lips with his left hand, and pushed himself out from the corner of the house and across the front yard toward the street.

As he moved out onto the front lawn, Bill then noticed Foudray's tow truck sitting in a shattered heap near the intersection. Black smoke spiraled up from the crushed hood of the old wrecker, the source of the third smoke plume he had seen earlier.

The cab was almost nonexistent, nothing but a twisted mass of metal and broken glass; the partially melted yellow light bar that had once sat on top of the cab now hung limply down, distorted by the heat of the gasoline-fed fire that had engulfed the majority of the truck. A faint hissing noise was evident, and Bill could smell the burning of rubber. He could only surmise that Roger and his dog had perished.

Crossing the street now, carefully scanning back and forth with his eyes, Glock at the low ready position, Bill saw from the corner of his eye as he passed Foudray's smoldering truck what he guessed was a portion of Roger's skull lying on the rear deck, a tuft of blond hair evident, apparently blown out the rear window. No time to dwell on that now. Bill moved at a quickened pace in a semi-crouch across the pavement toward the rear of the bus.

He dropped into a deep-knee crouched position at the sound of an explosion in the distance. He guessed it came from the area of the city utility shop, but he couldn't be sure; it could have been Joe's Diner or Mac's Union 76 filling station.

The huge fireball and oily black smoke that Bill saw rising off to the south told him it was Mac's gas station.

Oh, God, the fire department—the Summitville Volunteer Fire Department. They will be responding, lights flashing and sirens blaring, right into whatever the hell is doing this. Then it struck Bill: *Why had they not responded here? The smoke plumes and the noise—surely someone would have noticed and called it in?* Various scenarios raced through Bill's mind, but he pushed them aside and, rising from his low crouch, moved toward the church bus. He did not have time to spare, he reckoned.

The bile rose in Bill's throat again as he stepped past the grisly potpourri heaped and splattered across both lanes of the street, stumbling and almost falling as his boot caught on a piece of asphalt sticking up from what he assumed was a bullet crater. Catching his balance, Bill moved all the way up to the rear of the burning bus, scanning bodies while trying to scan 360 for his own safety. No Jenny.

A quick glance inside the bus told the graphic story of what happened to the girls trapped inside. Bill estimated that maybe two had not made it out, their remains evident in the aisle that ran down the center of the bus interior between the seat rows. The bus was filled with swarms of flies and smelled of burning flesh, seat vinyl, rubber, and gasoline. The inside of the bus was filled with bits and pieces of the foam padding material that once filled the seat cushions. Some of those pieces were red-tinged.

Bill blinked then turned on his heel and headed back toward the side of the street, making for the park, where trees and foliage would afford him some cover.

On his way, he glanced into what was still left of the driver's area of the bus to see if maybe Jenny had died up there and the girls had tried to escape out the back on their own. He could see no indication of human remains and continued toward Mitchell Park.

Although he knew it was probably useless, Bill reached up to the mic attached to his uniform shoulder and tried to raise dispatch again. Nothing but dead air.

At that instant, three blocks away, a patrolling AUCV stopped momentarily, its artificial brain recognizing the brief burst of electromagnetic energy generated from Bill's walkie-talkie when he keyed up to call dispatch. The armored-metal and high-strength synthetic monster skittered out of the side street and headed toward the source of the signal it had detected.

Bill noticed, to his horror, as he ran to the rear of the park through the debris field that had once been playground equipment, that all of the houses in the surrounding neighborhood showed signs of ballistic impact. All of them.

The siding of every house he looked at bore huge patterns of holes as if hit by giant shotgun blasts. That was why nobody called the fire department—there was no one to make the call and likely no firemen to respond. Anyone left alive would have had trouble calling anyway, given the communications failure.

Bill ran toward the alley where he had parked his police car, again detecting a slight electrical buzzing sound and a tingling of his arm hair. Glancing around as he ran, he saw nothing that constituted a threat. As Bill rounded the corner of the yellow-sided house with the destroyed lawn tractor in front, he glimpsed a blur of something between the houses adjacent to the yellow one. He knew that could not be anything good, so he broke into a full sprint toward his car.

Arriving at his police unit, Bill quickly checked both ways down the alley then jumped in. Bill started the vehicle up and dropped it in gear, moved forward, and then carefully nudged it out into the street from the alleyway, looking back and forth for any sign of danger. Seeing nothing, he shot out into the roadway and headed toward the police station at the town hall building.

Bill did not see the AUCV that careened around the corner next to the park, seeking the source of the electromagnetic signal it had detected a few minutes earlier. The AUCV stopped and remained motionless, waiting like the predator it was for the next telltale sign of prey.

Bill zipped down several back streets and, to his absolute horror, saw off to his right about a block away, across the open expanse of the Miller Elementary School ball fields, what appeared to be a military vehicle. It was about twice the size of the army's Bradley fighting vehicle, something Bill was familiar with from his own days of military service in the reserves. There was no resemblance to anything Bill was familiar with in the United States arsenal, however. What he saw was almost featureless, low-slung, drab, with an obvious cannon mounted on top. He noticed that the vehicle had no visible wheels or tracks but seemed to hover just above the ground surface. Air cushion, maybe? It was hard to tell from that distance.

Bill had, against his best judgment, slowed his car and was still staring at the strange combat vehicle when his eyes detected movement to the immediate south. He quickly identified that movement as another of the combat vehicles—and then another. *Holy crap, how many of them are there?*

Common sense and reason now filtering back through Bill's curiosity and fascination with the strange combat vehicles, he hit the gas and headed on toward the town hall, hoping the things had not noticed him. They had but were presently occupied with hosing down one of the town's three fire engines with high-velocity cannon fire.

Someone must have gotten a call in to the personal number of one of the volunteer firefighters, as the little department had, indeed, bravely responded to the turmoil that had engulfed the small rural municipality. Those who had shown up to answer the call of duty had died almost immediately upon exiting the firehouse in their trucks, confronted by two of the AUCVs that were positioned in the street just yards from the overhead bay doors of the firehouse.

One of the men whose body lay among the twisted remains of the lead engine, mulched by the cannon fire, was William "Wil" Forry, Summitville's fire chief of twenty-one years.

Officer Hill floored the Crown Vic police unit and, disregarding stop signs, headed toward the alleyway that ran behind the town hall, which was where the rear door to the police department was located, next to a small, fenced parking area for the cops.

Bill wheeled the big Ford into the alley and headed toward the town hall building a half block in front of him. He had to coast the last couple of yards as his engine cut out suddenly, as did all the vehicle's electrical power. The thought that maybe those odd combat vehicles were equipped with some sort of electromagnetic pulse weapon briefly flitted through his consciousness, but Bill had no time to dwell on that sort of crap. He needed to get his ass inside now. *Are those things manned? Who do they belong to?* Bill's mind quaked with uncertainty and anxiety.

Bill jumped out the driver-side door, leaving it hanging open, and bounded up to the heavy metal pedestrian door that gave access to the rear of the police department. Fumbling with the keys, he managed to insert the right one into the door and rush inside, slamming the door secure behind him.

For whatever reason—software glitch, deleterious effects of the time portalling, hand of God—the overhead UAV net only now decided that Officer Hill's patrol car was interesting and decided to engage. This was great news for Officer Hill, although he had no idea there were aerial vehicles deployed above his town.

Had the UAV net decided earlier to focus on Hill's car, he would have been blasted from existence early on. As it was, Hill managed to pull his car up to the rear of the police department and just make it inside before a hail of projectiles from multiple-air bursting munitions shredded the Crown Vic like a Kleenex.

Hill startled at the horrendous noise made by the destruction of his police car, loud even inside the building. Running to the front of the tiny police office suite, he could see over the old fashioned front desk and outside onto Main Street through the front door glass.

He arrived at the back of the glassed-in front desk in the police station lobby just in time to see a AUCV fire off some sort of missile from somewhere on its hull; a flash and a streak of light arcing skyward was all that he saw, but that was enough. It was now pretty clear to Officer Hill that the entire town of Summitville—and maybe the whole country—was a combat zone and that he was pretty much alone when it came to doing anything about it. How or why this situation existed, he had no clue.

AUCVs were excellent multi-taskers, as Officer Hill was finding out. Simultaneous to the missile launch, the cannon on top of the hull swiveled smoothly toward the front door of the police station and fired a short burst, having detected Hill inside the structure.

Upon seeing the AUCV fire the missile, and milliseconds before the cannon fire, Hill had thrown himself to the left and down to the floor behind the department's refrigerator, as that was all he was able to do in the time he figured he had, which was nearly none.

It wasn't the flimsy metal of the refrigerator that saved him. Oddly enough, it was Troop 16 of the Girl Scouts of America.

The evening before, the Girl Scouts had attended a career day at the town hall, and the old bathtub in the restroom—whose door was located next to where the refrigerator stood—was filled with ice to keep the sodas cold for the kids' event.

This morning, the tub was still filled up with an icy slurry, and it was that cold tub full of ice water that Hill rolled next to after diving past the refrigerator. The icy mix masked Hill's thermal signature, and the cannon's rounds instead zeroed in on the most prominent heat source in the little station, which was the electric motor of the departmental refrigerator.

SAINEN'S NISSAN GT-R, PARKING LOT IN THE DAAN DISTRICT, TAIPEI

Sainen leaned against the door of his sleek street machine with the smart phone pressed to his right ear. He was casually inspecting the emerald-studded ring that adorned his free hand. This was the second phone conversation he had had with Je-Ju Lee in recent times.

He knew what she wanted to talk about.

"This labor-driven people's revolution that Ijinashi is spearheading…it is, I think, his shot at both some semblance of atonement as well as an attempt at possibly mitigating the damage to our existence—the very planet's existence—that he feels responsible for. He feels like he was part of the corruption that spiraled out of control, that the terrible things happening to people all over the world are partially his fault and his responsibility to try to make right."

"Sainen, we have made a fortune—several fortunes—from this knowledge, from this unholy technology from the past. We live lives that most couldn't conceptualize. If we want to continue thriving as we have become accustomed to, and have a world to live in, we must consider that we have to take action. Direct action. Not necessarily locked hand in hand with Iji-nashi but something to help put this evil genie back in the bottle and maybe minimalize its future abuse."

"We could, of course, simply use our swords to leave, but there is no guarantee that where—when—we wind up won't also be corrupted…maybe worse."

"This isn't just idle worry. Based on conversations I have had with some very intelligent people, the space-time aberrations that have been manifesting all over the planet may be indications that there has been serious disruption done to the entire fabric of space-time—that maybe, just maybe, the multiverse has been hosed beyond repair. This is stuff that would make Einstein's head swim."

"We should, first and foremost, consider that we have a trail of people who could easily orchestrate our undoing. People in Tokyo, Seoul and at AVI come to mind. More in Taipei and Manila. People in McLean, Virginia, in the US.

"We should clean things up."

"Yes, Je-Ju, you are correct, and I don't dispute a single word you have uttered. This situation is as you have described it."

"We started a widespread and bloody Asian street gang war pitting the Chinese, Japanese, and Koreans against each other. This little gang shoot 'em up has claimed many lives."

"We did this as a calculated means of obscuring our hand in killing a handful of individuals whose knowledge could have jeopardized our mercenary endeavors—our manipulation of the sword technology and our alignment with AVI and others, in and out of government, who had a hand in causing the calamities that are sweeping the globe."

"We allowed technicians and those advanced research projects guys—both government and corporate—as well as elements of organized crime, Yakuza, and companies that they influence to examine, test, and image the technology of our swords. Then there is AVI; we gave them the same opportunities to exploit the sword technology. We were instrumental in coopting United States senators and members of their House of Representatives—

congressmen—so that we could further profit from that technology and the scientific leap forward its examination afforded."

"Yes, Je-Ju, you are correct. We are certainly responsible for exposing the technology so that the scientific—quantum—principles it employs became apparent to governments, segments of the private sector, and, of course, elements of international organized crime. That is true. And those people were quick to put that new knowledge together with secret knowledge of the past—what the Nazis did—and exploit it."

"The subsequent experimentation with the technology, coupled with a growing understanding of the principles involved, permitted those with sufficient financial backing to execute a couple of trans-dimensional—temporal—trips. Those test 'flights,' for lack of a better term, allowed those people to fully grasp this new capability."

"Warfare, of course, was the driving factor among the governmental elements. Profit was the underlying motivator for the others. Us, for example."

"Not to be left out of the conversation is the acquisition of that vehicle… that clam-shell-shaped temporal vessel that they were able to get and then exploit via the technological advances we made possible. Added to what they already had available to them, they were able to advance their capabilities by ten thousand fold—maybe more. That clam-shell 'saucer' is, by the way, one and the same as those described in Jopon legend. You know, the ones Ijinashi said he once saw."

"This newfound understanding led, of course, to the temporal anomalies currently plaguing the planet."

"Some who have died are innocent bystanders. Others who have suffered were just plain, ordinary people trying to live their lives. These anomalies that are threatening the very fabric of reality are more than just partially our doing. They are directly attributable either to our actions or to the actions of those we enabled with the technology. If found out and properly connected to this matrix of events, we stand to do the rest of our lives in prison—or worse. And I doubt Ijinashi disclosed much about his sword. I just doubt that he did. His guilt stems from giving us—me—the knowledge."

"I like this world, Je-Ju. I like this time. I like my lifestyle, my freedom. I do not wish to see it all destroyed. Do not mistake that as altruism. I simply like it here and enjoy the life I have established here in this…this timeline."

"Make no mistake, if the situation degenerates to the point where I see it as prudent to unass, I will do so without hesitation. Along those lines, I suggest you make plans for your own survival. Until that point, I agree that we should begin the process of securing ourselves. Beyond that—actually simultaneously—we can do something to stem the tide in regard to the growing utilization of the technology."

"We will do this ourselves. Just us. No one from the Yakusa, no one from any of the Tongs or Triads, and no one from any of the Korean groups. We do this solo. We certainly don't tell any of the AVI goons or government shitheads. No witnesses."

"I will make flight arrangements tonight."

SUMMITVILLE

G olden shafts of sunlight, streaming in through what remained of the front glass, illuminated the dust and atomized contents of the refrigerator that hung in the air, the clouds of tiny particulates eddied according to the vagaries of the morning breeze now freely flowing into the shattered police station lobby.

Officer Hill lay motionless next to the tub, barely allowing himself to breathe as he listened, attempting to divine what the mechanical monster a few yards away was doing. The hair on his arms tingled, and he sensed a light buzzing emanating from outside.

Bill wasn't sure how long he stayed curled on the bathroom floor, afraid to rise above the protective bulk of the ice-water-filled tub.

The tingling on his skin and the electrical buzzing noise had dissipated several minutes ago. Hearing nothing outside, Bill cautiously—and a bit reluctantly—rose up into a sitting position, listening intently for any tell-tale indication that the machine had detected his movement. After a long minute, he pushed himself up and stood, surveying for the first time the destruction the machine's weapon had wrought.

Bill moved as silently as he could through the broken glass and debris strewn across the floor, cringing each time something crunched under his boots. Making his way to the front, he carefully checked the street in front of the police department for any sign of the machine. Seeing none, he surreptitiously poked his head through the shattered remains of the front double doors and quickly glanced both ways down the street. No sign of the AUCVs, just the incongruous and absurd image of burning vehicles and ugly smoke plumes rising into the sky in a scene more appropriate to Afghanistan than to central Indiana.

As Bill withdrew his head back into the station, his consciousness registered that, besides the burning vehicles and demolished buildings, the scene also included bodies here and there along the street and sidewalks—bodies of people Bill knew. The imagery was so surreal that his mind refused to dwell upon it. That would come later, he feared.

Bill moved back across the lobby to the closet in the squad room that served as the department's armory. Unlocking the door with a key from his squad car's key ring, he withdrew a Remington 870 twelve-gauge riot gun and a box of shells, placing them on one of the squad room desks. He reached back to the rack and removed a second weapon, this one a 5.56 M4 assault carbine, along with several boxes of ammo.

Bill retrieved two more fifteen-round magazines for his Glock service pistol and a couple boxes of nine-millimeter. Bill knew that these firearms would have no effect on the armored skin of the combat vehicles he was up against, but they would be useful against their occupants—if there were occupants.

Bill had a suspicion that the things were robotic, unmanned fighting vehicles. He had not seen any hatches, windows, periscopes, or camera apertures on the AUCVs. He was no expert on military combat vehicles, and he did not want to just make the assumption that there were no human foes involved in whatever was going on here. Better to be prepared the best he could.

Bill pulled his backpack from his locker, unzipped it, and dumped its contents onto the nearest desk, shoving the granola bars and bottled water back into the bag. He also retrieved the bottle of Tylenol and tossed it back into the bag as well. He moved over to where he had put the long guns and extra ammo and threw all the ammunition into the backpack, except for one box of nine-millimeter.

Bill took the box of nine-millimeter HP+P rounds over to his desk and began loading the two extra Glock magazines to capacity. When finished, he tossed the two loaded mags into the backpack with the rest of the ammo before returning to the armory closet where he loaded the 870's extended tube magazine with high brass 00-buckshot rounds interspersed with sabot slug rounds.

Bill grabbed three loaded thirty-round magazines of 5.56 NATO for the M4, slapped one into the magazine well of the weapon, chambered a round, and safed the weapon before putting it with the 870 scattergun.

As he was assembling the equipment and items he might need until help arrived, Bill thought of his fellow officers, wondering how many might have survived and where they were—protecting their homes and families?

Bill's thoughts moved to his own family, his parents and sister in Muncie. *Is this…this invasion a widespread thing? Are those hideous machines in Muncie, too? Is this a full-scope invasion of the United States? By whom? Who the hell are they? Why Summitville, for cryin' out loud?*

Bill wondered who the county and state had up there. He couldn't know that the missile he witnessed streaking upward from the AUCV that ravaged his police station had found and obliterated the sheriff's unit and that another munition fired from an AUCV several blocks away had destroyed the ISP car. Had Bill had the overhead vantage of the UAV loitering south of town, he would have seen the burnt-out and shredded frames of the two police cruisers, still steaming and hissing where they sat broken in the traveled portion of CR200E.

Bill nearly pissed his pants when the bang on the metal rear door caused him to drop the extra Motorola walkie-talkie batteries on the floor. In a flash of motion that surprised even him, he unsnapped his safety holster and extracted his Glock service pistol.

"Please, let us in…please! Is anyone in there?"

A woman's voice.

Bill angled over to the wall adjacent to the door in a defensive posture and positioned his weapon so he could quickly bring it to bear on whoever was on the other side of the door when he opened it.

After getting his breathing back under some semblance of control, Bill reached out with his free hand and quickly turned the knob, unsecuring the door. He immediately released his grip on the knob and moved his left hand up to support his Glock in a two-handed combat hold.

The shocked look on Bill's face was probably quite apparent to Jenny as she rushed inside the station, ushering three dirty and frazzled-looking Girl Scouts in ahead of her. Close on Jenny's heels, crab-walking backward through the doorway and covering their "six" with a handgun was Roger Clark, Bill's SPD colleague. Officer Clark pulled the door closed as he moved across the threshold.

Bill was overjoyed at the sight of other human beings, especially Jenny and his fellow officer. He was surprised but happy that three of the scouts had made it out of that bus with Jenny.

Bill quickly scanned the forms of his five new companions and asked, "is anyone was hurt?" Clark, a reserve police officer with the Summitville Police Department, answered "we are all okay—nothing other than a few scratches and bruises, at least physically."

Bill gave Jenny's arm a light squeeze, and he and Roger Clark exchanged a quick embrace. Bill looked more closely at the three "tween-age" girls standing alongside Jenny, seeing the nervousness—the fear— in their eyes. He could not think of anything halfway intelligent to say that would be in any way comforting, so he belayed that thought and turned to Jenny.

"I saw the bus and, uh, I, uh…" Bill couldn't think of what he should say about the horrific scene he had encountered at the bus and decided just to stop talking, at a loss for words. They had been there—lived it; he didn't need to describe it to them.

Roger spoke up. "I came across Jenny here and the girls over at the middle school. They were loading nonperishables from the school cafeteria pantry into a backpack when I noticed them through a window as I was passing by the building, making my way here."

Bill then noticed the Green Bay Packers backpack sitting at Jenny's feet, thinking to himself that provisioning food items was a smart move. But, then again, they were *scouts*, after all.

Jenny spoke up. "Whose combat vehicles are those? Are they Chinese? Russian? What is happening, Bill? They...they murdered all those poor—"

She paused to get her emotions back in check before continuing.

"The whole town—the entire damn town—has been shot to hell. There are victims littering the streets, yards, driveways. It's like something from a low-rent horror movie."

The three Girl Scouts looked up at Jenny but said nothing. They didn't have to. It was reflected in their faces.

Roger said, "I was only able to grab a couple items and run from my house before all hell broke loose in the neighborhood. I managed to grab my service weapon, one extra mag, my combat folder, and my duty vest as far as gear is concerned. I have my cell phone, but it appears to be disabled."

"I wouldn't have been able to grab that much had I not already been up, dressed, and preparing to walk out of the house to head over to the store."

Roger's full-time job was as manager of the Ace Hardware in Summit-ville. He worked one weekend a month as a reserve policeman, helping to augment the handful of regular officers employed at the Summitville Police Department. Roger was a solid officer, even-tempered and a good guy to have your back.

Looking up to the lobby through the open squad room door, Roger surveyed the damage to the police station. Turning to Bill, he asked, "Do you have any idea what is going on? Are we at war?"

"I don't know, Rog. I have been wondering the same things myself. I can tell you this: those fucking machines—uh, sorry, girls—are everywhere, and they have pretty much annihilated Summitville from what I can tell. My assessment—guess—is that those are advanced ground combat vehi-cles, possibly unmanned automatons. As to whose military they belong to, I haven't a clue. For all I know, they are from our own US inventory."

"Any idea how the hell they got to Summitville?" Roger asked.

"None whatsoever. It does not make sense. Why little Summitville? We have no industry, no National Guard armory, no airport, no major interstate interchange, nothing to make this little burg a target that I can think of."

Roger looked down at the floor and asked, "How many of the PD are, uh, have survived?"

"You are the only other officer I have seen from any agency. From what I can tell, the fire department and EMS service was decimated before they got much past the firehouse driveway. Most of SPD was likely caught, like the general public, at home and totally unprepared. I have to assume that they are casualties. We are quite possibly it."

"State and county?" Roger asked.

"Nothing. All the radios are dead, and I haven't seen any other units anywhere in town. In fact, I haven't seen any operating motor vehicles of any kind anywhere. Nothing."

"Military aircraft?" Jenny asked.

"Nope. None observed. It has just been me and those things out there, playing cat and mouse.

"I can tell you this," Bill continued. "Those combat vehicles have outstanding sensor capabilities and appear to have multifaceted weapons suites. They are smart…almost *cunning.*

"While we're on the subject of those things, I don't think we should stay here in the PD, given this building houses the center of government for the town and has a big-ass radio tower and all. This structure is a natural target. I think we should find another site where we can shelter until we can formulate a plan to take us out of Summitville. We need to find others…get to help."

"Okay, Bill, I agree. Let's get together what we need and get rolling. I don't want to be here if those things return to finish this place off. I saw what they are capable of."

"Yeah," Jenny said, "I don't want to be anywhere those things may take interest in." At that, one of the Girl Scouts began softly sobbing. Not knowing what else to do, Jenny simply pulled the girl close to her and patted her shoulder. What was there to say? She had already—they all had—endured and seen far more than any kid, or anyone at any age, should ever have to witness.

"Let's get this stuff together and be ready to move. We need to figure out where we want to move to, so we don't waste time. We need to have a clear destination in mind and choose the most secure route so we can minimize our exposure," Bill said.

With that, they began assembling gear and supplies in preparation for departure.

Roger was one of the defensive tactics instructors for the police department, certified in krav maga, and a part-time assistant instructor at the little taekwondo dojang that had operated in Summitville for more than two decades.

Fred Wallser was the chief instructor and owner over there, a fourth dan in taekwondo and a former Golden Gloves boxer. Roger, along with Wallser, taught a self-defense course at the little martial arts studio that utilized krav maga as the core discipline. The police department took advantage of that local resource, and Roger helped keep the officers up to speed with street survival and hand-to-hand tactics.

Thinking of Wallser—his friend and teacher—Roger wondered how Fred had fared in this horror show. It then occurred to him that the little taekwondo dojang had a semi-finished basement where the weight equipment was set up.

"The studio's basement might be a good place to hole up, Roger said, until we can figure a route of egress from town. There are two doors, one leading up a flight of cement steps to the outside and the other up into the main workout area of the studio. Two ways in and out, so we wouldn't be trapped if one escape route were to be blocked. There is also a cooler full of bottled water, PowerAde, and a supply of energy bars."

"Jenny, what do you think?" Bill asked.

"Sounds as good as anyplace I can think of," she answered.

"Yeah, I agree," Bill said. So, we all agree?"

The screeching of tires outside in the alley got everyone's attention, causing Roger to visibly jump. Apparently whatever had disabled his squad car earlier was no longer in play, Bill thought. The sound of a key in the rear door brought everyone's eyes to focus on the doorway. A half second later, the door shot open, and the chief of police rushed in.

Dave Millen, at fifty-three years of age, was graying and slightly overweight. He was, however, not a man to be trifled with, his reputation as a brawler during his younger years on the force still fresh in the memories of many of the town's middle-aged ne'er-do-wells, most now respectable citizens.

Dave was wearing blue jeans, a ratty old cotton shirt, scuffed cowboy boots, and had his departmental vest on with his gold shield affixed to the Velcro badge holder on the front panel. Millen's departmental Glock ninemillimeter was in a pancake holster on his right side.

Dave slammed the door closed and looked around, nodding to the five people staring at him in the squad room, two with guns in their hands. Bill and Roger holstered their pistols and went over to slap him on the back and shake his hand, both pleased to see that he had survived.

"Sonofabitch, it is hell on earth out there, boys." Sweat glistened on Dave's forehead, and stress was clearly visible in his face. "Jenny, honey, I am glad to see you are okay. I saw your bus earlier this morning. Folks, I don't know where to start or what to say other than this is a waking nightmare, and there are a lot of good people dead here in town."

Looking over at the three Girl Scouts clustered around Jenny, Chief Millen smiled. "You are the McFarren girl, aren't ya? And you two, you are the Albrecht sisters, right?"

The three Girl Scouts all nodded. Millen knew most of the kids in town. Being from such a small community, he knew pretty much everyone who lived in town and the surrounding rural township. Dave Millen had lived in Summitville all his life.

"I reckon we three are likely the only surviving members of the department, boys. I have seen none of the others, and I have been out for a couple hours, dodging those demonic machines, and have been in most sections of town. Nadda. Zip. No sign of anyone else from the PD, the fire department, or anyone from any other law enforcement agency."

Melissa McFarren spoke up at that point. "Daddy is a fireman. Are the firemen okay?"

After a short pause, Chief Millen spoke. "Sweetie, I wish I could tell you something positive, but I, uh, I just don't know. I just don't know, honey."

Chief Millen then turned back to Bill and Roger.

"Either of you have any idea as to what is happening…who is operating those damn army vehicles that are blasting the place to hell?"

"No, Chief, we have no clear idea as to what, or who, is doing this," Bill answered. Then Bill and Roger began briefing their chief on their planned movement to another site.

After several minutes of going over their egress plans, comparing notes on what they had observed and tossing around some ideas on what might be going on, the three policemen turned back to Jenny and the scouts. Chief Millen explained that they were opting to go on foot, fearing the vehicle, while faster, might draw the unwanted attention of the AUCVs.

With a plan in mind and with Chief Millen in the lead, the six cautiously exited the back door of the police station and into the bright sunlight.

Skirting the downtown area, keeping to the alleys and side streets whenever they could, they made their way to Wallser's taekwondo school, which was a small storefront business on the far end of the main business district three blocks from the town hall building.

Wrapping around the backside of the businesses, the group used the rear yards of the residences adjacent to the business district to approach their destination, keeping clear of even the alleys when they could. Chief Millen and Roger had the point, with Jenny and the three scouts in the middle of the string and Bill bringing up the rear.

They stopped every few yards to listen and to survey their surroundings, staying alert for any sign of the AUCVs, using cover and concealment whenever possible.

They were a block away from where Wallser's studio was located, crouched near a picket fence in someone's backyard, when the hair on the back of Bill's neck stood up. He looked all around, peering into the shaded spaces between the houses, but saw nothing. Jenny looked visibly disturbed and turned to Bill, whispering that she had a bad feeling, like someone was watching them.

Bill told Jenny to keep an eye out behind them and carefully moved the short distance to the front of the group to convey his uneasiness to Roger and Chief Millen.

As he knelt down next to Roger, two feet away from Dave Millen, he heard what sounded like fabric tearing. The sound was brief and muted, difficult to isolate. It sounded like someone had quickly torn a piece of bed linen in two.

Bill did not have time to mull over the origin of the strange tearing sound. At the same instant he detected the noise, Dave Millen's back virtually exploded.

Perceived in almost slow motion by Bill and Roger, tangled threads from Dave's ballistic vest panel, intermixed with greasy-looking strands of shredded entrails, pulverized intestinal contents, and glistening chunks of internal organs blew outward in a bright red spray from Millen's lower back.

Being just to the rear and slightly to the side of Millen, Bill watched in frozen horror as the cone of aerosolized gore blew past his left side, some of the outriding splatter catching on his vest.

It was as if a silent grenade had exploded inside of Dave, blowing the contents of his torso out through the rear panel of his bulletproof vest. The protective vest might as well have been made of rice paper.

Breaking their frozen trance, both Bill and Roger frantically scanned all around them but saw no sign of any of the AUCVs. Nothing. Absolutely nothing seemed out of order.

Looking back to where their chief had crumpled to the ground, one leg grotesquely bent under his body, they had no doubt that Millen was dead.

Bill scooted forward on his knees and pulled Millen over, checking for any sign of life while Roger covered the group with the M4 carbine. Jenny pulled the three girls to her and quietly repeated to them the need to keep as quiet as possible. The girls were beyond frightened, huddled in a quivering mass, staring blankly at the fallen police chief.

Bill saw that a ragged, fist-sized hole was evident low on the chief's front vest panel, almost missing the vest panel altogether. That would be the entry wound, meaning the shot—or whatever it was—came from in front of them. There was no pulse, no breath, and the chief's open eyes were already acquiring that glassy look one saw in the recently deceased.

Chrissy Albrecht vomited all over Jenny, her sister, Michelle, and Melissa McFarren. Immediately after vomiting, Chrissy began hysterically sobbing and emitting little gulping sounds, strings of snot dangling from her nose as she stared wide-eyed at the front of her Girl Scout uniform.

Jenny saw that the spray of gore blown from the back of Chief Millen had struck the front of Chrissy's shirt, spackling it with a spaghetti-like smear of mulched human entrails.

There was no time to mourn over the chief. Something they could not see had just killed him in broad daylight while he was less than a yard from them. Bill reached over the chief's corpse and grabbed the Remington 870 shotgun still gripped in Millen's right hand, pulling it free.

Rising to a low crouch in unison, Bill and Roger ordered Jenny and the girls to stand up and follow them. Jenny shook Chrissy, looking her in the eyes, "you have to keep quiet and keep up with the rest of us or you will likely die. Do you understand?" It was harsh, but they needed to move and move right now.

They ran like the devil himself was chasing them.

Unable to kick in the robust rear security door at Wallser's Taekwondo, the group had to send Roger to the flimsier front door, risking detection on the main drag in the downtown district. Roger booted the front door in on his third try, closed it behind him, and waited, watching for any sort of response from the AUCVs. After a few minutes of tense waiting, Roger went downstairs to the rear door and opened it, allowing the others inside the building.

After Jenny cleaned up the Albrecht girl the best she could in the studio's tiny basement bathroom, she and the still-shaken scout rejoined the others, who were sitting on the weight machines that occupied most of the basement's limited space.

Bill spoke first. "Okay, we were all there, so I won't regurgitate what we all experienced. But I want to draw everyone's attention to the fact that neither Roger or I—nor Dave, as far as we could tell—saw anything out of order in that backyard or in the alley. It is broad daylight out there, and we saw nothing."

"But I did hear a strange sound—a very muted sound that was a bit like fabric tearing, like what you would hear if you ripped a piece of cloth in two. It was just perceptible and lasted only a split second."

"Roger here said he does not recall hearing anything. Jenny, did you or the girls hear anything?"

"No, I did not hear a thing. Girls, did any of you hear anything strange back there?"

"No, Jen," said Michelle. Both Melissa and Chrissy shook their heads.

"Okay, I was the only one, unless, uh, Dave maybe heard something. I have been thinking about this, and a couple things stand out, so I am going to run those by all of you."

"First, whenever I was near one of those vehicles, I felt a tingling of the hair on my arms. There was no such tingling back there in that yard when… when it happened. Also, I could hear a humming sound when the vehicle was nearby. There was no humming this time."

"Secondly, the sound, the ripping noise I described, was very low-key, almost imperceptible among the background noise of the breeze in the trees. The rapid-fire cannon on top of the combat vehicle that fired at me back at the station earlier this morning made a similar sound but much louder—very noticeable."

"Jenny, Roger and I need to talk privately for a minute to discuss some tactical issues." Bill and Roger walked over by the cooler and spoke in hushed tones.

"So, Roger, I think that maybe these things—these combat vehicles—have an assortment of armament. Maybe we have only experienced a little of what they have available in their onboard arsenals. Whatever this last weapon was, it was more small-arms-like. The, uh, effect was inconsistent with the large auto cannon mounted on top of the vehicles. What I saw back there with Dave—it was nothing like what I saw with the other casualties."

"Yeah, I agree, man. I saw a couple casualties this morning as I was making my way over to the middle school and again when moving from the school to the town hall. Most of the victims appeared to be blown apart, completely obliterated. My take was they were hit by a weapon likely designed to be used against other armored vehicles. I think what hit Dave was fired from more of an anti-personnel weapon, a small arm."

"This is just a guess, Rog, but my sense is that the blast that took out Dave was more like a column of shot from a shotgun, fleshettes maybe. The entry wound was ragged around the edges, like it was not one projectile but many bunched together, like with a shotgun. And the exit wound was huge, very consistent with what one might find with a fist-sized group of fleshettes exiting or maybe a very rapid-fire string of individual rounds hitting nearly simultaneously."

"My concern is this, Rog… we didn't see a vehicle. Only one of us heard anything. The wound Dave sustained was inconsistent with what we have seen on other casualties. Either those things have some sort of means of remotely reaching out with a small-arms type of munition of some sort, or, uh, that round or burst or whatever the fuck was not fired from one of those vehicles."

"So what are you saying, man? Are you saying what I think you're sayin'? That Dave was hit by a *man-portable* weapon, a small arm such as would be employed by an individual combatant?"

"Yep, that would be what I am sayin', Rog. We have to open our minds to the fact that we may have enemy ground combatants involved besides those super tanks."

"Okay, Bill, I hear ya, but I have a problem with that theory. We did not see shit. No movement. No nothin'. If there had been someone—an enemy foot soldier, for instance—firing on us, we likely would have seen something."

"Also, man, the angle of the shot was not consistent with a round fired from a sniper in some elevated firing position, like from concealment from an upper-story window or something. The projectile or projectiles appeared to impact and exit on a level plane. The exit wound would have been angled somewhat downward had the shot been fired from an elevated position."

"You have a point, Rog. I guess we just need to stay alert for any range of threat, vehicular and otherwise."

"Roger that. I agree a hundred fuckin' percent, man."

"Okay, we need to discuss how and when we should unass and head out of town. We can't just stay here indefinitely. Who knows how long it will be before any sort of help arrives? Plus, if this is a military invasion, the opposing forces may conduct door-to-door searches at some point once they believe they have secured the area sufficiently to dismount, providing there are ground troops involved in this attack."

"Okay, then let's go back over to Jenny and her girls and get our plan of action put together. We need to get the hell out of Summitville. We can't, as much as we may like to, loiter and try to carry on some sort of guerilla action. We can't hurt those things with what we have, and we can't hazard Jenny and the girls that way."

After a nearly sleepless night in the basement of the martial arts studio, the little group of five departed just as the sun was coming up the next morning. They had briefly discussed leaving under cover of darkness, but the girls were terrified at the thought of going out into the night with the machines roaming around out there. Bill and Roger decided they would wait until dawn and leave then. At least they could see what was around them that way.

This time, Bill took point and Roger brought up the rear with Jenny and her scouts in the middle. They moved southeast from the taekwondo studio, heading quickly out of the business district and into the surrounding residential neighborhoods, using the shrubbery and backyard fencing, along with the closely built houses, as cover.

They made it to the edge of town. The open farm fields were not good egress options, but there was a wooded tract that would afford them concealment and a means of putting distance between themselves and the town. The woods followed a creek that would take them a good two miles before they would have to deal with open fields.

The small, two-story house whose backyard they were kneeling in showed signs of being hit by the AUCVs, the screened-in front porch hanging in shreds, pieces of screen and wood gently swaying in the breeze. Most of the windows on the front side were blown out, and the siding showed signs of being hit by multiple projectiles, just like most homes in town.

Bill was just getting ready to signal their movement to the trees along the creek to begin their exit from town when a dog chained in the backyard of the house next door began barking frantically. All five of them startled when dozens of birds burst into the air from the trees in several of the back-yards, including the one they were in.

Bill could see the dog, a German Shepard, snarling and pulling against the chain that tied him to a doghouse. He was turning his head back to address the group when his vision picked up the vaguest hint of movement near the trees in the backyard where the dog was tied.

Bill couldn't even be sure he saw something. It was what? It was fleeting and undefined. Just movement.

He stared at the space where he thought he saw something, and whispered to the others, "I think I saw something over there in that backyard where the dog is carrying on. I'm not sure. But I thought I saw movement. Be ready...be ready to go."

Bill focused his vision and attention on where he thought he saw the movement. His heart was pounding, making it hard for him to listen to his surroundings. He blinked and focused again on where he thought he saw something, wiping sweat from his forehead and from his left eye, which was stinging from the sweat rolling down from his brow.

The dog was crouched low to the ground, chewing at the chain. The hair on the animal's back was standing straight up. All the birds that had rock-eted upward from the neighborhood trees were now gone. Other than the low growling of the dog, it was dead quiet. Scary quiet.

Roger gasped just as Bill saw it again: the faintest hint of movement just about midway between the now-yipping dog and a large oak tree in the rear of the yard. Bill blinked again and looked back as Roger whispered, "Did you see that?"

There it was again…it was like a translucent outline that one could see through. "What the fuck is that?" Bill whispered.

Just then the dog yelped and disappeared in a hideous puff of red mist. There had been no sound.

Bill and Roger both brought their weapons up at the same instant—Roger with the M4 automatic carbine and Bill with the 870 riot gun—and simultaneously let loose a brief, controlled volley of fire toward where they had seen the wavering outline in the air.

For absolutely no reason that Bill or Roger could divine, the occupant of the home with the dog burst from the back door and ran screaming at the top of his lungs to the side of the house.

The man, who was in his sixties and wearing pajamas, grabbed a garden hose from a reel mounted on the house and, reeling out the hose as he ran toward where they had seen the outline in the air, began spraying water toward the image's last-observed location.

There was a sparkling in the air, and the transparent image reappeared and began to waver and turn colors. It reminded Bill of the transporter scenes on the old *Star Trek* series, an outline of a person flickering into form as it materialized from thin air.

Wavering as if being viewed through heat waves, the image that came into view was defined enough for Bill, Roger, Jenny, and the three Girl Scouts to see its form.

The spindly, bipedal form had a triangular head, like that of a venomous snake. The head reminded Bill of a pit viper's.

There were a series of black orbs arrayed on the head, which Bill took to be eyes or visual sensors. It was, Roger estimated, seven feet tall, give or take.

The body was smooth and featureless. The thing appeared to be made of a dull material. The arms were thin, except for the forearms, which were noticeably thicker than the rest of the limb.

There appeared to be protrusions extending from the inside of the forearms. Their purpose was not a mystery for long, for the thing—the being—whatever it was, turned toward the still-shrieking man with the hose and, raising one arm, blew him nearly in two. The man's torso exploded in a storm of ripped flesh, surrounded by a misty cloud of blood that hung momentarily in the air after the ruined body fell to the ground.

Roger emptied his M4 magazine into the thing as Bill racked off several rounds of 00-buckshot and sabot slugs. The thing, apparently unfazed, turned its ugly snake head toward them and raised both arms. There was very little noise.

The only thing going through Bill's mind as he racked off round after round from the Remington was, *we are occupied.*

HILTON DUBAI JUMEIRAH UAE

"I think, Je-Ju, that we should not afford Ijinashi a first-strike advantage. We should make his neutralization a priority."

"No...I can't. I see your logic, and it is sound. But I can't wrap my head around killing Ijinashi right now. Give me some time, Sainen. I need to think things through, to weigh options."

"Time is Ijinashi's ally, as it affords him the option of letting us grow lax while he picks a time and place of his choosing to settle things with us. Ijinashi is the last human being on the planet that we wish to give any advantage to, Je-Ju."

"Yes, you are right. I know it. I am not a fool. Ijinashi Tamna is cunning, brilliant, and as adept a killer as has ever trod the earth."

"So you are willing to entertain my proposition?"

"Yes, I am willing to consider it. Yes, dammit."

"There is a restaurant I like over in the hotel near the beach. Let's run over there for something to eat later, and afterward we can return here, sit out by the water, and get a plan together."

"I need to do this now, Sainen. I don't want to wait and allow doubt and uncertainty to creep into my thinking. Let's do it now, please."

"Okay, I'll have room service bring us something, and we will work out our plan."

"Sainen, I know you, and I agreed early on to keep this confined to just the two of us. But I want you to hear me out before you object. Let me lay out my idea, okay?

"I know someone—a zealot and a political crusader—who could potentially take care of this thing with Ijinashi so that we are not directly involved. I am not suggesting this because I have no stomach for getting Ijinashi before he can get us. We offer this guy and his cause enough cash money, he may set aside his politics for pragmatism.

"This man, he is not Yakuza, Triad, Korean mob, or AVI. He was never in the chain of people whom we dealt with regarding the technology. He is a detached third party who, I believe, could not only get close to Ijinashi but could take him out.

"Through my business dealings in Manila, I had occasion to hear of this man and of his skills. I have never met him. He does not know you or me or anyone within our respective crews. Let me reach out to this person—securely, of course—and ascertain if employing him might be a viable option for us. If it turns out that he is not of utility, we can easily press ahead on our own unilaterally."

"I trust your judgment and your instincts, Je-Ju."

"Thank you. Besides, if we can get this guy to deal with Ijinashi, we can focus on those businessmen in McLean.

Think about it. If they are out of the picture then not only have we seriously degraded a keynote government contractor critical to the exploitation of the technology, but at the same time we will have eliminated two individuals who possess direct knowledge of our role in the grand configuration of things."

"Make your calls, Je-Ju. We will see what you can turn up with this guy. One condition, though. I want his name and location. That is my sole caveat. You agree?"

"Sure. His name is Remy Sanchez. He is a Filipino. He can be reached in Manila."

OUR LADY OF MT. CARMEL PARISH, QUEZON CITY, PHILIPPINES

R emy thought that it must be providence—something preordained in the master scheme of the universe.

His friend Osvaldo Prio Torrado had just phoned him last week, asking him to meet a colleague in the movement, the leader of the New Weathermen faction in America.

Now, this message from Manila, from the local queen of crime, who was reputed to be high up in the Cloud Dragon criminal enterprise, commissioning him to kill the New Weathermen leader. A significant sum of much-needed money would be transferred to an account of his choice for use by his New Katipunan movement.

Was it some elaborate setup—maybe a test of his revolutionary dedication?—or was it a divine sign that he was supposed to seek out this Ijinashi and take his rightful place in the revolutionary struggle?

Remy believed it was an orchestrated plan, put together by the command tier of the global people's revolution with the help of the Cuban intelligence service. Due to compartmentalization, Remy could not know the whole operational plan.

He would not make it a complicated thing and would not allow himself to dwell on and fret over the decision. He had spent nearly two hours inside Our Lady of Mt. Carmel, praying for his path to be revealed, his destiny clarified. He would follow his heart.

The sun felt good as Remy strolled through the growing numbers of pedestrians beginning to fill the sidewalks on this gorgeous morning.

He reflected upon the targeting materials that he had received clandestinely through the local Cloud Dragon network. It was thorough but beautiful in its stark simplicity, appearing to be nothing other than one more street crime in a neighborhood accustomed to violent crimes against individuals.

Although the mechanics of the encounter were left to him, Remy was given very precise instructions on how he was to exfil from the scene.

Following this sequence, Remy was told, would permit colleagues in the movement to aid in his safe escape from the country and his ultimate return to the Philippine Islands.

The service Remy was providing, he was assured, was crucial to the survival of the movement. His subject, the leader of the New Weathermen, had been corrupted, he was told. The man was an impediment to the revolution.

It was Remy's sacred duty. His destiny. The revolution needed him.

Remy assumed that his good friend Osvaldo Torrado was a key advisor in the scheme and had probably recommended Remy for this important role because of his unwavering devotion to the cause.

Of course, adherence to proper tradecraft would prevent Remy from openly discussing this with Osvaldo.

Someday, though, he thought, he would express his gratitude to his Cuban friend for the confidence shown in him and the honor of being selected for such an important task.

Remy would be wrong about that.

NORTHERN VIRGINIA

Sainen and Je-Ju knew the two men's patterns of life like the backs of their hands, having put surveillance on their place of business, movements, and activities for three weeks straight. They knew who the key holders were at their SeriusCrux corporate office building, when employees came and went, what the building's lighting pattern looked like, day and night, and the patrol pattern of the lone security officer on premises after hours.

Sainen and Je-Ju had followed both principal targets home and had documented the comings and goings of both men's respective families. They had done the same for their neighbors on both sides in event that utilization of a neighboring residence was required.

There was little about the lives of Dr. James Randolph and Dr. Michael Nelson, their families, and the operation of their company that Sainen and Je-Ju didn't know by heart.

They knew, for instance, that a delivery truck arrived at the company headquarters on Tuesdays at the rear loading dock and that the front receptionist who sat in the round marble kiosk in the ground floor elevator lobby arrived promptly at seven-thirty Monday through Friday. They knew that

Randolph's daughter went to fencing lessons every Wednesday afternoon in Chantilly and that Nelson's wife volunteered at a local church.

So it was that they knew that, twice a week, Jim Randolph ate at the Taco Bell in Vienna, not far down State Route 123 from SeriusCrux Inc., apparently favoring Mondays and Thursdays. They knew that Randolph used the drive-thru and, rather than fight with trying to cross the busy traffic lanes of 123 to make a left out of the restaurant lot, instead made a much more convenient right into the flow and went to the next light, turning right on Glyndon Street to go around the block so he could get back onto 123 at another automatic signal a block down from the Taco Bell, in the direction he wanted to go.

It was this detour down residential streets that was of interest to Sainen and Je-Ju.

The narrow little tree-lined lane that paralleled 123 was lightly traveled. The residents of the stately older homes along this little strip of asphalt had had speed bumps installed to keep the speeds down, rendering their little street relatively unpopular as a cut through to most everyone except James Randolph.

By Sainen's watch, it took Randolph exactly two minutes to traverse the strip of road while slowing for two speed bumps along the way. The speed-deterring humps of asphalt were positioned just before and just after what would be considered midblock. Given that the street was not very long, that kept speeds very modest, except for the occasional teenage driver doing burnouts between the bumps in a display of defiance.

It was decided that the easternmost speed bump afforded the best location, one of the homes at that spot sporting several large shade trees in the front yard as well as a conveniently placed decorative shrub line.

What made things even better was that on Mondays, Dr. Michael Nelson joined Randolph for lunch, apparently using the drive to Taco Bell as a mechanism for getting some time outside the office together to privately discuss matters of mutual interest. Sainen and Je-Ju deduced this during their surveillance, as the two men always appeared to be engaged in heavy conversation during their lunchtime ride to and from Taco Bell. That meant that they were distracted, their minds occupied and engaged. Perfect.

It was a beautiful, sunny day, even though it was Monday, a day typically not at the top of most people's popularity charts.

Randolph turned onto the pleasant, tree-lined little street, partially engrossed in watching two bright red cardinals chase each other from yard to yard as he nudged the Mercedes up to twenty miles per hour, his driver-side window down a few inches so he could hear the birds and smell the fresh air. It was good to be away from the stuffy, canned office atmosphere.

"This exploitation has taken some surprising—and unfortunate—turns, I'll give you that. That having been said, we can't allow the fantastical nature of these, uh, anomalies, to shake up—to deter—us from keeping our eyes on the ball. What choice do we have, anyway? We can't just bag ass, right?"

"You know, Mike, we are prosperous even by Washington standards. We—our families—live a good life here in Northern Virginia. The USG's security apparatus and the mighty DoD will cover things at least to the extent that SeriusCrux won't become publicly known as a player. It is, after all, a highly classified and compartmented project… its public disclosure would be terribly inconvenient for the government. It would be nothing short of a debacle for them, not to mention the careers of more than one congressman."

"Yes, Jim, I know—"

"Whoa…who is that?"

Both men shifted their attention to the young woman staggering from the shrubbery into the street, bent over and holding her stomach. Jim brought the car to a stop, straddling the speed bump he had just begun to ease over.

The woman—girl, it appeared—with long blond hair mouthed the words "help me," her face twisted in apparent pain.

Randolph brought the Mercedes to a stop, both men focused on the female; neither saw the tall, redheaded man in the Baltimore Ravens jersey step up to the driver's side and insert his right hand through the partially rolled down window.

Jim felt a prick on the left side of his neck, startled to see a man standing at his window as his head jerked around. "What the fuck—" was Dr. Randolph's final utterance as his body jerked and spasmed violently, his fingers and toes contorting painfully as the blackness closed in.

The man stretched his arm in, reached past Jim's still form, and put the car in park.

Mike Nelson was shocked at the speed at which the young blond girl covered the distance to his door, which he had just begun opening so he could exit the car and help her. His mind was unable to process the significance of the tiny aerosol canister the girl shoved into his face or the brief puff of odorless mist that shot into his eyes.

The girl had to grasp Mike's shoulder and forcefully shove his violently twitching form back into the Mercedes' passenger seat, frothy foam bubbling from his parted lips.

The blond girl retrieved a set of drug paraphernalia from her fanny pack and tossed it onto the car's center console as the man in the Ravens jersey pulled several gay porn magazines from a backpack and threw them onto the floorboards.

It wasn't until they were a block away on another secluded side street that Sainen and Je-Ju pulled off their wigs and removed their sunglasses, leisurely driving out of town on this gloriously beautiful day in Virginia.

SUMMITVILLE

Whether it was a malfunction attributable to prolonged detachment from its timeline—a vagary of temporal travel—or it simply ran out of ammunition, no one would know. Whatever the causative factors, Bill, Roger, Jenny, and the McFarren and Albrecht girls all owed their lives to whatever aberration caused the cybernetic figure's weapons systems to fail.

Bill, Roger, Jenny, and the girls stared in a blend of terror and awe as the entirety of their surroundings began wavering, the outline of every object taking on a halo-like shimmering.

Bill jerked awake, the twitter of song birds audible through the partially raised bedroom window, golden rays of light from the morning sun streaming in.

Bill was gripped by anxiety so severe that it felt like a ball of lead in the center of his chest. He struggled to align his thoughts. *Was that a dream?* He was flabbergasted at the vivid imagery fresh in his mind, the feeling that it had actually happened…that he had lived it. At the same time, he was relieved—relieved that he and Summitville were still around, as they had been.

Still trying to clear the cobwebs from his head, Bill launched out of bed and rushed to the window, jerking the curtains aside, peering out at his neighborhood, looking exactly as it should, the B&M refuse truck grinding down the next street over.

Fighting the anxiety that was now to the point of scaring him, Bill ran to the front room, still in his underwear and the same t-shirt he had been wearing underneath his vest for his night shift in the…*dream? What the…?*

His car keys were on the coffee table, just as they should be. Running back to his bedroom, Bill saw the departmental vest on the carpet next to the closet door where he had dumped it, the jumbled tangle of his duty gun belt next to it. All normal.

This…this ain't right. It's is as if I woke up the morning after the end of the night shift I dreamt about, and the dreamed events didn't happen. Of course they didn't. I can't remember! I remember getting home and getting into bed. What time is it? Why did I wake up, what, two hours after getting in bed after a graveyard shift?

Wow, damn, that dream rattled me. I've never had such a surreal dream experience.

He wished the anxiety would subside.

Bill ran to the closet, grabbed his cargo shorts from the dirty clothes pile, and, jumping into them as he hopped across the carpet, ran to the front door and out onto the porch into the crisp morning air.

Bill could hear Roy Hudlin starting up his lawn tractor a quarter-block down, just as it should be. The newspaper was on the step, as it should be.

Starting to calm down a little, breathing in the fresh morning air, Bill was surprised when the restored candy apple red Chevy Nova screeched to a stop in front of his house.

Roger stepped out of the car and, moving like he was in a trance, walked slowly up the walkway to Bill's porch. That was odd; Bill and Roger hadn't worked together in a month due to annual vacation leave, and Roger had never come to his house before.

A cold chill went up Bill's spine as he saw the look on Roger's face—in his eyes—a look of disoriented…what? Horror?

Roger stammered, "I need you to tell me…I had a dream or some sort of…of…psychological event…about a military takeover or invasion of town. Strange machines. Dave got killed."

The anxiety that now seized Bill's entire being buckled his knees, dropping him onto his porch, bitter bile rising in his throat.

Roger began sobbing. "Did you…did you have it too?"

LOGANSPORT STATE HOSPITAL, ISAAC RAY TREATMENT CENTER

D ave, Bill, Roger, and Jenny, along with the McFarren and Albrecht girls and their respective parents, all sat in a circle in the pastel blue team room with the specially assigned psychological counseling team they had been meeting with twice a week for months now.

In similar team rooms, also painted in soothing color schemes, sat Roy Hudlin, his wife and daughter beside him, along with wrecker driver Roger Foudray and his dog, Elroy. Also present were Danny Day, Mike Brewer, Joey Donahue, and Mark Mason from B&M Refuse, along with their counselors, also specially assigned to the Logansport facility through the CDC.

In yet another team room sat the rest of Girl Scout Troop 16 and their parents. In other rooms were assembled the rest of the Summitville Police Department officers, both regular and reserve, and the entire compliment of the Summitville Volunteer Fire Department and EMS.

The entire grounds of the Logansport State Hospital and Isaac Ray Treatment Center—plus several offsite locations commandeered by the US government under special provisions of the Patriot Act—were crowded with prefab FEMA trailers that had been converted into team rooms to handle the population of Summitville, Indiana. Every living soul in the town had been assigned to a team of counselors. The MCSD and ISP officers were there too.

Everyone had been horrified, but quite relieved, when the CDC and Homeland Security responders had told them that they had been exposed to a psychotropic antipersonnel chemical agent employed by a terrorist group.

The government teams, consisting of leading experts in chemical warfare, had assured the people that the residual psychedelic effects of the chemical weapon would dissipate over time.

They were informed that the terrorist cell responsible, a radical Islamic splinter group, had been killed while resisting capture.

Specially trained technologists seconded from DARPA were on hand to assist the US Army psychological warfare experts in conducting the debriefing of the victims.

Of particular interest to these teams of experts were the hallucinations suffered by those exposed to the chemical agent, especially details about the technologies manifested in those "hallucinations." How very odd.

Eventually, selected individuals were moved out of their original therapy groups and placed in segregated team environments with special counselors assigned.

Bill observed that those pulled into the special groups were all those who were "killed" during the "event," Dave Millen, chief of Summitville Police Department, included.

Bill had occasion to note one day, while standing in the hallway during a session break, a lady wearing a staff ID badge that he recognized. He had seen her image on the cover jacket of a book on the shelves at Barnes & Noble. She was an expert on NDEs, near-death experiences.

Bill didn't buy a fucking word of any of it.

CHICAGO, ILLINOIS, SOUTH SIDE

The front door to the apartment complex was on a relatively well-lit city street. Immediately adjacent to the entrance to the residential building was a construction area, the worksite blocked off from pedestrian traffic by plywood sheeting erected along the sidewalk. The section of the sidewalk that ran through the construction area had a metal scaffolding overhead with canvas tarp to shield pedestrians from debris.

Although the covered portion of the sidewalk was lit by a series of open bulb lights hung from the overhead, the site was shrouded in shadow and much darker than the street and sidewalk outside the work area.

It will do, thought Sainen as he surveyed where Remy would be doing the deed. Sainen had, in fact, put together much of the information that Remy would use to do the job.

Being a resident of Manila, Sainen reasoned, Remy should be accustomed to street altercations in congested, poorly lit areas, that description fitting a significant percentage of the urban environment in his native Philippines.

The targeting package Remy had been provided indicated that his subject would be attending a meeting in one of the apartment residences on a particular night. A time bracket was provided, along with estimated arrival and departure times.

Except for emergency exits mandated by the city fire code, residents of the building came and went via the large, awning-protected front doors.

The target information Remy was provided even included a meteorological report for the calendar date selected for the operation. Remy was impressed when he saw it.

Remy's target subject was expected to arrive by taxi, but the subject could, being security conscious, approach the location on foot after being dropped a distance away. The subject could be expected to employ counter-surveillance tactics prior to approaching the apartment structure, as well as after departing.

The material Remy had been supplied also included basic information such as physical descriptors, assessments of the subject's weapons and hand-to-hand skills, etc.

The package concluded with suggested egress methods and routes, along with a synopsis of the country exfil plan that had been extensively briefed in previous instructions clandestinely provided to Remy.

The package also cautioned him not to dispose of the weapons used within fifteen blocks of the scene unless required to do so under imminent threat of discovery and arrest.

1900 S. MICHIGAN AVENUE NEAR THE 18ᵀᴴ STREET TRANSIT STATION

The light rain that had been forecast in the meteorological segment of Remy's targeting package was, indeed, falling, a faint odor of ozone present in the air as Ijinashi made his way up the poorly maintained, crumbling concrete steps of the old public library a few blocks from the apartment building identified in Remy's intelligence material.

Ijinashi went to the circular arrangement of cheap vinyl couches arrayed around a chipped and cracked coffee table under the windows at the rear of the library. Newspapers and periodicals were displayed on racks and shelves positioned next to the reading area.

Ijinashi removed his raincoat, shaking the moisture from the garment before laying it over the arm of one of the decrepit couches. Pulling the most current edition of *Popular Mechanics* from the shelves, Ijinashi plopped down on the couch.

Three minutes after he sat down, Remy retrieved a *Chicago Tribune* from the rack and sat down on the couch across from Ijinashi, opening the paper to the financial section.

"I gather you detected no indication of surveillance on your way here," Ijinashi said as he turned the page of the magazine.

"None, sir. No tails evident anywhere along my route here. I am a professional and quite thorough," Remy boasted.

"Outstanding. So tell me about the methodology utilized in reaching out to you and anything you were able to deduce vis-à-vis the identities of those who brokered your assignment."

After listening to Remy talk for about fifteen minutes, paging through the *Popular Mechanics* as he did so, Ijinashi looked up at Remy and, smiling warmly, thanked him for the extraordinarily professional report, for his devotion to the cause, and for his loyalty to his brothers in arms. Ijinashi praised him as hero of the revolution.

Remy, a dedicated believer in the socialist revolution, lapped it up. He believed Ijinashi to be one of those "chosen" to lead the downtrodden workers' rebellion to victory over the money-grubbing oppressors.

Remy also believed that his friend Osvaldo was privy to the secret machinations Remy was embroiled in and that Osvaldo was quietly monitoring things from the background, relying on Remy to champion their cause and help protect its leaders.

Remy was convinced that he was doing the right thing by warning the New Weathermen leader, his proletarian brother, of a plot he believed was designed to demoralize the workers' revolution.

In that, Remy was dead wrong. It was simpler than that. It was just ruthless people covering their asses.

Remy was also convinced that he was a chosen warrior-savior figure, destined to play a keynote role in saving the revolution from evil capitalist conspirators bent on its destruction.

He had been quite easy to manipulate, both by the Cuban case officer he knew as Osvaldo who he erroneously believed to be his friend and by Je-Ju Lee and her Cloud Dragon cohorts in Manila.

A proficient martial artist and committed revolutionary, Remy was also, quite frankly, crazy.

It was a pity, Ijinashi thought, as he looked up into the earnest eyes and gullible face of Remy Sanchez.

Standing, Ijinashi put on his raincoat and tugged on his black gloves in preparation for venturing back out into the cold, misty rain that continued to fall this drab Chicago day.

"Give me about five minutes to get out of the library and on my way then make your own way out. Stay alert for surveillance. I suggest you use the 'L' to make your departure from the area; the Eighteenth Street transit station is just down the block. Get off a couple of stops down and take a cab from there. We can't be too careful."

The intense, near maniacal gleam of the true zealot was evident in Remy's eyes as Ijinashi walked past him and put the magazine back on the shelf.

Ijinashi brutally cranked the head, using both hands and all his core strength, breaking Remy's neck with a sickening pop before walking to the front of the library, past the aging librarian, and out into the drizzle.

Watching from the second-floor window across the street, Sainen knew he would have to take care of this himself, just as he had thought.

Sitting low in the rusted and faded Honda Civic parked down the block, Je-Ju thought of Remy. *Idiot. Goddammit.*

Sainen's cautionary words resonating in her head, Je-Ju knew he would not taunt her with "I told you so," but he would be thinking it. She also knew as she watched Ijinashi disappear around a corner a half block down that she and Sainen would, indeed, need to deal with Ijinashi themselves, as Sainen had said.

MANHATTAN BEACH, CALIFORNIA, CONGRESSIONAL OFFICES OF AVERY "BUSTER" WAVERLY, THIRTY-THIRD CONGRESSIONAL DISTRICT OF CALIFORNIA

Sainen swept into the congressional offices of Buster Waverly with flourish, long hair fluttering in his draft and a wicked grin plastered across his face.

Having attached a special blocking device on the doors, Sainen knew he not only had a captive audience but, far more importantly, that nobody could enter the offices from the street unexpectedly.

Without missing a beat as he strutted across the lobby, he shot the good congressman's security agent square in the forehead, dropping him as if pole axed before the ill-prepared officer could extract his sidearm.

Sainen grabbed up the office manager as she stared dumbstruck at what had just occurred, pulling her to him and kissing her roughly on the lips before shoving her hard away and putting three quick rounds into her—ugly, dark holes stitching in a diagonal up the side of her beige blazer as she crumpled toward the carpet, shock permanently frozen on eyes already glazing over.

A male staffer bolted toward the front reception kiosk in a valiant effort to hit the panic alarm button but instead ran solidly into Sainen's rising knee, his testicles crushing an instant before Sainen pistol-slapped him across his temple. In a smooth flow, Sainen grabbed the stunned intern's hair and cracked his head on the granite counter of the receptionist's kiosk. Coughing bloody froth and bits of broken teeth, the intern cascaded down the front of the kiosk and onto the carpeting.

Having hardly broken stride since entering the front door, Sainen whipped around the right side of the kiosk and flowed toward the rear office spaces like a rushing torrent of angry flood water, bowling over the receptionist who was running out the women's restroom door, smashing her nose and right orbital with a downward-hooking left elbow. As the woman slumped to her knees, Sainen smoothly exchanged the magazine in his pistol for a fresh one retrieved from his pocket.

Sainen opened and whisked through the heavy ornate door into the congressman's private office, surprising the politician as he talked on the phone, unaware of what had transpired up front due to the superb sound-muting qualities of his decorative door.

The fact that Sainen's pistol was equipped with a high-grade suppressor prevented anyone out on the street or elsewhere in the building from being alerted by the shots.

A look of total shock and confusion spread across Buster's face, eyes widening as he gazed upon the grinning apparition that had just invaded his office, pistol in hand.

Another congressional staffer, tapping away on a smart tablet when Sainen burst into the office, also froze in shock and surprise. The young man recovered quickly, however, and jumped from his chair to confront the intruder.

Sainen's vicious side kick caught the staffer's weighted knee as the kid planted his foot to stand from the seated position, buckling the leg and causing the staffer to cant sideways, his upper body carried forward by gravity and momentum.

Taking advantage of the man's broken structure and loss of balance, Sainen shot a short arc elbow horizontally into his face, the full force of his twisting torso behind the blow. The staffer sagged unconscious onto the intricately woven Afghan rug that adorned the congressman's office floor, leaving Buster still staring slack-jawed at the wicked-looking pistol in Sainen's hand.

Sainen walked over to a small antique table in the corner of the congressman's office and withdrew a Cuban cigar from a carved humidor while covering Buster, who still sat behind his desk. Briefly inspecting the cigar, Sainen strolled over to where Buster was seated.

"Light," Sainen said, raising an eyebrow as he held his suppressed Kimber .45 on the tip of Buster's bulbous nose, red from too much booze. Buster fumbled with a fancy silver lighter, finally managing to get it open and lit, holding it toward Sainen, unable to reach the cigar and afraid to lean forward toward him.

Sainen took the lighter and touched the flame to the cigar, puffing it to life before tossing the still-flaming lighter into Buster's lap. Buster banged his knees into the underside of his oversized wood desk as he struggled to retrieve the lighter from his crotch, where it was searing the congressman's expensively tailored suit trousers.

Buster was breathing heavily from fear and too many years of sedentary, privileged lifestyle, his brow glistening with sweat.

His laughter subsiding, Sainen sneered at the terrified congressman, his trademark wicked grin curling across his face. "You goat-fucking vomit sack, you've pissed your pants."

A spreading dark spot was evident on the congressman's trousers.

"You got a hidden security video system running in here, Buster? Don't lie, Buster. See, if you lie, I'll have to hurt you—bad."

"No, no, there is no security camera in here."

Waving the specially customized Kimber Super Carry Ultra+ .45 ACP menacingly at Buster's quivering face, Sainen grinned again and said, "The number, Buster. The one in the Caymans where you funnel the riches you make from your special relationship with the AVI, Yakuza, and Triad boys.

"Get it for me now, Buster. If you fuck around, I will blow your right kneecap off." Sainen canted the suppressor-elongated pistol toward Buster's leg.

"Oh, yeah, Buster, there is nobody conscious out in your front office, so no one will hear you scream. And, as you can see, this superb handgun is nicely suppressed."

Buster shakily drew open his center desk drawer and withdrew his cell phone from where he kept it while working at his desk.

"It's in here, stored on my phone," Buster said as he held the phone out to Sainen.

"What the fuck are you doing, dickhead? Bring up the damn number and write it down for me—now. You have congressional business cards, you arrogant fuck? Write it on one of those; that way I will know where I got it.

"And, hey, don't get any of your stinking sweat on the card."

Sainen pocketed the number, briefly examining the fancy embossed congressional business card before doing so. He then turned his attention back to the quaking congressman, who appeared on the verge of keeling over.

"Outstanding, Buster."

Sainen shot him just above the left eye, the subsonic semi-jacketed hollow-point round blowing out the back of the congressman's head.

Walking back through the congressional offices to the front lobby, Sainen put one round into the head of each of the still-unconscious people on the floor and, for good measure, shot each of the previously shot people again before exchanging his magazines and putting the weapon underneath his stylish blue blazer.

Arriving at the front doors, he removed the blocking device and walked out.

Sainen stopped and got one of In-N-Out Burger's famous double-double cheeseburgers at the In-N-Out Burger on Branch Avenue in Arroyo Grande on his way out of town.

"Buster has been dealt with, along with his aides, who may have seen or heard something regarding the good congressman's side businesses." Although it was a minor divergence from good COMSEC, Sainen was utilizing the Blue-Tooth-linked in-dash cellular feature in his vehicle.

"Understood. I am on the other coast preparing to pay a visit to a small enterprise in Jersey."

Sainen and Je-Ju broke their connection as Je-Ju pulled away from the airport rental car agency and headed toward New Jersey.

After a random and circuitous route around the LA metro area following his departure from Manhattan Beach, Sainen headed toward Long Beach.

LOFT APARTMENTS, 5ᵀᴴ AND ALAMITOS, LONG BEACH, CALIFORNIA

S ainen parked near where the Queen Mary is permanently docked and walked along the beach among bikinied roller bladers and joggers before crossing the road and peeling off into the neighborhoods on the east side of Pacific Coast Highway. Once into the shaded, lightly trafficked residential area, Sainen did a quick clothing change out of the small backpack he was carrying.

Five blocks inland from the beach, alert to his surroundings, Sainen walked down the alley that ran immediately adjacent to the small, three-unit loft apartment building at 5ᵗʰ Street and Alamitos. The loft of interest to Sainen was the one closest to the alleyway.

Sainen glanced up to the taller apartment building that rose a few yards to the south of the lofts. Seeing none of the residents out on their decks, which overlooked the patios of the loft apartments, Sainen walked on north before swinging left out of the alley to head west along the walkway that fronted the lofts.

Putting on the hard hat he had been carrying in his left hand, he knocked on the door of apartment number three.

The resident, seeing an electric company logo on a white hard hat when he peeked through the security peephole, threw back the deadbolt and opened the door a few inches. A tall Asian male wearing blue coveralls smiled and apologized for the intrusion.

"I'm very sorry to bother you this morning, sir, but a recent power surge requires us to check with residents who live in this neighborhood. It will only take a few minutes of your time to answer a couple questions for my survey form, and I'll be out of here. Again, I apologize for disturbing you this morning."

After a brief pause, the man stepped back and opened the door up the rest of the way so Sainen could step into the apartment's tiny foyer.

Sidney Winchester was a special aide to the recently deceased Congressman Buster Waverly. More of interest to Sainen was Sidney's role as Buster's accountant, for the talented Mr. Winchester expertly massaged Buster's nefarious financial activities. More than any other staff employee, Sidney was the one most responsible for keeping the congressman out of the federal slammer. How very unfortunate for the slightly built, mild-mannered Mr. Winchester.

Looking around the small apartment's interior, Sainen saw a suitable spot. *Most accidents occur in the home*, he thought, suppressing a laugh.

As Winchester invited him into the living room space under the overhead loft, Sainen took advantage of the man's momentarily turned back and grabbed him from behind, quickly snaking his arms around the accountant's neck and sinking in a textbook rear naked choke before Sidney could call out.

Arching the man's back rearward as he half stepped back, Sainen used his constricting arms to quickly cut off the blood supply to Sidney's brain, rendering him unconscious.

Sainen held the choke tightly in place for several long minutes until satisfied that the man was dead, ignoring the urine that dampened Sidney's pastel-green golf pants.

Pulling the lifeless Mr. Winchester over to the bottom of the wooden ladder that led up to the loft bedroom, Sainen turned the body around to face north, as if he had been coming down the stairs when he tripped and fell.

Sainen slammed Sidney's head into the metal HVAC panel cover that was located on the south-facing wall at the bottom of the loft steps. He then positioned Winchester's body in a stretched-out posture at the foot of the steps, head on the floor against the HVAC unit cover and feet angled up the stairway and hooked through the open spaces between the steps.

Excellent. Looks like poor Sidney inadvertently hooked a foot through the open steps and fell to his untimely death. Pity. Home accidents, particularly falls, account for a number of fatalities every year.

Quickly but thoroughly scanning the apartment for any sign of a video-equipped home security system, Sainen returned to the foyer, carefully removing the plastic booties that had gone unnoticed by Mr. Winchester.

Sainen pocketed the booties and then opened the door, locked it from the inside, stepped outside, and closed the door behind him, the lock engaging as he pulled it shut. He then removed his thin, flesh-toned gloves, pocketing those with the booties.

Sainen walked west along the sidewalk that ran in front of the lofts. Stepping into a shaded space between the lofts and a green stucco residence that bordered them on the west, Sainen removed his hard hat and coveralls. He retrieved a plastic bag from his pocket and stuffed the overalls in, compressing them into as compact a bundle as he could manage.

Inside both arms of the coveralls were layers of foam rubber that Sainen had fitted into the clothing. He hoped the foam-lined sleeves would minimize any bruising to Winchester's neck that would indicate strangulation to investigating police and medical examiner personnel.

No need to make things easy to investigate, which is why Sainen had taped a bright red flyer on the front receptionist's kiosk in Buster's congressional office lobby—a flyer that was boldly emblazoned with the trademark clenched fist logo of the New Weathermen movement.

Nearby, in Belmont Shores, just down the Pacific Coast Highway from the Long Beach neighborhood where Sidney Winchester had resided, was a gourmet eatery that served up burgers with peanut butter on them that Sainen quite liked. This was turning out to be a real burger orgy sort of day.

NEW JERSEY

The business park was fairly nondescript, a cookie-cutter replica of dozens of other business parks that dotted the outskirts along the periphery of Parisipanny, New Jersey.

The Jordan Shyman Executive Plaza was accessible via a single roadway that ran off a busy six-lane divided highway, the intersection controlled by an automatic signal. The access road looped around back into itself, the big circle drive accommodating roughly twenty-seven businesses, two ponds with picnic tables, and a host of mom-and-pop delis and grills sprinkled throughout the park.

Trident Dart Imports, 123370 Whiteboard Parkway, Parisippany, New Jersey, 07054, was located about halfway around the loop on the south side of Whiteboard Parkway.

Trident Dart Imports had red brick fronting and an upscale appearance, its parking lot littered with high-end automobiles.

Je-Ju sat in her rental car, windows down, watching a construction crane swing around in the distance, yet another commercial structure rising from what used to be farmland.

Burnt out from too much coffee, Je-Ju was ready to call it a day and head back to her hotel, having satisfactorily completed her three-day casing of the import company and the patterns of its employees.

Bright and early the next morning, well rested from a good night's sleep, Je-Ju Lee bounced into the front lobby of Trident Dart Imports.

"Good morning. I'm Faith with Mid Atlantic Enterprises. I'm a demographics analyst conducting a survey of this business park and some others in the Parisippany area. Mid Atlantic has been contracted to determine whether a health and fitness center—a gym—would fly here. Wondering if you would have a minute to answer a couple questions for me?"

The young Asian man with the ponytail behind the counter of the small, well-appointed lobby looked at the attractive young girl in front of him and nodded. "Sure, yeah, what do you need to know?"

"Let me get my tablet out, okay? This will only take a couple of minutes, I promise," Je-Ju said cheerfully as she set her backpack on the floor and unzipped the pack's main compartment.

Unable to see the pack over the counter, Ponytail had no warning when Je-Ju stood up with a Daewoo K7 suppressed subgun instead of an iPad.

The great thing about the Daewoo Precision Industries K7 nine-millimeter submachine gun was that it sported a permanent, integral factory suppressor. A versatile weapon, the K7 would accept high-capacity magazines from both the Uzi and the Beretta PM12. Designed for the South Korean Special Forces, the weapon was only 620 millimeters long with the stock retracted and had a rate of fire of eleven hundred rounds per minute.

Je-Ju fired a burst of nine millimeter Parabellum square into the center of the man's chest, dropping him instantly. Reaching back down to the backpack, she retrieved a black nylon bandolier that contained several loaded Daewoo magazines and slung it over her left shoulder.

Surprised that no one had come to the lobby to investigate the thud made by counter boy hitting the floor, Je-Ju pushed through the double swinging doors into the warehouse that made up the bulk of the leased commercial space occupied by Trident Dart Imports.

Sitting around a card table with a pall of cigarette smoke hanging overhead were five Chinese men, young street gangsters mostly in their twenties engrossed in a poker game.

Je-Ju cat walked forward, the K7 extended in both hands at eye level, firing controlled bursts into the group of card players as she glided toward them. A spray of blood, bone, poker chips, and shattered beer bottles exploded from the table as she closed on the hapless men. Not one got to his weapon in time.

From the corner of her eye, Je-Ju saw the lone figure start down the staircase from the second-floor office, pistol in hand. From her days on the other coast of the United States, she recognized Bobby Shing, Triad button man.

Jerking the K7 up and to her right, Je-Ju let go a quick burst at Shing, pelting the staircase and wall inches in front of him. Bobby cranked off three rapid-fire rounds at Je-Ju, one she felt burn through her hair on the side of her head, a very near miss.

Bobby Shing, veteran of numerous gangland firefights, racked off another string of three rounds one-handed as he bounded down the steps, jumping the last three and diving behind a forklift as Je-Ju's extended burst ate up the wall, ricocheted off the staircase railing, and followed him to the forklift. Bobby narrowly got behind it in time.

Goddamn, that was fucking close, Bobby thought as he quickly calculated the number of rounds he had left in his handgun, having no spare magazine on him. *Fuck!* Being at a tactical disadvantage in a gunfight was not a situation Bobby was accustomed to.

The K7's magazine exhausted, Je-Ju pulled her Chiappa Rhino .357 Magnum from under her shirt and fired off a round in Bobby's direction to cover her retreat across the warehouse floor to a stack of wooden shipping crates, where she could exchange magazines in the subgun from behind cover.

Someone in an adjacent unit must have heard the exchange of gunfire and called the police, as both Je-Ju and Bobby Shing could now hear the wail of sirens in the distance.

This is your lucky fuckin' day, Bobby Shing, Je-Ju thought as she bolted across the ten feet of open space between her and the swinging doors to the lobby, firing another extended burst at Bobby's hiding place to cover her retreat.

Entering the lobby, Je-Ju knew she had only seconds to unass the scene before the cops arrived and she was the one who was fucked. She quickly dropped the bandolier next to the dead lobby guy and then placed the K7 submachine gun down near his hand. She then quickly ran out the front door and rocketed down the sidewalk away from the scene, tearing her gloves off as she ran.

Je-Ju knew that the responding police units were nearly on scene, their sirens having cut off; the police would traverse the last block or so silently, no lights or sirens.

Cutting through a gap between buildings, Je-Ju ran across an expanse of manicured lawn behind the businesses before scaling a chain-link fence at the edge of the industrial park property, entering a field high with weeds and un-mown grass.

Je-Ju arrived at the small cul-de-sac in the sea of townhomes and condominiums where she had parked her rental car, allowing herself time to sit in the vehicle for a minute to catch her breath before driving off.

Bobby Shing ran up the steps to the office and grabbed his jacket, cell phone, and keys before unlocking and exiting the heavy rear door that opened onto the stairs that ran down the back wall of the business. There was nothing he could do for his colleagues. If any were still alive, he didn't have time to help them, anyway. Five-O would be coming through the front door any second.

Bobby rode his Kawasaki Ninja 300 behind the row of business units until he arrived at where the circle drive reconnected with itself, a half block from the light at the main highway.

Seeing no more responding police cars and assuming the cops were all now occupied at Trident Dart, Bobby gunned his bike onto Whiteboard Parkway and rode up to the light, turned left and entered the flow of the traffic heading out of town.

The wind whistling by his dark visored helmet, Bobby wondered just what in the hell Je-Ju Lee was doing shooting up his New Jersey crew.

A week later, Je-Ju and Bobby Shin were back in Southern California, Je-Ju discussing the East Coast debacle with Sainen while Bobby Shing did the same with his Triad boss.

LOS ANGELES

"It was Bobby Shing I saw at Trident Dart in Jersey, Sainen. For one, we did not know that Shing's crew was involved with the import front. They must have assumed control of it from Hung's crowd in a quiet deal of some sort, given we heard nothing about it. And, secondly, Shing is still alive."

"Yup. That is not good, Je-Ju. Shing is no one to fuck with. Worse, his boss is about as significant a Triad boss as you can find in America. Abso-fucking-lutely not somebody you want to idly fuck with. Any chance he was arrested, caught by the cops before he could escape the building?"

"No. Bobby is too smart for that. He had time to get out, same as I did. No, he wasn't wrapped up by the cops. My bet is he is back here in California… likely back up in 'Frisco, where his boss is headquartered."

"Well, Je-Ju, one thing we can count on then: we will be seein' ol' Bobby again. His crowd won't take kindly to you wasting those boys out in Jersey, especially if that operation was a big money maker or key logistical link for the Triad."

"Yeah, I know. I know."

CHINATOWN, SAN FRANCISCO

In the backroom of an Internet-order Chinese herbal medicine warehouse, tucked away in a warren of narrow side streets and crowded alleyways in San Francisco's sprawling Chinatown, sat Bobby Shing and his boss.

Bobby seldom got his ass chewed, and he didn't like it. His boss was fuming, asking why in the hell that bitch Lee was still alive. Bobby had no good answer other than he missed. It was really simple. She was alive because he had not taken her out of the picture in Jersey.

Spittle flew as Triad kingpin Jason Mark Wen raged, bordering on an arm-waving tantrum. His rage was not directed toward Shing, however, but toward Je-Ju Lee.

"That fucking bitch Lee! And that goddamn son of a bitch Sainen Chinhung is a known associate. Yakuza cocksuckers! That Jersey thing was important, and she—they—fucked it. Fucked it all to hell!"

"I have no idea why they—or the Yaks—would want to hose one of our operations, sir."

"I don't give a flyin' fuck why—not a flying fuck, hear me!"

"Yessir."

"That little street shoot 'em up that we and the Yaks and the fucking Koreans got into a while back is cooled. Normalcy returned to everyone's business following the negotiations, and everyone was getting on with making fucking money. So why the fuck would a Cloud Dragon or fucking Yakuza or whoever the fuck she represents hose down our boys?"

"I have no answer, sir."

"Here is what we are fucking going to do, Bobby. I am going to call a couple Koreans I know up in LA to see if they know any fucking thing, then I will phone the sosai of Sumiyoshi-Kai in Japan about that bitch Je-Ju Lee, followed by that old bastard in Kobe who runs the Yamaguchi-gumi that Sainen Chinhung was working for before the start of that Cloud Dragon shit."

"Yessir."

"You give me a bit to make those calls, talk to a few people. Once I have assessed the answers I get from the Koreans and the Yaks, I want to make another call to Hong Kong, talk to old man Chen."

"Right, sir."

"It will take me a day or so to get all that done. Then I will tell you whether to proceed or not."

"Got it."

"You and the boys, you scope out that Je-Ju bitch and her fucking Yak buddy Sainen and get a handle on where they are laying their heads. Watch 'em. I want to know what they eat for fucking breakfast and when they take a shit, understand?"

"I do, sir. But, uh, why are we connecting Chinhung to Je-Ju? It was just Lee I saw out in New Jersey."

"Mr. Chen told me a couple months back that there was speculation that Je-Ju Lee and Sainen Chinhung had semi-detached their operations from the Yakuza, going off on their own with independent enterprises."

"Okay, that would be very, uh, unorthodox, sir."

"It would, yes. While connections between Chinhung, Lee, and their respective Yak organizations do, of course, still exist, the two seem to have set up their own empires, loosely linked to each other. Chinhung is reportedly operating out of Taiwan, and Lee out of the Philippines. They have somehow accumulated incredible power, acquiring sufficient status to operate solo without Yak interference. As you say, Bobby, very unorthodox...very unorthodox indeed.

"So, Bobby, it is my belief that this Je-Ju Lee and Sainen Chinhung are, as we here in America say, in cahoots."

"I see."

"And, Bobby?"

"Yessir?"

"One other thing. Mr. Chen also told me that there appears to be a connection between Je-Ju Lee and that Korean guy who runs the New Weathermen radical group, Ijinashi-Tamna. The intelligence connecting them is tenuous, at best. But Mr. Chen thought that there had been, at some point in the past, a definite connection between Lee and this Ijinashi.

"What I am getting at is this: I want all bases covered this time around with no fucking loopholes. I want this Ijinashi dickhead taken out along with the bitch Lee and that Sainen guy, okay?"

"Yessir, it will be handled."

"You and your crew be prepared to whack 'em all whenever I say, you hear? No fucking mistakes this time. You be ready. Triad has been around for centuries. We are not—*not*—going to allow some shithead newbies to run us out of town."

"Understood, sir. I will await your orders." Bobby Shing bowed respectfully and took his leave.

MALIBU

Most people familiar with Sainen Chinhung would consider being face to face with him akin to touching noses with a cobra. Not so, however, for Je-Ju Lee, for they were lovers.

The house they leased in Malibu was as upscale as they come, and it was a frequent layover when they were together in LA attending to their mutual Cloud Dragon business interests.

The beach home had been done with an Old Hollywood retro look in mind, the interior designer doing a first-rate job of it. Given Chinhung and Lee's fortunes, no expense had been spared.

Leased in alias, with all the utilities, taxes, records, and bills associated with the house also being in alias, none of their real Hollywood neighbors knew anything about the occasional residents, seeing them only rarely. Most could not describe them, if asked, other than to say that they appeared to be a young Asian couple, the male being abnormally tall for an Asian.

The cars occasionally seen parked in the drive were no different than the expensive rides parked in all the other drives of the rich, upscale neighborhood peppered with famous names and faces. The couple was occasionally seen out on their deck that overlooked the ocean, just like the other residents with oceanfront property.

They were typical, which was, of course, by design.

From a security standpoint, the properties were not butted up against each other, but they were close enough that gunshots, breaking glass, screams, and the sounds of violent altercation would be detectable by neighbors.

The fronts of most Malibu properties were protected by walls, and all had gated driveways. Views of the homes and their occupants from the public road were obscured by decorative foliage.

The rear sides of the homes that faced the ocean were more open, with the beach line essentially unobstructed for aesthetic purposes, this being environmentally conscious and nature-friendly Southern California.

Bobby Shing's crew was experienced, street savvy, and cautious—not prone to amateurish mistakes. They were methodical and professional in the conduct of their business, which was killing people.

Most of Shing's inner circle had been with Bobby—and Wen's Triad organization—for upward of a decade. They were solidly loyal and highly capable, to a man.

Their surveillance of Je-Ju and Sainen, discovery of their Malibu residence, and subsequent casing of the property was thorough, their activities going unnoticed.

Given the relatively frequent sheriff's patrols and the top-of-the-line home security systems favored by the neighborhood's well-heeled and security-conscious residents, Bobby and his team came to the conclusion that maybe the Malibu residence would not be the optimal choice for the conduct of their business. Adding to the risk were the private security patrols that roamed the neighborhood in addition to the random county police drive-throughs.

What did look promising was a couple of the other LA locations Chinhung and Lee tended to frequent: Terminal Island and San Pedro. The expanse of commercial seafront and the associated industrial sprawl created by the side-by-side ports of Long Beach and Los Angeles afforded many enticing possibilities.

SAFEWAY

Kenny Wong, Mike Li, and Billy Cheong were shopping in the Safeway supermarket near the Pacific Coast Highway in downtown Long Beach, sent there by Bobby Shing to purchase food supplies for their surveillance activities.

They were in the store less than five minutes when Sainen, who had entered the same store to replenish his supply of Tylenol, made them, immediately recognizing two of the three Triad gangsters. Silently cursing his bad luck, Sainen attempted to leave without drawing attention to himself.

Quickly turning down an aisle to avoid detection by Kenny Wong and Mike Li, Sainen ran smack into Billy Cheong. A momentary look of shock crossed Cheong's face, as Sainen was the last person he expected to run into in the Safeway store.

With nothing else to do, Sainen smiled at Billy.

"Why is your punk-ass smiling, Chinhung?"

Grin widening, he said, "Because I know that nobody will be able to get here fast enough to save you."

Before the look in Sainen's deadpan eyes could start a chill up Billy's spine, Sainen's movement forward into a bow stance and double hand taiji push sent him flying violently backward, crashing into the glass doors of the packaged seafood cooler, cracking his head against the heavy glass, spider-webbing the pane.

Momentarily dazed, Billy slid down the front of the cooler, his slumping body almost making it to the floor before Sainen's karambit cut into the front of his throat and ripped viciously out the side of the neck. Blood spurted from the ruptured artery onto what appeared to be the freshly mopped tile floor of the grocery aisle. *Sorry about that shit.*

Hearing the commotion an aisle over, Kenny Wong and Mike Li rushed over to check on Cheong, finding him sprawled in the aisle nearly bled out, head canted at an unnatural angle against the frozen foods cooler. Billy's piece was still in his waistband.

"What the fuck?"

Looking at each other, Kenny and Mike bolted down the frozen foods aisle toward the front of the store, their motivations torn between finding Cheong's assailant and getting the hell out of there before a customer stumbled onto Billy's body and started screaming.

Sometimes shit just happens, like Chinhung, Cheong, Li and Wong all coming together in a supermarket. Murphy's Law.

And Murphy loves nothing better than fucking with people already in compromising situations. As Sainen reached the front of the supermarket, two situations awaited him.

Store management was trying to negotiate with an intoxicated homeless woman at the counter where lottery tickets were sold, and Loomis Armored was making a cash pickup, two of its armed uniformed guards standing in front of the store's office door.

As the Loomis guards warily eyed the homeless lady—her slurred and angry voice rising in volume—Sainen noticed the employee behind the counter pick up the phone, likely calling the cops. *Fuck.*

Making a quick judgment call, Sainen elected not to walk past the guards and store personnel to get out the front doors. He didn't need anyone pro-viding a good description of the tall, long-haired Asian guy to the Long

Beach Police Department when the stiff was discovered in the frozen foods aisle.

Turning around and choosing a different aisle than he came up, Sainen headed back toward the rear of the store, hoping to escape out the rear employee exit.

Wong and Li, like Sainen, having decided against parading past the armored car guards and store personnel clustered up front, also headed quickly toward the back of the store.

Sainen rounded the corner of the dairy aisle just in time to run into Li and Wong, all of them heading for the employees-only door to access the store's loading dock area and, ultimately, the rear employee parking lot and safety.

Fortunately, at this hour, the store was nearly vacant of customers; but, as fate would have it, one of the handful that was shopping apparently had just entered the frozen foods aisle, based on the blood-curdling scream that echoed through the store.

That high-pitched screech momentarily diverted the attention of Kenny and Mike, already surprised by their unexpected face-to-face encounter with Sainen Chinhung at the back of the store.

That was all the diversion that Sainen needed.

Head-butting Kenny square in the face, Sainen elbowed the man across the Adam's apple and thrust his left knee upward into his groin. Sainen then shoved the gasping and rattled Kenny Wong into Mike Li, knocking Li off balance and preventing him from completing the draw of his pistol from the small of his back.

Stepping quickly at an angle past Wong's falling body, now entangled with Li's, Sainen came alongside Li's left side and drove a horizontal elbow into his temple. Torquing his torso around to his left, Sainen blasted Li in the temple again with the opposite elbow.

In a smooth, coordinated movement taken from Filipino arnis, Sainen raked the karambit in his right hand across the side of Li's neck, severing the artery. Sainen used his left hand, which was closely following behind his right, to shield his eyes from the spray of blood from Li's neck, all simultaneous with his torso's rotation back to the right. Sainen then drove his left knee into Li's testicles and, reaching in an arc around the side of Li's head, drew the hooked blade of the karambit laterally across both of his eyes, destroying them both.

Sainen turned his attention from the doomed Mike Li and stomped the exposed neck of the downed Kenny Wong, crushing the vertebra with his heel.

"Cleanup, aisle five," Sainen muttered as he breezed through the employee door on his way out of the Safeway.

MARINA DEL REY

As she exited the Sport Chalet, shopping bag in hand, Je-Ju noted the same beige BMW parked a few doors down on Maxella Avenue that she had seen on Colorado Avenue over in Santa Monica earlier that morning when she was leaving the Tiato Kitchen Bar Garden restaurant.

More than once over the span of an hour and a half, nearly five miles and multiple road changes, is not a coincidence. It is surveillance.

Using the extraction and feigned fumbling of her car keys from her purse as an excuse to stop and surreptitiously look back at the Beemer again, Je-Ju saw that the car appeared to have three occupants, the two up front likely Asian males, from what she could tell with the bright sun glinting in her eyes, its rays only partly mitigated by her Giorgio Armani shades.

It was hard to be sure, given the glare of the sun, but the front passenger bore a resemblance to her one-time street partner Animal Mother. If that was the case, this was not good. Not good at all. Mother had only one skill set.

Je-Ju pulled her bright yellow Camaro SS away from the curb and into traffic on Maxella Avenue, her dark sunglasses shielding the fact that her eyes were repeatedly darting to the outside rear view, keeping track of the beige Beemer, now also pulling into traffic several cars behind her.

Fucking sonofabitch, Je-Ju thought as she capitalized on slowing for a pedestrian in the crosswalk to more closely peer at the Beemer's occupants, concluding that it was, indeed, her former partner and Triad shooter in the beige BMW. "Yup, that's Mother, all right. Damn."

Furtively retrieving her Chiappa Rhino .357 from under the seat, Je-Ju began formulating a plan of action. First and foremost, she needed to decide on a route of travel most advantageous to her and least accommodating to the likely hit team trailing her.

SIERRA MIKE ONE

When it needed salty professionals and a degree of disassociation, the US government utilized contract help. These folks, whose salaries tended to be more attractive than those of general-schedule government staff employees, also tended to have superior skill sets, honed from years of experience.

That was the case with Sierra Mike One, a small, elite team whose claim to fame was its ability to eradicate unwanted human pathogens deemed too troublesome to allow continued existence. In short, Sierra Mike One whacked people who had pissed off the government.

Sometimes, Sierra Mike's targets hadn't really pissed anyone off. They were just liabilities. That was not lost on the members of Sierra Mike One.

Sierra Mike One—abbreviated as SM1 on the few government and cleared industrial contractor documents that even mentioned them—was typically provided heavily sanitized targeting packages.

These carefully prepared, concise documents provided only what material the team would need to accomplish its mission and were meticulously cleansed of any information that could link the government to SM1's extra-legal activities. This was the case with the Ijinashi Tamna targeting portfolio.

SM1's members, as professional as they were, could not know that they had competition on this job. Their competition, while not made up of former Special Forces commandos, were nonetheless just as lethal. It was a fact that the Triad boys had far less restrictive bureaucracy to contend with and virtually no rules to speak of. Combat experience is the anvil on which all warriors are forged, and the Triad boys had lots of experience with the purveyance of violence.

It could also be argued that the Triad guys were more highly motivated, the price of failure in their case generally being such that it was never really a rational option.

The SM1 team didn't know it, but that was actually the situation in their case as well.

BURTON CHACE PARK

Je-Ju, being a very experienced and savvy street warrior, had begun laying on an escape plan immediately upon her return to California from New Jersey, motivated to do so after being forced by circumstances to leave Bobby Shing alive back at Trident Dart Imports.

Chance truly does favor the prepared mind, and Je-Ju had not remained alive this long through lack of preparation or by taking unnecessary chances. She was well aware of the ramifications of shooting up one of Wen's Triad operations and leaving a witness behind to tell about it. It wasn't rocket science, for crying out loud.

Je-Ju regretted not telling Sainen about the precautions she had taken after her return to Southern California but figured that he likely had taken or was taking similar steps for self-preservation. They were lovers and business partners, not a married couple.

Je-Ju had purchased a well-maintained 2012 Donzi 35 ZRO speedboat for $229,000 and had leased dock space for it in Marina Del Rey's Burton Chace Park. She had the boat fueled and had laid on a supply of nonperishable camp foods and potable water. The boat was prepped and ready to go whenever it might be needed.

Always one for detail, Je-Ju even had the boat tied up with its starboard side against the south side of the pier so that its bow was pointed toward open water for a quick departure. Every second counted in an emergency.

Je-Ju, knowing that she would have pursuers if she ever needed to—when she needed to—utilize the ZRO for escape, had placed a small but powerful plastic explosive charge under the pier a few yards down from where her boat was docked.

The package was weatherized and equipped for remote command detonation via a number dialed from her cell phone. The explosion would be sufficient to blow out several feet of the pier, discouraging any pursuers on foot who happened to be on that section of the pier.

In preparation for a hasty departure, Je-Ju kept a small bug-out kit in the trunk of her Camaro that contained a cocked and locked Wilson Sentinel compact nine-millimeter, ammo, spare magazines, combat folder, a clean cell, money, clean credit cards, passport, and a few clothing items. She also carried her Jopon sword with her now, everywhere she went, if possible.

A similar kit was also stored onboard the Donzi, along with a Kalashnikov AKMS with folding buttstock she had stored in the cockpit.

As she drove, Je-Ju reached over to the passenger floorboard and unzipped the colorful fabric suitcase that filled most of the space. Keeping one eye on the road while keeping watch on where the Beemer was behind her, Je-Ju threw the flap back and positioned the contents of the suitcase for easy extraction.

She doubted that Mother and his pals in the BMW were prepared for what she was about to dish up for them.

She was, she reasoned, as prepared as she could be. Most importantly, she had a plan.

PIER 7

J e-Ju figured that, given the urban environment, the Beemer boys would opt to wait until she led them to a more suitable location for an ambush. Gunfire in the midst of the beautiful people in stylish seaside communities just wouldn't do.

Je-Ju was counting on Mother and company liking the treed little expanse of Burton Chace Park that adorned the north side of Marina Del Rey's Pier 7.

If any of them survived the little picnic she had planned for the park, she would light them up with the charge waiting underneath the pier.

The Donzi ZRO's speed and the extra fuel bladder installed in the speedboat would permit her to put many miles between her and the carnage she planned to leave behind in sunny Marina Del Rey this fine California morning.

Just as she had counted on, Mother and his Beemer butt buddies were more than happy to follow her into the marina area. She imagined they were checking their weapons and preparing to engage as soon as the opportune moment presented itself. *Dickheads.*

They were now on Via Dolce, the street that completely ringed the marina except for the channel opening. Pier 7 and the park were at the southeast end of the marina area.

Turning from Via Dolce Street onto the narrower access road to the piers, Je-Ju then chose the lane that went directly through Burton Chace Park, adjacent to Pier 7, where her Donzi was waiting. As she knew it would, the Beemer sped up as soon as they drew into the park's wooded area, rapidly closing the distance to her Camaro. *Excellent, boys, excellent.*

Je-Ju made one final check to ensure that the items in the suitcase were ready and brought the Camaro to a stop in the middle of the lane, angling it slightly so she could utilize the vehicle for cover.

Seeing Je-Ju's Camaro abruptly stop, Animal Mother—actual name Jason Yu—bolted out the passenger-side door of the Beemer before it had come to a complete stop, knowing that all kinds of hell was about to visit them.

Mother made sure he had as much of the Beemer's engine compartment as possible between him and what he knew would be coming his way from Je-Ju. Bringing his ARES FMG submachine gun to bear, he let loose a blast at Je-Ju's car, silver-ringed holes stitching across its trunk and right rear quarter where the nine-millimeter rounds blew the yellow paint away as they punched through the car's body.

Je-Ju drew two weapons through the open flap of the suitcase, one an AKM Russian assault carbine with a GP-25 forty-millimeter underbarrel grenade launcher attached. The other was a specially chopped Benelli M3 twelve-gauge semi-auto shotgun that she had had custom made in Italy.

Crouching behind the angled shelter of her vehicle, Je-Ju swung the AKM up and fired a quick burst at Mother, shattering the Beemer's windshield and pock-marking the passenger door with a staggered line of holes. Shifting the weapon to the right, she fired a second burst through the driver-side windshield.

Mother retreated down the side of the BMW to a position where more of the car was between him and Je-Ju, seeing the interior door panel of the passenger door he was previously behind explode in a spray of fractured plastic and faux wood.

It was funny, Je-ju thought, the things the mind focuses on in times of stress. She could swear that Mother was wearing some sort of snakeskin patterned cowboy boots. *Brother.*

The driver, having only partially exited the vehicle before Je-Ju fired, caught two of the 7.62X39 Russian AK rounds in his right chest and shoulder. Knocked back against the door jamb, he struggled to extricate himself from the doorway so he could make it around to the more protected area at the rear of the Beemer. Too late. Je-Ju, seeing him vulnerable, cranked off another quick burst, this time all the rounds finding center mass, dropping one very dead Mr. Gao like a sack of bricks to the pavement beside the Beemer.

The exchange having taken place so suddenly, the idiot in the backseat of the BMW was trying to shoot out the windshield so he could fire on Je-Ju from inside the car. He must have seen that shit in a movie or something.

Backseat Idiot—a Mr. Liang originally from Guangxi Province, China— never got a chance to draw a bead on his intended target, succeeding only in rendering himself effectively deaf from repeatedly firing his nine-millimeter inside the Beemer. But that did not matter a bit.

Je-Ju let loose another quick burst to her left to keep Mother occupied then leveled the AKM at the BMW and fired the GP-25, launching a high-explosive forty-millimeter grenade into the interior of the doomed vehicle. The explosion literally caused the Beemer to bounce, levitating its crumpled form several inches into the air before gravity slammed it back to the roadway, its top flayed open. Bits and pieces of the late Mr. Liang drifted to earth along with Beemer parts.

Je-Ju emptied the remaining rounds in the AKM's magazine in Mother's direction, not seeing him anymore but not wanting to assume the explosion killed him. If he was pressed against the vehicle body for cover, he was likely history. However, Je-Ju knew assumption was the mother of all fuckups.

With no time to dawdle, Je-Ju dropped the AKM to the ground and, using the Benelli to cover the threat from a still-unseen Mother, leaned into the Camaro and snatched her sword from the suitcase. Since she had another, duplicate bug-out kit in the Donzi, she elected to leave the one in the

Camaro's trunk and be on her way before LA's finest showed up. Besides, both of the Camaro's rear tires were deflated from bullet strikes. The gunfire, and especially the explosion, would have the local citizenry dialing their phones. She needed to run and run fast.

Sprinting across the short stretch of beautifully manicured lawn between her and the pier, Je-Ju could now hear sirens in the distance. All she needed was for one of LAPD's choppers to arrive on scene before she could get clear of the marina and out into open water. Hopefully, there would be no witnesses to provide a description of her boat for the Coast Guard. But she couldn't worry about all that right now; she first needed to get her ass to the boat and get out of Dodge.

Animal Mother's left leg, both upper and lower left arm, and part of his left side were peppered with shrapnel from the explosion. Luckily, in an effort to cut through the park and flank Je-Ju's position, he had moved several yards away from the car prior to the grenade's detonation. The force of the blast still knocked him on his ass, but his injuries were not life-threatening. Hampered only by a slight limp, Mother was making good time as he headed toward the marina in pursuit of Je-Ju, loading a fresh magazine into his ARES FMG subgun.

Je-Ju, panting slightly from her all-out dash to Pier 7, pounded down the pier, covering the final few yards to her boat, her high-speed ticket to safety. Glancing back toward the pall of smoke rising from the burning BMW, she saw Mother racing toward her, his submachine gun raised, a stream of smoke trailing from its muzzle. Bits and pieces of the wooden pier planking kicking up around her, Je-Ju ducked and brought her Benelli to bear, firing off two twelve-gauge rounds in quick succession toward Mother, knowing that the 00-buckshot would spread too widely before reaching him, given the distance that still separated them.

Je-Ju hurriedly knelt and untied the aft line then ran forward, keeping Mother in sight, and began undoing the forward line on the Donzi, one-handedly firing off another round toward Mother as another burst from his subgun stuttered across the pier, two of the rounds striking her boat.

Mother slowed his pace, now wounded a bit more severely from one of the .33-inch lead pellets of 00-buck that found his lower abdomen, although it did no immediately fatal damage.

Dropping his exhausted submachine gun to the ground, Mother retrieved his .45-caliber Sig Sauer from his inside-the-waistband hideout holster and popped off a semi-aimed shot in Je-Ju's direction, splintering the wood on a pier pylon next to her boat.

Tossing the Benelli and her sword into the boat's cockpit, Je-Ju pulled her Chiappa Rhino and, taking careful aim, fired off one round of 125-grain semi-jacketed HP .357 Magnum at Mother before she climbed aboard the now-untied speedboat.

Mother spun partially around and, knees buckling, dropped to the ground, a gaping wound in his right shoulder where the .357 slug smashed into him, the hollow-point bullet blowing out a ragged chunk of flesh as it exited. Dazed and bleary-eyed, the effects of shock creeping in, Mother slumped forward, wanting to vomit.

The Donzi coughed to life, and Je-Ju began turning the wheel to start pulling away from the pier. Looking back over her shoulder toward Mother, she saw that he was trying to stand, apparently her .357 round having found its target. She retrieved her revolver from the waistband of her jeans and fired another round at him, wanting to give herself time to clear the dock and put some open water between her and Mother.

That round, fired hastily, missed its target, kicking up a piece of turf next to Mother, who had just managed to assume a standing posture on wobbly legs.

Mother had dropped his Sig when Je-Ju's round took him in the shoulder, and he had to retrieve it from the ground with his left hand, his right inca-pacitated from Je-Ju's .357 slug.

Seeing Je-Ju pulling away from the pier, blue exhaust and frothing water bubbling at the speedboat's stern, Jason "Animal Mother" Yu mustered every ounce of strength and will he had left in his being, pushing one foot in front of the other as he transitioned from a stumble to an unsteady jog, trying to cover the last few yards that separated him from Je-Ju's departing boat.

Unable to throttle up until she hit deeper water, Je-Ju looked back to see where Mother was, surprised to see him heading down the length of Pier 7, pistol raised in his left hand.

Mother's shots were falling short of the rapidly diminishing target presented by Je-Ju's departing boat. She would still have been within effective pistol range had Mother's right arm been operable. As it was, his weak-hand shooting left much to be desired. In his defense, most men would have already collapsed from the wounds he had sustained. The fact that Mother was still functional was a testimony to his stamina and resolve.

Je-Ju put her Chiappa down and, pulling her cell phone from her right front jean pocket, went to favorites and speed-dialed the number marked "seven."

The sharp explosion of the plastic explosives affixed to the underside of Pier 7 reverberated out across the water, sending a geyser of shattered wood planking skyward. Je-Ju felt the slight increase in atmospheric pressure as the explosion's shock wave passed over her.

Looking back toward Pier 7, Je-Ju thought she caught sight of a booted leg as it twirled through the air.

Je-Ju Lee, whose adopted name sounded in English like "Jay Jew," was escaping danger in a fast boat in a place with trees—palm trees—like those that grew in Southern China, just as Ijinashi-Tamna had said so very long ago, in another time.

BUG OUT

Now alerted to the forces arrayed against him, Sainen wasted no time in unassing Long Beach. After his departure from the Safeway supermarket, Sainen made his way immediately to a small self-storage business on Argonault in Aliso Viejo, California.

Opening the padlock that secured his unit, Sainen entered and grabbed up the bug-out bag he kept prepacked in case of emergency, a very similar precaution to what Je-Ju had taken.

Checking the bag's contents, Sainen made sure it was as he had left it. Satisfied, he zipped the bag closed and set it by the door.

If interrupted, he could grab the bag and go in a pinch, able to get along with just what was contained in the bag.

Also in the self-storage space were nonperishable food stocks, cases of bottled water, several long guns, ample stocks of ammunition for his array of weaponry, and various other items that might be valuable to someone needing to unass in a hurry.

Sainen closed the door and, clicking on the small overhead light, pulled fresh clothes from a rack and began changing, getting out of the attire he had on during the Safeway incident.

Dressed in clean jeans and a comfortable t-shirt bearing the image of Bruce Lee, Sainen pulled on a pair of Oboz trail shoes.

A passport, driver's license, Social Security card, and other identity papers were in his bug-out bag, as was a Beretta PSX Storm in .45 ACP. Sainen favored the compact Beretta, finding them well made, reliable, and accurate right out of the box.

As with Je-Ju's emergency kit, Sainen's bag also included a high-end smart phone, money, clean credit cards, additional alternative passports, a couple of knives, and a few clothing items.

Moving over to the far left rear corner of the storage unit, Sainen moved an old green military foot locker aside and, brushing the dust away with his hand, used the tip of his karambit to gently pry up a special panel he had personally installed in the flooring of the unit. Pulling a long Pelican case from the hidden compartment, Sainen sat it on the deck, unlocked the heavy-duty security locks, and pulled his sword—the Four Dragons Sword—from the foam-padded and felt-lined interior.

Sainen selected a Kel-Tec composite framed pocket pistol from the shelf and made sure the little .32 was loaded and ready, pushing the tiny gun into his jeans pocket, using an Uncle Mike's nylon holster to prevent it from "printing," revealing the outline of a pistol to a trained observer.

Although thought by most to be underpowered, the little .32 ACP with modern rounds would put the hurts on you at close range, which is precisely what it was designed for. The attached Crimson Trace laser sight made it so that only the most incompetent shooter could miss. Its true utility to Sainen was that it was easily concealed; it literally fit in a pocket.

Sainen removed from the shelf another Beretta PSX Storm, this one also chambered for the venerable .45 ACP cartridge, and pulled a specially made CrossBreed concealable holster from the bins of firearms-related materials arrayed on the shelving.

This wasn't the first time Sainen had performed this drill, so he proceeded through his checkout list quickly and readied himself to head out, making sure his karambit was clipped to his jeans before leaving the storage unit.

Having loaded all his gear into the car, Sainen climbed into his Mustang 500 GT and began his bug-out route.

Sainen being Sainen and somewhat crazy, there was one little detour he wanted to make before taking his leave from California. Picking up the Pacific Coast Highway in Laguna Beach, he headed north.

VANCOUVER, BRITISH COLUMBIA, CANADA

Ijinashi deplaned and, upon clearing Canadian Customs, headed directly to the rental car kiosks, having only carry-on and no need to stand with the crowds around the carousels watching checked luggage go round and round.

Because of his utilization of commercial air travel, Ijinashi was totally unarmed when he departed the international airport, so he needed to make a stop in Vancouver's sprawling Chinatown to procure a few items before continuing his journey. Having made arrangements before leaving Chicago, he made sure the items he required had already been provisioned by his Vancouver contact and were conveniently prepositioned at a safe location. All Ijinashi had to do was drive there and get them.

Ijinashi had taken every precaution as he traveled from Illinois to British Columbia, acutely aware that Je-Ju Lee and Sainen Chinhung were very dangerous opponents.

In fact, Ijinashi was covering his exfil from the United States with all the professional competence that he could muster. After finishing the Remy Sanchez business on the South Side of Chicago, Ijinashi had caught a glimpse of a female sitting in a Honda as he rounded a corner down from the library. That female looked quite a bit like Je-Ju Lee. Not believing in coincidences, Ijinashi just took it for granted that both Je-Ju and Sainen had been surveilling him and began planning his personal security measures accordingly.

Before leaving Chicago, Ijinashi had paid a visit to the Chicago Foreign Missions district, seeking out the commercial office of a deep-cover Cuban intelligence officer illegally operating in the United States under the alias of Osvaldo Torrado.

Following a short interview session that Amnesty International would most certainly classify as torture, Ijinashi had extracted what he needed from Torrado, leaving his lifeless body slumped in his leather-bound chair.

Being intimately familiar with Triad operations, Ijinashi recognized the likely work of Chinhung and Lee when he watched the news coverage of a suspected organized crime shooting in Parisippany, New Jersey. Had he not known that Sainen and Je-Ju had business dealings with Jason Wen and that Wen had a shop operating in New Jersey, he might not have tied it together. As it was, it wasn't high math for him to piece together that Sainen and Je-Ju were trying to cover their trail in preparation for a bug out, which was probably why they had hired poor Remy to kill him as well.

Maybe he was off on a detail or two, but Ijinashi figured he had enough of the picture to recognize when he needed to go defensive. Time to get out. He had done what he could do with the New Weather movement. Self-preservation concerns had to take precedence. Had Ijinashi been aware of Bobby Shing's crew and of the Sierra Mike One team, he would have taken even more extravagant precautions.

SIERRA MIKE ONE

"Yup, Gary, it looks like our package has left CONUS and has arrived in Vancouver, British Columbia. The government resources available to us confirm that he got off in Vancouver."

"Okay, guys, let's get packed up and ready to roll. Mark, you and Harrison make the travel arrangements, same platform as last time."

KEEFER STREET, VANCOUVER CHINATOWN NIGHT MARKET

S ituated around Vancouver's Chinatown Plaza at Keefer and Columbia Streets, with crowds of patrons oftentimes spilling out onto Main, East Pender, and East Georgia Streets, is Chinatown's famous night market.

Every Friday, Saturday, and Sunday, May to September, row upon row of tented booths sporting bright red, yellow, and green tops line Keefer Street between Main and Columbia.

An extravaganza of Asian foods and handicrafts, clothes, CDs, DVDs, folk dances, martial arts demonstrations, lion dances, and live bands, the hundred or so booths are open for business from 6:00 p.m. to 11:00 p.m., drawing throngs of tourists and locals alike.

Ijinashi had known Charlie Deng for a number of years now. When circumstances allowed, he would visit Deng a couple times a year. Attending the night market festivities in Vancouver's Chinatown with his friend Deng was one of the treats that Ijinashi looked forward to.

Deng would always treat Ijinashi to a potato tornado, one of the famous local snacks available at the night market. Deng was a performer at the Shaolin Hung Gar Kung Fu Night at the night market and a well-known and respected sifu.

Deng was also an expert on creative finances, forged documents, counterfeit passports, procurement of sterile cell phone SIM cards, and provision of various weaponry. It was Deng who had prepositioned a stash of supplies and equipment for Ijinashi at his cousin's booth at the market.

Deng had come by his illicit skills honestly, truth be known. He had been specially trained while serving in the People's Liberation Army as a young man in China. Very bright, Deng was put in a special PLA program that afforded him considerable expertise in a variety of "shadow" arts.

Deng did not stay in the military, instead he opted to pursue a career in the film industry in Hong Kong, where he became a successful second unit director and stunt coordinator. Retiring to Vancouver to be near his daughter, nowadays Deng devoted most of his time to operating his kung fu school.

Deng, at Ijinashi's request, had arranged for the package stashed at the night market booth to include a key to Deng's hung gar kwoon, where Deng had rendered the back storeroom into a mini-apartment for Ijinashi, complete with a camp cot, dorm-size fridge, and a microwave. The storeroom was close to the kung fu studio's restrooms and showers. There also was an emergency back door exit that was quickly accessible from the back room. Everything was perfect for Ijinashi's needs during his stay in British Columbia.

Deng had argued for Ijinashi to be his house guest, but Ijinashi explained that it would be safer for everyone if he stayed at a separate location, the kung fu kwoon being an excellent choice.

Deng told Ijinashi that, if he was going to deny him the honor of being a guest at his home, he would not accept Ijinashi's refusal of his help in regard to the current "difficulties." Begrudgingly, Ijinashi agreed.

At the same time that Ijinashi was collecting his package at the night market booth, Sierra Mike One was checking into the Fairmont Pacific Rim hotel in Vancouver's historic port district.

LOS ANGELES, LINDLEY STREET

Sainen drove up to LA and began trolling the areas where he knew half-assed hoodlum and Triad wannabe Joey Wang liked to hang. Joey was too young and too stupid to be involved in any real Triad work, but his uncle was Jason Wen, who certainly had his finger on the pulse of Triad doings in both Northern and Southern California, as well as Nevada and Arizona.

Wen likely maintained decent OPSEC in his conduct of business, but his idiot nephew was a nosy little bastard and, being family, might have had occasion to overhear something he shouldn't have.

From Sainen's previous dealings with Wen's Triad group, he knew that Joey had the access and that many of Wen's inner circle—so used to seeing him—treated him like a piece of furniture, discussing sensitive matters within his earshot.

More significantly, Joey was eager to brag about his connections, especially to impress the girls with his insider knowledge. Joey had all the trappings: hot car, hot girls, fancy iron stuffed jauntily in his pants, just no brains. As far as Sainen was concerned, Joey was the perfect means by which to locate Bobby Shing and his crew—or what was left of it.

Joey occasionally frequented high-end nightclubs like the SkyBar and Ecco Lounge on the Sunset Strip, but he most often could be found in the parking lot of a lower-end bar on Lindley near the California State University Northridge Campus. Joey knew that the bar was a favorite of young college girls.

Sainen spotted Joey, as he suspected he might, leaning against his 'Vette amid a bevy of CSUN girls in the bar parking lot on Lindley, likely talking shit. Sainen drove by to make sure it was Joey and to see if he had any of his fellow wannabe gangsters with him before pulling off and parking a block down. Better to approach on foot, as he wanted to be upon Joey before the little shithead had a chance to jump in his car and bolt.

It would be better to wait for Joey to leave and contact him in a less-crowded venue, but who knew how long Joey might loiter in the lot, or if he would leave with a carload of girls? Besides, Sainen did not have the luxury of time nor the patience to wait.

Sainen strode into the little crowd of adoring gangster worshippers and sidled up to Joey, planting himself against Joey's Corvette right next to him before Joey's dumb ass could react. Several of the girls whispered and giggled, Sainen cutting an impressive figure. Joey was both annoyed and scared—even his low-wattage brain registering that he was potentially in deep shit.

Leaning over to Joey and sporting a conspiratorial grin for appearances sake, Sainen whispered in his ear, barely audible.

"You are going to smile, tell your little bitch fan club that you have urgent business to attend to, and then you and I are going to get into your car and leave. If you hesitate or protest, I will hurt you in front of these girls. I will, in fact, make you scream like a little girl and probably cause a few of these gals to blow their groceries, understand?"

"Okay, G-money, no need for any unpleasantness here, okay?"

Sainen could smell the stress-induced perspiration that was beginning to bead up on Joey and detected a slight tremor in his voice as the kid acknowledged his instructions.

Joey flashed his best forced smile at his fan club as he quickly excused himself, pulling his car door open as he did.

"I gots bizniz, ladies," Joey crowed, looking back over his shoulder at the crowd, trying to sound all gangsta as he slid into the Corvette. Sainen smiled at the chattering and still-giggling cluster of girls as he rounded the car and dropped into Joey's passenger seat.

"We need to talk, Joey. Here's what I need you to do. Turn around and head up the street to that parking garage sign on the right up there."

"Okay, dude, you got it. What's this about, anyway?"

"Some urgent business I am trying to take care of for your uncle, Joey— very important."

If Joey knows about his uncle's hit, he will know I'm lying, Sainen thought. *But, fuck it, maybe he's not privy to the specifics of his uncle's orders to Shing's crew but knows something important like where Shing and his boys are hanging while down here in LA from San Francisco.*

"Okay, Joey, pull in here and head up to the third deck."

The parking garage was relatively new, a plain white cement structure with four parking levels, counting the rooftop. Due to a revitalization effort in the area, the garage was surrounded by mostly vacant buildings, either under construction or renovation. Less likely to harbor witnesses, Sainen reasoned.

The third deck, Sainen hoped, would not be totally parked up, and there would be at least one open space left. He preferred to park under the view-blocking fourth deck roof so there wasn't an unobstructed view of what might take place there that evening.

Besides hoping that Joey was not aware of his uncle's hit on him, Sainen hoped that he was dull enough not to realize that, logically, his uncle would have told Sainen precisely where and how to reach Bobby if he had tasked Sainen with passing urgent word to him.

Hoping for the best, Sainen popped the question.

"Joey, I need to get urgent word to Bobby Shing to relay new instructions from your uncle. Do you know where I can reach him?"

"Uh, I, uh…sure, I know where Mr. Shing—Bobby—is at, man."

"I knew you were plugged in, Joey, and I apologize for the tough talk back there. It's just that this is really important shit, you know."

"Yeah, uh, sure, man, no problem."

"Here's the thing, Joey. I need to hook up with Bobby, like, right now. So can you help a brother out?"

"Bobby and a few of his guys are, you know, staying at old man Xue's shop, in the back. That is, uh, right at Alpine and Broadway in Chinatown, Xue's Golden Buddha. The shop has that funky gold-painted dragon in the front window. Why it ain't a golden Buddha like the store's name, I don't know. You can't miss it, man."

"That is excellent, Joey. I really appreciate it. Do you happen to know—I know you hang with the crew some—whether there is a rear entrance? I don't want to disturb Mr. Xue or any of his customers. I would rather just slip in and tell Bobby what your uncle needs him to know and, like, take off."

"Yeah, dude, there is a rear door. The alley behind the store you reach by walking the cement strip between Xue's shop and the building to the west…it is a tight squeeze, kinda. Anyway, the rear door to the shop faces north onto the east-west alley that runs behind the store. There's, like, a small apartment back there that old man Xue's sister stays in when she visits from San Francisco."

Sainen had decided several minutes before that he wasn't going to kill Joey. Joey was almost too stupid to talk to, let alone take the trouble of killing. Besides, when Wen found out that this moron led him to Bobby, he would probably kill Joey himself.

"Joey, this is very, very important. I need you to keep your mouth shut about this, savvy?"

"No problem, man, you got it."

"Okay, Joey, I'm going to ask you to drive me back down to the first level and to let me out at the sidewalk in front of the garage. My car is nearby."

"Sure, no worries."

Sainen didn't, of course, tell Joey that the reason he parked out on the street was so he would not have to negotiate the parking garage levels and ramps if he had found it necessary to shoot him. Besides, many modern commercial parking facilities had surveillance cameras. As it was, this was Joey's lucky day—maybe among his last once his uncle found out who dimed out Bobby and his crew.

XUE'S GOLDEN BUDDHA STORE

Putting the pick kit back in his pocket and pushing the door open just enough to pass through, Sainen slid inside, entering into a poorly lit—almost dark—back room of some sort. Immediately brushing against what felt like a stack of cardboard boxes, Sainen recoiled slightly, bumping into a metal shelf sagging under the weight of way too many ceramic Buddhas. Of course, all that shit shifted, and one fell to the floor, shattering on the aged—and hard as rock—wood floor.

Quickly crushing out his cigarette, Bobby Shing spun around and opened the door that led into the rear storage room, pulling his pistol from his pants as he ducked through the doorway.

Sid Hwang and Anthony Lim were right on Bobby's coattails, but—eager to back up their boss—they stumbled over the door jamb as they attempted to simultaneously pass through the narrow doorway, Hwang inadvertently tripping into Shing's back and Lim hooking a foot on one of Hwang's legs and falling sideways into a metal trash can. Shing had to take a big step forward to catch his balance, and Hwang cut his hand on an exposed metal screw when he grabbed at some shelving to regain his balance. What a circus.

Proof that Murphy indeed had a great sense of humor, four armed—and opposing—gangsters now found themselves in a dark, cramped, obstacle-rich environment. For reasons he couldn't fathom, Sainen did not enter with his gun in hand. It would have been so simple if he had. *Idiot*, he thought to himself.

Like all real street fights, it wasn't pretty or stylish but instead a vicious flurry of arms and legs, each combatant trying to take out the other any which way he could. The fighter with the calm mind, who was able to "see" the fight, generally had an edge, many martial artists would tell you. Calm minds tend to go to hell in a handcart when the fists start flying.

Absolutely nothing was ever guaranteed in life, especially in hand-to-hand combat. That had held true for centuries, and that was the case there that night. It had the makings of a full-scale, world-class goat fuck.

Seeing Bobby Shing's form silhouetted in the light from the doorway, and seeing a gun in his hand, Sainen shot out a left hook that caught Bobby square on the cheek, missing the jaw but jacking Shing's head to the side hard enough to send saliva flying.

Shing's off-balance uppercut response grazed off Sainen's chin—close but no cigar. Shing's pistol had gone clattering across the floor, Bobby's gun hand having cracked against a shelf edge when Sainen slugged him, which was the only reason Sainen wasn't dead.

Having no time to pull his own gun now, Sainen unleashed a jumping knee, driving Bobby backward and sending him careening into Hwang, who in turn fell over Lim, who was struggling to get to his feet, hindered when the trash can he had his arm braced on rolled out from under him.

Following Shing's back-stepping retreat, Sainen pressed in and hit him with a right cross that connected, contorting Bobby's face, his mouth twisting at a funny angle as the blow stretched the flesh.

Screaming at his idiot colleagues to get the fuck up, Shing fired a straight left that Sainen narrowly avoided, catching the fist as it landed. Holding Shing's fist tightly to his shoulder with both hands, Sainen violently twisted Bobby's trapped wrist in a basic qinna joint manipulation maneuver, attempting to use his core strength against Shing's limb to painfully wrench the isolated joint, forcing Shing off balance and to the ground. Stuff like that always worked in the movies.

Sweat-slick hands allowed Shing to free himself, but—balance disrupted—Bobby's horizontal elbow counter was evaded by Sainen, who subsequently landed a solid overhand right, cutting Shing just above his left eyebrow and causing blood to flow distractingly into Bobby's eye. To his credit, Shing recovered immediately, clearing the blood from his eye with a flick of his head, quickly finding his feet, and getting both hands up into a defensive posture, chin tucked down.

Bobby fired a straight right that Sainen slipped with a slight movement forward and to the side, rolling enough to give his counter punch some power, hitting Shing in the neck with a resounding smack. Sainen immediately ducked under and clutched the stunned Shing around the waist, lifting him up slightly before canting him to the side and slamming him to the floor. Shing's head banged off several flimsy metal shelves on his way down.

Releasing his hold before Shing hit the floor and letting gravity do the rest, Sainen kicked backward with a vicious heel kick, catching Anthony Lim in the solar plexus, dumping him back to where he had been on the floor, this time fighting for breath.

Gravity hits hard, and Bobby had collided with the floor without the benefit of a breakfall, cracking the back of his head on the hard surface as he hit. Shing was severely dazed, and his head lolled as he fought to regain his bearings. Blood stinging his eye from the eyebrow cut, he was flailing his left arm about on the floor, trying to find his goddamn gun.

Sid "Big Sid" Hwang was a brute, huge and muscular. Having regained his feet, he had been biding his time and waiting for the right moment to move. Too unsure of his skills to use his handgun in such close proximity to his colleagues in poor light, Hwang rushed in and grabbed Sainen from behind, damn near caving in Sainen's ribcage as he did.

Locking his hands around Sainen's waist, Hwang hoisted upward with a grunt. Lifting Sainen up and over in a smooth arc, Big Sid drove him toward the floor with all the strength he could muster. Sainen realized that if Big Sid got to pile drive him into the flooring, it was all she wrote.

Keeping his eyes on the approaching floor as Sid executed his brutal takedown, Sainen had readied his arms to help break the fall, managing to survive the jarring impact without breaking anything, although both hands were numb. Unfortunately, former high-school wrestler that he was, Big Sid followed Sainen to the floor, deftly acquiring superior positioning immediately upon landing.

Seeing out of the corner of his eye that Bobby was starting to regain his feet and that Lim was getting some color back and stirring, Sainen knew he had to do something quick, or he was a goner. He certainly couldn't allow Bobby to retrieve his gun because Bobby—not having the inferiority complex of his cohort—would start blazing immediately upon getting the weapon back in his hand.

Rotating his hips and torso hard to his right, Sainen sank on his left arm, extended his right arm out in front of his face, and struck up and back with his right elbow, smacking Big Sid in the right temple. The blow allowed Sainen to escape Big Sid's grip, roll away, and scramble up, banging into a shelf full of lion dance crap as he did.

Had this little brouhaha not occurred in a crowded, poorly lit storage room piled with boxes and crates, Sainen would likely not have survived as long as he had, given that he was up against three competent opponents, all with guns.

Lim suddenly gained enough juice back to flick his jumbled sport coat back and grab his nine-millimeter as he rose up on one knee. Shakily pointing the weapon in Sainen's general direction, he cranked off five fast rounds, blowing several Buddhas into dust, perforating the wall next to the outside door, and shattering an orange 1970s vintage ceramic lamp.

"Goddamn sonuvabitch, stop fucking shooting, you moron! You just damn near shot my ass, you fucking idiot," Bobby snarled as he frantically scooted across the floor and scrunched up against a set of shelving in an attempt to get clear of Lim's maniacal shooting binge.

Lim, looking confused, focused again on Sainen, who by then was rocketing across the confined space in an effort to get behind a stack of boxes that he hoped were full of something substantial. Firing three more fast shots, Lim stitched the stack of boxes that Sainen had just dove behind, sending Styrofoam peanuts soaring out the open top of one of them.

"Jesus, Tony, did you fuckin' hit him?" Bobby was again scrambling around on the floor, looking frantically for his lost gun.

Big Sid was now propped up on one arm, trying to shift to his other side so he could retrieve his own handgun, still rattled from the elbow shot.

Sainen, still miraculously free of gunshot wounds, shoved the stack of boxes he was behind forward, toppling them right on top of Tony Lim, prompting Lim to immediately begin firing again, this time wildly blasting away in a swinging arc covering the area of the storeroom where he last knew Sainen to be, smoking brass casings bouncing around on the floor and pinging off the metal shelving next to Lim.

Angling off to his left after shoving the boxes over, Sainen finally was able to retrieve his own sidearm. Bringing the Beretta Storm .45 up and into a good two-handed isosceles hold, he angled his aim back to his right as he ran and double tapped Lim in the chest. Lim slumped forward, his smoking pistol's slide half out of battery from a stovepipe jam.

Big Sid had now shifted his weight to his left arm and had his pistol in his right hand, trying to cover Sainen as he fought to get from his knee to a standing position. Had he remained in a kneeling position and simply engaged Sainen from there, he might have fared better.

As it was, Big Sid took a .45 round square in the middle of his forehead, Sainen snapping off the shot as he swung back toward Sid after killing Tony Lim. Big Sid fell over sideways, dead eyes looking up at the ceiling.

Sainen knew he had to address Bobby and do so right then.

Where the fuck is he? Sainen scanned the room once then twice—no Bobby. *What the fuck?* Then he heard the unmistakable rack of a pump-action shotgun emanate from the door leading into the store. Shing had scrambled out of the storeroom and now apparently had a shotgun, Sainen reasoned.

Sainen did not have time to formulate another thought because Bobby began pumping twelve-gauge rounds through the door into the cramped storeroom, shredding boxes and peppering the entire space with number-four shot. Motivated by self-preservation and acting on instinct alone, Sainen dove the three feet separating him from the still-ajar rear door.

Hitting the alley surface in a front roll breakfall, Sainen popped up, spun around, and racked off a string of shots through the doorway he had just dove through, hearing the pinging of metal and the breaking of glass.

Sainen sidled sideways out of the cone of dim yellow light spilling out of the open door into the alley, keeping his weapon aimed at the doorway. The shotgun blasts had stopped, but Sainen was not about to stick his head inside to see whether he had hit Bobby or not.

Well, no time to worry about Shing now. I need to roll on outta here before the cops arrive to see what all the shooting was about, Sainen thought to himself as he carefully backed away from the rear of the store and made his way down the alley. He had some driving to do.

VANCOUVER

"Iji, my associates tell me that the police responded to a shooting down in Los Angeles yesterday evening. I think you may know some of the people involved. According to what I was told, two of Jason Wen's Triad boys—Sidney Hwang and Anthony Lim—were killed at a shop in LA's Chinatown. Both were shot with a forty-five-caliber pistol cartridge, I believe they said. A third man—Wen's enforcer, Bobby Shing—was also involved and took a round in his left forearm."

"The police have made no arrests and apparently there are no suspects. Shing, being Wen's henchman, was treated by Triad physicians, his gunshot wound never reported to authorities."

"That is very interesting indeed, Charlie. I do know those names. Bobby is a dangerous piece of work, and his boss, Wen, is considered by some to be somewhat—how should I say? Unstable. I must say, Charlie, that I did not realize that your, uh, connections were so extensive and far reaching. Do you know who shot them?"

"Yes, Iji, I do know. At least I know what my associates have told me. Apparently Wen's young nephew was beaten within an inch of his life by Wen himself. Come to find out, young Joey—that's Wen's nephew—had provided Sainen Chinhung with the location where Bobby and his crew were staying while down in LA. It is believed that Chinhung is the one who killed Hwang and Lim and winged Bobby Shing."

"Ah, I see. Yes, that would make sense. I believe Sainen and his occasional partner, Je-Ju Lee, were attempting to clean up a trail of inconvenient people who were witting to their involvement in some very dangerous business deals."

"So it was a gangster-on-gangster dispute then?"

"Yes, Charlie, I believe you could safely say that was the case here."

"Were you close to any of them? Were any of them people you might care about, Iji?"

"No, none of them are of concern to me. They are casualties of the business they have chosen to be in. No more."

"Are you curious about the rest of the story, my friend?"

"Sure, yes, tell me the story you have heard."

"It appears that another Wen crew, headed up by the somewhat infamous Animal Mother—he's another of Wen's street henchmen—got themselves killed down in Marina Del Rey, actually at the marina, in fact. The facts are somewhat sketchy as to specifics. However, some fairly impressive weaponry was apparently involved, including, I'm told, a grenade launcher and even some prepositioned plastic explosives."

"Je-Ju Lee."

"Why, yes, Iji, you are correct. My sources tell me it was apparently the handiwork of a Ms. Je-Ju Lee, who made her escape in a speedboat like in a James Bond movie... hahahahaha. Ms. Lee's current whereabouts are unknown."

"Figures. What about Sainen?"

"Well, my friend, informed sources say that he disappeared from the scene of the LA Chinatown shoot 'em up, assumed to have left the country. His whereabouts are not known."

"I see."

"Iji, my friend, there is a bit more to the story, I'm afraid. My well-informed sources tell me that Wen had three teams deployed. One team was to go after our Ms. Lee; things didn't work out too well for that team. A second team was dispatched from Wen's base in San Francisco down to LA to take care of Sainen Chinhung, and that is the team that I first told you about that was shot up at the shop in Chinatown, Bobby Shing surviving with a non-life-threatening wound to his arm. And, my friend, apparently the third team—hit squad—was to find you."

"That is somewhat unexpected but not too surprising. I knew that Sainen and Je-Ju thought that they would be better off—safer—if I was out of the picture. But I was not aware that the Triad was also trying to have me removed. I suspected that there could be some wires crossed, given all the moving parts, but I did not know that Wen—or maybe his 'Uncle' Chen in Hong Kong—had issued any orders to kill me."

"There is more, but first let me finish telling you about the third team— the one sent after you. Apparently, and I have this on very good authority, Wen called back the third team after the debacles with the other two teams. There is considerable heat from the police now being focused on Mr. Wen and his operations. He has decided, it seems, to take a lower profile, for a while at least."

"And the rest of the story?"

"My people in Seattle and here in British Columbia—old associates— tell me that there are indications that another team of men has been dis-patched to, well, murder you, Iji. This group of men—alleged to be three in number—is a private-sector entity not associated with the Triad. These men, former military specialists that work as contract help for various US government and shady corporate concerns, have been tasked with your neutralization, to quote a source."

"Okay. I imagine that my recent activities likely scared some important people within the American government, not to mention some powerful industrialists."

"Well, word has it that these men have followed you here to Vancouver. They are staying in a hotel in the historic port district, the Fairmont Pacific Rim."

"Okay, guess I had better—"

"Now, Iji, before you start telling me how you need to leave to spare me the danger, let me continue, okay?"

"Okay."

"There are a couple of very competent men keeping watch on these guys at their hotel. These guys won't do anything or go anywhere without me knowing about it."

"I appreciate what you are doing for me, Charlie. You are a good friend, a true friend. I am honored by your friendship."

"And I by yours. Now, if you will allow me, I have a plan."

HUNG GAR KWOON, VANCOUVER

"You see, Ijinashi, my friend, there is no need for you to flee the city, nor is there a need for you to face those three men on your own, although you are certainly capable. My senior students—very capable students—are quite capable of mitigating this situation without drawing the attention of the Canadian authorities. Well, I should rephrase that; my students will not draw attention to themselves but may well draw attention to the three men."

"I don't see why you do not wish to more fully explain just how your, uh, senior students will be handling this. But I respect your wishes and will not pester you for information you do not wish to divulge."

"Excellent! I am very glad, my friend, that you have come to that decision. My people will take care of it. You should do as you always do when visiting and take your 'tourist' stroll through our famous night market. I will give you the address of a friend who has an apartment down there. You can pop in if you like; she will give you tea and let you watch the goings on comfortably from her second-floor bay window."

"As you wish, Charlie."

THE PANDA

The alley—actually a side street—was very narrow, so most people considered it an alleyway rather than a street proper. It seldom bore any vehicular traffic, mainly accommodating pedestrians who were residents of Vancouver's thriving Chinatown. Few tourists were aware of it, sticking to the main night market venue for the most part. The crowds were mostly local Chinese and, oftentimes, the families of residents visiting from China and Taiwan.

The street—formally named Panda Path by the city but known simply as The Panda by locals—was congested with booths and food stands year round but was horrendously congested during night market, which drew foreign relatives of the population. Every commercial concern one could imagine was competing for space. Booths selling everything imaginable and food stands serving all variety of Asian food were all crammed together, occupying every inch of concrete in the pandemonium that was The Panda.

Colorful overhead lanterns swung in the breeze, which carried charcoal grill and tobacco smoke blended with the aroma of exotic spices over the teeming crowds of jostling shoppers and merchants. Trinket and souvenir kiosks were parked willy-nilly in the traveled portion, already reduced to a path barely two feet in width, its serpentine length clogged every few feet by throngs of diners crowding around the open-flame grills.

Bright red canvas overhangs shielded alcoves set into the alley's brick walls, each jammed full of clothing racks and stacks of wares that would not fit in the sales booths of The Panda's merchants.

Multicolored Chinese signage created an artificial forest of painted and neon advertising along the length of The Panda. Spaced among that forest were the windows of second-story apartments that lined the little alley, some with swing-out windows open to the night air.

Also evident were numerous old-fashioned fire escapes, some of the landings converted by apartment residents into mini-decks crowded with potted plants and flowers, contrary to city code. Many of the older denizens sat out on these landings of an evening, smoking and chatting as they took in the local color from their vantage points above.

It was from one of these vantage points that Ijinashi sat on a lawn chair, sipping tea, watching the undulating throngs of people snaking down The Panda as the sun went down.

SIERRA MIKE ONE

The paper flyers stuck under the wiper blades of all the cars on level three of the hotel parking garage advertised a martial arts extravaganza to be held at the night market.

The flyers had color photos of several masters who would be performing and provided a short bio on each of the experts. The flyers indicated that the show would be held in the street and that the masters would be available afterward to answer questions. The printed portion of the ads stated that the venue could only accommodate one hundred attendees, due to space restrictions in Chinatown.

One of the masters whose image appeared on the flyer was Ijinashi, whose picture adorned the top center of the ad format.

Directions indicated that attendees should enter the venue by way of Panda Path and arrive no later than 7:00 p.m. A street map was conveniently provided on the reverse side of the flyer.

Deng's people waited until the Americans noticed and read the flyer left on their rental before going around and removing the rest of the fake flyers from the other vehicles on level three of the Fairmont Pacific Rim hotel, disposing of them in a dumpster a few blocks away.

Charlie Deng's senior hung gar students hoped that the Americans followed the directions precisely.

Raphael Wang, Mark Qingjian, Robert Peng, and Sophia Oh drove down to the night market to get set up.

DIAN XUE

G ary Mitchell, Mark Brewer, and Harrison Franks wound through the jostling crowds along The Panda, heading toward what they believed to be completion of yet another successful, and profitable, Sierra Mike One job.

In the crowded venue of The Panda, Raphael, Mark, Robert, and Sophia were simply four more Asian faces in a constantly changing tidal flow of Asian faces. That made it relatively easy, particularly with the aid of a few friendly elements within the crowd, to manipulate the paths of the three Caucasians. Thus, Deng's students were able to regulate the timing of the round eyes' progress through the sea of booths and food stands, predetermining where the three men were along The Panda at any given time.

Wang, Qingjian, and Peng's initial function was to funnel the men of Sierra Mike One to their deaths. Once they had managed that portion of their assignment, they ducked into the shadows behind a clothing booth to quickly change their clothing.

Sophia Oh was dressed in a comfortable blouse and pants consistent with current popular fashion—attire that fit in but allowed her adequate freedom of movement. Sophia, while an attractive young woman, was not dressed to attract attention this evening. Amid the waves of pedestrians that jammed The Panda, it was Sophia's intent to blend in like one more eddy in a rippling river.

Sophia Oh was one of the most gifted practitioners of dian zue—dim mak—that Master Deng had ever produced. She was phenomenally subtle.

Approaching the Americans from the opposite direction, Sophia was not particularly discernable among the giggling pod of young Asian girls with smart phones glued to their ears. To the three men of Sierra Mike One, the little gaggle of young women were totally indistinguishable from the legions of similar young people looking at, tapping on, or talking into cell phones as they threaded their way through the crowds.

Harrison Franks' eyes barely lingered half a second on the approaching girls, chattering away among themselves and on their phones. Harrison did not take notice of Sophia at all.

Sophia struck out with her right hand and, using her thumb along with her four extended fingers, hit Harrison in the cavity below his Adam's apple. Her fingers struck in and around the cavity while her thumb hit a point on Harrison's chest below and to the side of the cavity. In the din of the crowded alleyway, the out and back movement went unseen.

Immediately excusing herself and giggling, Sophia continued on, carried in the surge of bodies that were flowing down The Panda. Harrison Franks barely even registered what she looked like.

Three steps further on, Franks felt a pressure and heaviness in his chest, along with a choking feeling. Another step and extreme weakness, shortness of breath, and dizziness set in.

Within two minutes of Sophia's passing by, profuse sweating and vomiting beset Harrison Franks, who now gave onlookers every impression that he was suffering from a heart attack.

Kneeling next to their colleague, Gary Mitchell and Mark Brewer tried to loosen his clothing and make him comfortable while waiting on EMS personnel to arrive. There were two ambulances posted to the night market at any given time, so it was not a surprise to bystanders when two young men in emergency medical technician uniforms quickly arrived on the scene.

After a cursory exam and application of an oxygen mask, the two EMTs loaded Harrison onto the stretcher they had brought and began maneuvering through the crowds, one of them talking quickly into the walkie-talkie microphone clipped to his epaulette.

Mitchell and Brewer decided that they would accompany their teammate to the ambulance, ascertain which hospital he was being transported to, and then finish their mission before checking back on the status of Franks.

The ambulance was parked on a poorly lit side street off of Keefer where The Panda intersected, the crowds almost nonexistent at that spot. That the thinning of the crowd at that spot was by design was not something that registered on the two SM1 operators, given that their mental focus was divided between the welfare of their colleague and the mission at hand. The fact that the paint scheme of the ambulance was not quite right was another detail that the two men failed to take note of.

The two SM1 men also did not notice that Franks was no longer breathing, having died en route to the ambulance.

Opening the rear doors of the ambulance, the EMTs hoisted the stretcher up and forward, its collapsible undercarriage folding up as the stretcher was pushed inside the rear bay of the ambulance. Instead of jumping in and beginning stabilization of their patient before transport to the emergency room, the two EMTs spun around, Raphael Wong and Robert Peng pouncing on Mitchell and Brewer before they could react. At the same time, Mark Qingjian exited the driver's door of the ambulance and came around to help his friends.

It wasn't much of a confrontation, over in seconds. It went unnoticed by the teeming crowds on The Panda and Keefer Street mere yards away.

Having been struck multiple times on sensitive acupressure points under their arms and on their faces, necks, and torsos by highly focused one- and two-knuckle blows delivered in rapid succession, the two men of SM1 had no chance to fight back against the three men assaulting them. Their twitching and convulsing bodies were unceremoniously loaded on top of their dead teammate in the bay of the ambulance.

Had anyone been able to observe and diagnose the final moments of the two doomed Sierra Mike One contract killers, they would have seen them beset by debilitating weakness, joint pain, muscle cramps, severe headache, vomiting, fever, rapid onset of dehydration, stomach pain, cough, diarrhea, and, within minutes, death.

The lifeless bodies of the former SM1 team were dumped along the curb of East Pender Street on the periphery of the night market, and the faux ambulance was deposited at a body shop across town, where it would be sanitized and repainted.

DENG RESIDENCE, NUTHATCH PLACE, NORTH VANCOUVER

Walking around the family room of Charlie Deng's home, Ijinashi was looking at the multitude of framed photographs, martial arts trophies, kung fu certifications, taijiquan push hand medals, and edged weapons that adorned the walls and shelves.

"I have never seen techniques like what your students used tonight, Charlie. From what I could see from the fire escape, they were bordering on supernatural, reminding me of the myths of Chinese masters with mystical powers."

Thinking of his adventures in ancient Japan during the time of the Jopon, Ijinashi said, "I have, of course, witnessed demonstrations of such, uh, capabilities before, but that was a long, long time ago. I have not encountered anything remotely like that in recent times."

He couldn't tell Charlie Deng that he found a means of exploiting the dragon lines, had traveled through time, and had actually seen these things eons ago; Charlie would have thought he had snapped under the pressure of recent events.

"Yes, Iji, my students are adepts at many of the ancient skills."

"I believe it. That does not, however, explain their capabilities, which were clearly above and beyond what could be called normal. It was like, well, watching a magic show or one of those old Hong Kong movies you used to make with all the wire work and special effects."

Laughing, he agreed. "Yes, Iji, it is true that Sophia, Raphael, Mark, and Robert are extraordinary martial artists."

Continuing to browse the huge array of swords and ancient Asian weaponry that Charlie collected from all over the world, Ijinashi stopped to examine a display case containing some beautiful old Chinese swords, some appearing to be examples of Middle Han Dynasty steel jian. *It is a very impressive collection*, Ijinashi thought.

Moving slowly from display to display as Deng chatted about his hun gar kwoon and the prowess of his prized students, Ijinashi came upon several examples of what he thought were very rare bronze jian of the Qin Dynasty, dating to 221 BC. Next to these was an artifact many museum proprietors would kill for, an example of a bronze sword that utilized chromium oxide as an anticorrosion protective coating, dating to somewhere around 700 BC. Fantastic. Deng's den was itself a museum.

Continuing to peruse the marvelous collection of blades that Deng had spent decades amassing, Ijinashi spotted a display containing steel-bladed swords of the Song Dynasty, dating to 960–1279 AD.

While looking at the beautiful artifacts in the Song Dynasty display, Ijinashi's eye caught a glint from an impressive-looking jian on a wood rack a few feet away and walked over to give it a look. It was a long jian whose blade almost glowed, Iji thought, as he stepped up closer to examine the beautiful sword.

Ijinashi gasped. His eyes, which had been fixated on the gorgeous blade, had drifted down to the ornate hilt and handle. He blinked, thinking he must have been seeing it wrong. But his eyes did not lie; the grip was adorned with an ancient Dogon design that he was very familiar with. The design, a rendering of a binary star system believed holy by the ancient Dogon of Mali, was exactly like the design on his Jopon sword.

Catching his breath, Ijinashi stared slack-jawed at the gleaming sword, mind racing as he struggled with the incongruity of what he was confronted with. As he gazed upon the ancient jian, he felt like he had seen the thing before—the entire weapon, not just the Dogon weave on the handle. There was an eerie feeling of familiarity.

"You have noticed the sword. It is familiar to you, yes?"

"How… how is this—" An icy chill gripped Iji, his blood turning to ice water. A shiver bordering on the convulsive racked his body.

"Well, you know, of course, the significance of the astronomical design on the handle. And you have seen this particular weapon before. You can feel it, I know."

"I, uh, yes, there is an almost déjà vu like feeling I get from it."

Deng's next words almost made Ijinashi's knees buckle.

"The young Chinese man who you met in Japan, the one who you believed to have mystical powers. It was a very long time ago, Ijinashi. The man who trained you in sword technique and ancient Chinese kung fu—properly called Chuanfa—that was his sword. It was then, as it is now, *my* sword."

Despite the look of dumbfounded disbelief on Ijinashi's face, Deng knew his friend was beginning to understand.

"You? It was… *you*. You were among the Jopon when I was there." Ijijan-shi was beyond being shocked.

"Yes. It was me. It is not coincidence that we have been friends over the years."

"So your students too?" Ijinashi managed to stammer out.

"No, they are not immortals or time travelers or whatever label people prefer to use in explaining such things. But they have achieved a grasp of the Tao, a very deep and profound grasp of the applications of taijiquan and traditional Chinese medicine."

"Okay," was all that Ijinashi could manage to say. His head was reeling.

"There is more, I am afraid. Won't you sit down, please? Please sit." Deng gently guided Ijinashi to a comfortable armchair.

"My name is not really Charlie Deng. I assumed that surname when I was, oh, maybe twenty-three while living in the People's Republic of China, prior to entering service in the PLA. I began using 'Charlie' when I moved to Hong Kong because I was dealing with English speakers.

"You may recall that the young man—that I—went by Zhuo. My real name is Zhuo Dong. If you express it in Western form, with the surname last, my name would be Dong Zhuo.

"I was, well, a warlord. I was a wicked young man, and I had a nickname—one still used by some of my close associates today. I was known as Dian Xue. 'Dian Xue' means 'death touch.' Today, a few of my senior students use that nickname because I focus on dim mak methods in my advanced classes. But back then the name derived from my many death matches and the means by which I won them.

"An arrogant and privileged young warrior with lots of riches and the ability to travel anywhere I wanted, whenever I wanted, I was on the road almost constantly. I had time to pursue my interest in martial arts, shamanism, and Taoism wherever and with whomever I chose. I did not, however, have time for a child."

"What?"

"Your real name, before you were adopted by Korean parents, was Cai… Cai *Zhuo*." Deng let that set in.

"Iji… you are my son."

It was several minutes before Ijinashi could speak.

"My mother?"

"A Westerner from what today would be France. Her given name was Amabel. She was, I believe, maybe a servant of some nature.

"I took the child—*you*—so that you would be raised in the East. You wound up, of course, in Korea. Life is strange, eh?"

"I need to go. I need to get my, uh, my being in balance. I will be back. Please forgive me. But for now, I need to go and get my head clear."

With that, Ijinashi got up and left.

Vancouver police files would reflect that the medical examiner's inquiry indicated the three male victims apparently died from severe organ damage. The medical examiner's report was inconclusive, however, as no external wounding or bruising was evident, making the internal damage hard to figure.

The horrid condition that the three bodies were found in was not released by authorities for fear that the details might spark a panic among the general public—fears of bio-terrorism and disease.

The victims were identified as Americans, names not released, whose presence in British Columbia—and their possession of illegal weapons—was under investigation by the Vancouver Police Department and Royal Canadian Mounted Police.

NORTH KOREA

Nobody would ever figure out exactly what happened with Kim Jong-un's command communications and control mechanism or why his fire order to his strategic rocket forces never made it to the field.

None of the fledgling nuclear power's arsenal made it into the air other than the half dozen medium-range mobile missiles that were launched in panic by a deployed mobile missile battery conducting field preventive maintenance and functional tests of their TELS twenty-five kilometers from the DMZ.

Of those six medium-range, nuclear-tipped missiles, one malfunctioned and fell to earth while still inside the DPRK, burning up in a rice field but leaving the remains of the unexploded nuclear warhead to later be recovered by North Korean forces.

Two of the missiles were destroyed in flight by jointly operating US and Japanese Navy anti-ballistic missile defense forces.

The remaining three missiles disappeared from radar in midflight, assumed portalled by the same time storm that had partially destroyed one of the missiles and its TEL, prompting the launches in the first place.

The missing—portalled—weapons posed the greatest problem.

OVER THE AMAZON

T he Sukhoi SU-30MK2 fighter banked left to come back around, having reached the edge of its patrol area as part of the joint 2014 South American Air Defense Exercise.

The pilot was disconcerted by the momentary visual aberration and somewhat confused by what seemed to be an instantaneous change of cloud configuration and his plane's orientation.

Checking his oxygen flow, the Venezuelan pilot began check-listing his instrumentation for functionality, alarmed by the drastic drop in flight level. Things just did not look or feel right.

The Mayan shaman looked up, briefly halting his climb up the stone steps of the huge pyramidal structure, transfixed by the screaming bird that brightly reflected the sun as it streaked overhead at a dizzying speed, angling into the jungle canopy.

Centuries later, UFO enthusiasts would attribute the golden, arguably delta-winged artifact retrieved by archaeologists as proof of alien visitation during ancient times. They couldn't have been more wrong, which is why several intelligence services pooled their resources and made sure that certain ancient texts of the Maya never came to light—the ones with the amazingly accurate description of the insignia their priests observed on the "carcass" of the shiny bird they found in the jungle.

TEN MILES WEST OF JODHPUR, INDIA

The last thing the population of Rajasthan, India, expected was for ten thousand suns to rise from the ground in the middle of their community, turning three square miles into a caldron of fire and death, reducing everything to superheated ash in an instant.

Vaporizing a half million people, the roiling, mushroom-shaped cloud of debris reared up high into the sky, a venomous, demonic apparition whose evil mark would still be discernable centuries later.

It was an incident so hideous that it was documented in the Mahabharata, described as having been delivered by an iron thunderbolt from the sky.

Twelve thousand years later, in the year 2014, the radioactive signature was still evident. That fact would, however, be kept suppressed, as would the findings of the special AVI-funded archaeological exploration that visited the site.

The ancient enigma would have been even more mind-bending had Indian historians known that the iron thunderbolt mentioned in the

Mahabharata was adorned with a red and blue flag insignia with a centered five-point red star inside a white circle—the national emblem of the Democratic People's Republic of Korea.

GUIANA SPACE CENTER, FRENCH GUIANA

French scientists studying data collected by the European Space Agency's Planck Space Observatory in elliptical (lissajous) orbit 930,000 miles from earth checked and rechecked their conclusions. The evidence, based on the preliminary results of their analysis, seemed to indicate that a Hiroshima-sized nuclear detonation occurred approximately two hundred million years ago in the Canis Major Dwarf Galaxy, which is situated roughly forty-two thousand light years from the galactic center of the Milky Way and about twenty-five thousand light years from earth.

That an explosion took place deep in space was not what had the astrophysicists excited. What excited them was that the atomic blast had taken place just above the surface of a large asteroid, something that would not occur naturally.

The world could read all about it via a link posted on the Twitter account of French scientist Francois Sauvage, a project scientist for a deep-space study group. Of course, few paid any real attention.

CONFRONTATION

Although AVI – Applied Violence International – was scattered at a number of locations around the globe, inhabiting a variety of front businesses, the main headquarters building was located in a bunker-like fortress on Rangiroa Atoll, 200 miles NNE of Tahiti in the Tuamotu Archipelago of French Polynesia. With a good natural harbor, it made for an excellent base of operations, hidden away in the great blue expanse of the South Pacific. It was here that AVI had secreted away their black technologies.

The black clad commando unit had assembled just off the beach, conducting last minute weapons checks and camouflaging the small craft they had arrived in, concealing it within the lush foliage. The team, led by Texas Special Operations Executive (SOE) operators, was comprised of SOE soldiers and Texas Rangers. A diesel submarine – one of two recently purchased by the new Republic of Texas – lay silently on the bottom a short distance off shore near where the sub had launched the commando team.

Based on intelligence generated by the new Texan military and the Texas Rangers, the Texas government had found the command complex AVI used to direct its nefarious worldwide operations. The Texas Secretary of Defense had acted quickly to get an elite force assembled and on site to put a stop to the unholy scientific research that threatened the planet – and potentially the entire universe.

The assault team's orders were simple – obliterate the complex, destroy the labs and kill everyone they encountered. As a secondary mission objective, they were to seize any of the time portalling technologies they could carry away with them. A team of scientists was standing by on the sub to render the artifacts safe for transport back to the Republic of Texas.

At 0233 hours local, the team began moving in on the complex, silently eliminating sentry patrols as they closed on the command bunker.

Justice had found AVI.

LABORATORY C13

Two levels underground in the complex's subbasement, a thin, tousle haired technician in a white lab coat frantically tapped on a keyboard as he watched the approaching assault team on a CCTV monitor.

The technician, no more than 25 years old, walked to a stainless steel examination table and picked up a long, rectangular shaped object festooned with wiring and exposed circuitry. Taking one last look a the security monitor, the technician flipped back a cover exposing a red toggle switch on the softly humming rectangular device. Beads of sweat forming on his forehead, the technician toggled the switch. A shimmering enveloped the man and an instant later, he was gone.

The smell of gunpowder and the pungent, metallic odor of spilled blood hung in the air of the shattered bunker as the black clad figure keyed his mic and the tactical comms link crackled to life, spurring the sub's radioman hundreds of meters away to press his headset to his ear.

In a heavy Texas accent, the baritone voice of the assault team leader boomed over the secure airwave, "Reef Shark, this is Mantis, over." "Go ahead, Mantis, this is Reef Shark." "Reef Shark, we are preparing to egress from target and demo the site. We have 17 confirmed KIA and two friendly casualties. We are unable to locate any hardware, but our forensics specialist managed to download what appears to be the engineering schematics for an artifact of interest."

"Mantis, this is Reef Shark Actual, proceed with demo and we will be preparing battle surface to retrieve your team per the established mission schedule." "Roger Reef Shark…setting the charges as we speak."

"Mantis, Austin Command is inquiring if all hostiles are accounted for." "Reef Shark, unable to advise, given we didn't know how many inhabitants we had to begin with."

"Roger that, Mantis."

"Mantis out."

As Brad Walker unkeyed his tactical mic, he reflected on the close call he had while clearing a debris strewn, poorly lit passageway in the subbasement less than twenty minutes earlier. Straining to peer through a pall of smoke and dust that hung in the dank air of the shadow filled space, he had not detected the armed paramilitary security officer – one of the mercenaries hired by AVI to guard its illegal operations. Brad recounted in his head how the shadowy form had leapt from a dark recess with unholy speed, ugly combat blade slashing through the air mere inches from his throat. What followed was almost surreal.

The one member of the assault force whose presence on the raid was Top Secret, appeared out of nowhere from behind. The vicious side kick and follow on spinning hook kick were blurs in the semi darkness. The spin kick caught the merc solidly on the side of the neck, killing him before he could recover from the side kick that had bent him over.

The knife clattered across the hall floor, the razor sharp tip sticking in the baseboard, stark testimony to what the results would have been had the blade made contact with his throat.

Chun Kuk Do expert and Texas Secretary of Defense Chuck Norris grinned at Brad and simply nodded before both men continued their cautious advance through the building.

The Texan military and police apparatus was small, but by Brad Walker's reckoning, there was none better anywhere, and he was proud to be counted amongst those valiant men and women.

His thoughts returning to the present, Brad crossed over to join Ranger Wall and the other raiders as they made ready to depart.

EASTER 2014

For no apparent reason, the reports of the temporal anomalies stopped coming in. They stopped cold. No explanation. Many who were following the incidents were baffled but pleased. It would keep government functionaries writing reports for months, years.

Some were not so baffled, only deeply concerned.

The Benedictine priest in the secret, hidden alcove within the Vatican stood, having completed his contemplation of Holy Scripture, Lectio Divina.

One of only a small cadre of priests and monks who truly understood the mystical realities, he was still deep in thought as he walked from the familiar prayer chamber, contrails of his musings still drifting in his consciousness.

Possessing even a snippet of the true knowledge—gnosis—was a considerable burden to some. While sobering, having an understanding of the true nature of the universe was liberating, thought the priest as he walked the passageway.

To be otherwise would mean that one was, well, *blind*. What a horrible thought.

The themes of Genesis 28:12, Deuteronomy 10:14, and Kings 8:27 lingering in his head, the priest prayed that Shamayi h'shamayim—"Heaven of Heavens"—would remain a spiritual realm traveled only by angels and God and would remain unmolested by mankind.

NAMKADING CAVE, NYALAM COUNTY, TIBET

The two monks from the Pengyeling Monastery sat in meditation within Namkading Cave, sometimes called Milarepa's Cave, eleven kilometers north of the town of Nyalam above the Matsang River, the sweet perfume of herbs and wild flowers scenting the air.

"It has stopped, Lama, yes?"

"Yes, Trapa, it has indeed stopped."

"It is a blessing, Superior One. The holy ceremony has slain the demons and brought good fortune."

"That it is a blessing, Trapa, there is no debate. But I fear there are many among humankind for whom blessings, beauty, and good health are not sufficient—they seek only wealth."

AUSTIN, REPUBLIC OF TEXAS

The global arrests—orchestrated with the help of the special task force operating under the auspices of the Texas State Guard Special Operations Executive and the famed Texas Rangers—were nearly complete. There were only a few stragglers left to round up here and there around the globe.

The operation had been a huge success. Those in the know would later comment that the worldwide temporal anomalies and associated disasters were significantly mitigated by the efforts of the special international police federation. The Rangers, Texas State Guard, and the SOE commandos had played a major role in that success. A very major role.

Oddly enough, historians would someday document that the efforts of a leftist, labor-driven radical group known as the New Weathermen had also played a significant role in mitigation of the disastrous temporal anomalies by raising the public's awareness of the nefarious activities of corrupt government and corporate leaders.

The Texan task force had been among the first organized efforts to combat the unholy alliance that had brought the temporal horrors upon the earth. Worried that the temporal anomalies would eventually impact the nascent Republic of Texas, the task force was the brainchild of the republic's secretary of defense, who had gotten the buy-in of the Texan president.

Mobilizing the best and the brightest they had within their fledgling national police, military, and intelligence apparatus, the Texan president and TXSECDEF had given them a simple mandate: find the bad guys and bring them to justice. John Wayne would have been proud.

The Texans had run a sophisticated operation, using members of the Texas National Guard that had been embedded in the US federal military forces to flesh out some of the key intelligence that Texas authorities needed to identify, hunt down, and nullify those responsible for a worldwide plague of corruption.

It was not without risk, for the US government would have arrested and imprisoned the Texas Guard members had they been discovered within the American military establishment after the formation of the Republic of Texas as a sovereign nation. Relations between the two nations were not exactly peachy in the aftermath of Texan separation from the United States, even though it had been bloodless.

Because the Texan succession from the United States had been driven by disgust with the godless and intrusive government role in its citizens' lives, many in the US population were sympathetic. Overregulated and treated like children, the people had gotten fed up. Texans, long known for thinking big, had done something about it.

As it turned out, following the conclusion of their roles in the operation against the criminals who were involved with proliferation of the temporal technology, the Republic of Texas recalled their men from Washington without any glitches or fanfare that might raise suspicion and cause relations between the Texan Republic and the United States to suffer.

Major Richard "Dick" Dombroski returned to rejoin SOE, having served within the US Defense Intelligence Agency as a Texas Guardsman in the Defense HUMINT Service.

Major Wayne Potter III returned to Texas and the SOE after serving within the US Army's INSCOM at Fort Meade in Maryland.

Special Agents Alika "Al" Hayato Akee and Bradley Jacob Walker continued in their roles with the Special Operations Executive (SOE), ascending to leadership positions.

Captain Bob "Lone Ranger" Wall of the Texas Rangers, Texas Department of Public Safety, and his partner, Ranger Bill Sanchez, continued to serve within the SOE, representing the Rangers and DPS, helping to form the nascent Republic's HUMINT intelligence and counterintelligence capabilities.

During a special recognition ceremony held in closed session at the seat of the newly formed national government in Austin, Texas Secretary of Defense Chuck Norris presented service awards to all the members of the special Texas task force.

The keynote speaker at the ceremony was the Honorable George Bush, president of the Republic of Texas, who congratulated the Rangers, SOE, Texas Guard, and DPS officers, shaking each of their hands.

After a short speech expressing the gratitude of the people of Texas, the president turned the podium over to his secretary of defense for the finishing comments.

"You boys went out there into harm's way, used your wits, and, at the end of the day, bested the bad guys—some of the world's worse. For security reasons, those of you who served on the actual assault team must remain unnamed, anonymous heroes.

"You pulled together disparate elements in far-flung agencies, getting them all to work together for a common cause—a noble goal. You led from the front—you were at the point of that spear, the vanguard.

"You were outmanned and usually outgunned. You went ahead anyway, traveling to the far corners of the world to bring justice to those whose greed stood to destroy the planet.

"You're real-life, honest-to-God heroes, every one of ya. You are a credit to law enforcement, to our military service, and to Texas. You are, in fact, a credit to humanity and all that is good.

"You exemplify what every kid aspires to grow up and be.

"God bless you…God bless every one of you. I'm proud to know ya."

Later, Bush said, "Hell, Carlos, you sound a lot like your old character from your popular TV series."

Laughing, the secretary replied, "I sure do, Mr. President, I sure do."

SKID ROW

The alley between the two decrepit, abandoned warehouses was littered with makeshift cardboard and plastic tarp hovels where dozens of homeless slept each night. Half a dozen fifty-five-gallon metal drums burned brightly, huddled forms warming their hands over the flames.

The old industrial district in the inner city had long since seen its better days. It was a dangerous place any time of day but especially at night. After dark, the laws of the jungle superseded those of civilized society. Many of the down-and-out denizens who called that alley home would debate whether society was in any way civilized. It was not the homeless population that made it a jungle. Mostly, those poor, forgotten souls were just the victims.

That was the case as the three street punks swaggered down the middle of the alley, kicking grocery carts of belongings over and punching holes in the cardboard sides of the cobbled-together shelters.

A grizzled Vietnam veteran stepped up to confront the thugs as one of them backhanded a gray-haired woman who had the misfortune to be in their way, dropping her to her knees on the hard pavement. The three predators swarmed over the lone veteran, beating him to the ground, kicking him into unconsciousness.

Finished with the former soldier who dared to challenge them, the laughing punks turned their attention back to the gray-haired woman.

The woman, lip bleeding from the backhand and one hand gripping the side of the grocery cart that contained the totality of her worldly possessions, strained to pull herself up onto wobbly legs.

"You fucking old bitch," one of the punks snarled, the hatred in his voice palpable.

As the arrogant little piece of human flotsam stepped forward to hammer the old woman back to the ground, a shadow rose from the blackness next to a rusted dumpster, brushing loose some of the ancient green paint flaking from its sides.

Without a sound or uttering a word, the form glided toward the three young gangsters. Clad in a dark hoodie and stained, baggie pants, the figure was upon them before they noticed its presence.

The gray-haired woman would later tell investigating police that all she heard was a gurgling and what sounded like muted slaps.

No, she had never seen the person in the hooded sweatshirt before. No, she did not know his name. No, she did not think that anyone else knew him either. Did she see a weapon: large knife or machete or something? No, she hadn't. But she commented to the officer, "But I 'sumed there wuz sumthun cuz them boys wuz cut up real bad."

The old woman had never seen three men killed like those three punks. She remembered the blood. There was so much blood. It was as if a storm of razor blades had hit them, dropping them in their tracks before they could even scream.

She did not feel sorry for them. They died horribly, but she did not feel a bit sorry. *Fuck them boys.*

A couple of months after the three street punks were killed in that alley, the old lady saw the man from the shadows who had saved her from their predations. She approached him and simply said thank you. "My name is Ginger. Thank you for helpin' me the way you did. I wish I could pay you back somehow. And thanks for helping that man who tried to stick up for me; his name is Stan."

The hooded figure raised his head so the old woman could see his face and said, "My name is Ijinashi—Ijinashi Tamna. It was my pleasure, ma'am."

MIDNIGHT — NEW MEXICO DESERT

The former Air Force sergeant, her light blue uniform blouse stained with dried blood and vomitus, snipped the final links in the chain link outer perimeter fencing required for her to squeeze her frame through the ragged, hastily cut hole. Behind her, bathed in the ghostly white of the high security compound's emergency lighting, lay the mangled bodies of what was once a US military special operations team.

Moonlight reflecting in her wide, hungry eyes, the lithe form slunk into the waiting embrace of the desert night.

SUB-SAHARAN AFRICA

The Dogon priest stood patiently on the dune, waiting for the shimmering to manifest.

The pale young man in the white lab coat with the tousled hair stared slack jawed at the robed African man that stood before him, intelligent, emerald green eyes boring into his. The young man tried to speak, but couldn't, as the priest slowly reached out and flipped the cover shut over the toggle switch on the humming rectangle in the man's trembling hands.

The man in the lab coat startled as the fleeting shadow of a circling hawk swept over the two men.

It was clear and sunny that day in West Africa, 5,000 BC.

MARCH 10, 1967

Eleven-year-old "SC" Allen awoke from his nap with a start, the afternoon sun slanting through the dining room windows, warming his face. SC had a habit of taking midday naps on the dining room carpet near the furnace grate. The sound of his mom humming as she baked one of his favorites—grape jelly turnovers—along with the heavenly smell of the pastries drifted in from the kitchen.

He struggled to remember the details of the vivid dream as the last vestiges of its recollection faded like tendrils of smoke in a breeze, leaving him only the unshakable feeling that the dream had been somehow profound in nature.

"SC," as his friends and family called him, was raised on a steady diet of pulp fiction adventure novels and TV shows. When he was a four-year-old, his parents had told him that he had picked the nickname "SC" from a story his mom had read him when he was very young. He never had any reason to doubt them and went along with the story that he had, indeed, gotten the two initials from some long-forgotten adventure story read to him long ago.

Try as he might, he really couldn't recall the book or story's title or any details of his mom's reading it to him. That occasionally bothered him. He was a proliferous reader of pulp novels but could not recollect ever running across a character with the initials or nickname "SC" in any of them. But why would his parents tell him that if it weren't true?

His older brother Steve, his parents, and his neighborhood pals Pat, Steve, and Scott called him SC. The nickname stuck. His parents never considered giving him another first name; SC was just fine. It was the one he had when they got him from the adoption agency.

Folks in town said the moniker fit the young boy's demeanor, jokingly saying that SC stood for "Super Charged," given his unbounded energy. Most folks likely assumed that "SC" Allen had been adopted at a very early age, his biological parents having been Asians.

Later that afternoon, having waited until his mom was occupied with housework and before his dad would get home from the day shift at the Johns Manville plant on the west edge of town, SC stole into the backyard, taking care not to let the screen door slam behind him.

SC knew, somehow, exactly where he wanted to dig—the shallow impression in the lawn at the end of the backyard sidewalk, glancing at it as he walked by on his way to the garage.

Archaeologists and treasure hunters were among SC's heroes, years before the movie character Indiana Jones became universally popular. The idea of digging for fabulous treasure was deeply appealing to SC and always had been, it seemed. SC couldn't wait to begin his very own treasure dig in the backyard.

SC's other heroes were gunfighters and soldiers, bold men of high adventure and deadly prowess.

SC idolized one hero above all others. Bruce Lee, who played the character Kato in the "Green Hornet" TV series, topped the heap of his heroes. While SC liked the Green Hornet character, it was the martial art of Bruce Lee as Kato that truly captured his awe and attention.

SC carefully opened the pedestrian door to the detached garage and crept inside, turning to his right and carefully climbing onto the ancient wooden workbench and cabinetry that lined the garage's south wall. He removed the small gardening spade from where it hung and gingerly climbed back down from the bench to the cement floor.

SC's mom, whistling to herself as she ran the canister-style vacuum cleaner over the bedroom carpet, thought that maybe it was time to tell him the truth about his nickname and his origins.

Having adopted the boy as an infant, the Allens had planned to tell him more about his true ethnic heritage when he was older and better able to understand. In Phyllis DeAnn Allen's estimation, that time was about now, she supposed. Although SC was still quite young, his advanced IQ made up for his years as far as intellectual comprehension went.

It wasn't rocket science to see that SC's features were Asian and not Caucasian. SC knew, of course, that she and Bud were not his biological parents. But they had never formally explained it to him; so now was the time, she thought as she swept the floor. It was time to tell him about his original surname. Everyone had a right to his true identity, she thought. It was way past time they talked to SC about this.

The people at the adoption agency had told them, during the course of the proceedings leading up to the legal adoption, that the boy's surname was Chinhung and that he went by "SC."

The adoption agency staff had never, she reflected, mentioned what the "S" in "SC" stood for. Funny that she and Bud never asked, she thought, as she ran the long tube of the vacuum underneath the bed, stopping to remove the gum wrapper that had just been loudly sucked into the head of the vacuum.

Funny, too, that she and Bud had never delved deeper into the account the adoption officials had given them of SC's rescue from an illegal immigrant operation at the Port of Baltimore.

Out in the backyard, less than five minutes into his dig, SC was looking at the soiled, intricately woven handle—tsuka—of what a learned hoplologist might mistakenly and quite inaccurately identify as being a shinogi-zukuri katana sword. This sword—a sword to which SC felt an inexplicable connection—was much, much more than just a katana.

The Alexandria, Indiana, city police cold case files, as well as the yellowing archived records of the *Alexandria Times-Tribune* newspaper and the Madison County Historical Society, all reflected that the Allen child had mysteriously gone missing from his backyard one afternoon in 1967, never to be seen or heard from again.

Well, that was sort of true.

EPILOGUE

Je-Ju and Sainen disappeared. They got away clean, leaving no trace.

Ijinashi returned to a life of drifting, moving from one place to another at random, oftentimes using the largely faceless homeless community as a conduit. Someday, he knew he would have to face down Sainen and Je-Ju Lee, as well as come to grips with his father. But that was another day.

ACKNOWLEDGEMENTS

The motivation for writing this book originated from my love of the martial arts. I am in debt to my big brother, Stephen Larry Humphries, Air Force veteran and career lawman, whose Black Belt and Karate Illustrated magazines first exposed a skinny young kid growing up in small town Indiana to that fascinating world. My brother Steve was the first to draw my attention to a dynamic Asian actor named Bruce Lee, whose exotic fighting skills captivated the imagination of a shy, very un-athletic Midwestern boy.

What a stroke of luck that was for me. I went on to eventually sign up for karate lessons and, consequently, had the good fortune to study at Goju-Ryu legend Glenn Keeney's Komakai Academy in Anderson, Indiana under the tutelage of stellar karate men the likes of Larry Davenport, who still teaches Goju-Ryu Karate in Anderson. Thanks, Larry.

As an impressionable teenager, I was blessed to have as heroes Chuck Norris, Jeff Smith, Bill Wallace and Joe Lewis. I can't imagine how my life would have turned out without the positive influence of the martial arts community and role models like Norris, Wallace, Smith, Lewis and, of course, Bruce Lee. To this day, I still watch reruns of The Green Hornet and have

"Enter the Dragon" and the rest of Lee's fabulous movies on DVD. Ditto for Chuck Norris' wonderful "Walker, Texas Ranger" TV series, which I never get tired of. Why? Because they champion the Good Guy.

The reader will notice that one of the few hero roles in "Legend of the Four Dragons Sword" was filled by martial arts legend Chuck Norris as Secretary of Defense for the newly formed Republic of Texas. I also swiped the name of another famous martial artist—Bob Wall—for the role of one of the Texas Rangers featured in the book. If a reader should feel compelled to identify with a character in this work of fiction, it should be Norris or Wall.

AUTHOR'S NOTE TO READERS

This book is a work of fiction—the characters, their personalities and their actions all products of my imagination. The main characters, while dynamic and beguiling, are criminals and should not be construed as being behavioral examples for anyone. Cold heartedness, murder, deceit and greed are not traits or actions to be romanticized or aspired to. We have enough of that in our world.

I was fortunate to have grown up with parents and an older brother who were truly excellent examples of decent human beings. My dad, Avery, a WWII veteran of the D-Day landing at Omaha Beach, and my older brother, Steve, a Viet Nam veteran and career law enforcement officer, were perfect male role models for a kid growing up in Small Town USA. My mom, Phyllis— smart, kind and good-natured—was the classic American mom. Because of their influence, I know the difference between right and wrong.

The actions of the main characters portrayed in this novel fall into the 'wrong' category. While a fun, exciting read, the fictional criminals portrayed in "Legend of the Four Dragons Sword" should not be emulated or held in esteem, for they certainly aren't worthy.

Finally, I am blessed to have my wife, Catherine, soul mate and fellow Cockatiel wrangler, whose influence in my life is 100% positive. She is by far the sweetest and kindest human being I have ever known.

THE MARTIAL ARTS, TACTICS & WEAPONS OF "LEGEND OF THE FOUR DRAGONS SWORD"

The hand-to-hand engagements, as well as the sword duels and gun-fights depicted in this story, are all products of the author's imagination and were not drawn from any actual experiences of the author or real world events. That said, the martial disciplines and weapons featured in the book are real.

This author has been fortunate over the years to train in a wide array of martial systems and to have studied with some superb martial artists. I drew the techniques depicted in the hand-to-hand combat scenes from real systems that I have studied or been exposed to over a 30 year love affair with martial arts. Any technical mistakes or misrepresentations are the author's alone, and do not reflect upon the skill of those outstanding professionals who have endeavored to train me.

In no particular order, the following martial arts professionals and institutions provided the author with the wherewithal to write a martial arts novel.

I took little bits from here and there, from this art and that system, to piece together the fight scenes in this book.

Wushu & Taijiquan master Lu Xiaolin is proficient in an incredible number of Chinese fighting systems, and I am honored to have her, along with her marvelous staff at O-Mei Wushu Center, as my teachers. A Wushu Gold Medalist, Lu Xiaolin's expertise is such that she was commissioned by the Chinese government in the 1980s to go to the famous Shaolin Temple to help re-establish the Shaolin training program. You can learn more about Master Lu Xiaolin and her Fairfax, Virginia Wushu school at http://www.omei-wushu.com.

Jeet Kune Do legend Gary Dill of Self Defense Systems International trained at Bruce Lee's Oakland School in the 1960s under Bruce's protégé, James Yimm Lee. Professor Dill's martial lineage traces directly back to the authentic Jun Fan material being taught in James Y. Lee's garage. Professor Dill – Shodai to his students – is a sought after JKD trainer and master instructor of Bushido Kempo based in Oklahoma. I had the privilege of obtaining a Black Belt in Kempo under Professor Dill's fine organization. You can check out Dill's organization at http://www.jkd-garydill.com/jkd/Home.html.

There are so many people who contributed to my martial arts education, and therefore contributed to my ability to write this book, it would be nearly impossible to list them all. To those I have left out, you have my sincerest apologies.

Larry Davenport of Goju-Ryu Karate was likely one of my very first martial arts instructors, teaching out of Glenn Keeney's Komakai Academy in Anderson, Indiana in the 1970s when I was a teenager just beginning what would wind up being a life-long obsession. Years later, one of Larry's black belts and a truly superb martial artist—Danny Ray—would work alongside me in law enforcement. Danny, also belted in Aikido under the legendary Steven Seagal, is one of the finest martial artists I have had the pleasure of knowing. Ray Sensei continues to wade into harm's way wearing a badge in Maryland.

Sifu Clarence Burris, attorney, police officer, executive protection agent and martial arts master teaches Chinese Kung Fu, Qinna and Kuntao at his

Chinese Martial Arts Institute in Virginia. I have had the pleasure of studying Qinna with Master Burris, as well as train with him in Filipino Arnis.

Soke Stephen Blackburn of Laohu Kenpo I owe for schooling me in Okinawa Kenpo Karate, White Crane and Tobosa Kali-Eskrima. A world traveler with multiple languages, Blackburn Sensei is one of the most learned martial artists I know. I am privileged to hold Shodan grade in Laohu Kenpo from his private Laohu Hombu Dojo in Sterling, VA.

For an introduction to the devastating Korean art of HapKiDo, I owe Master Sam Kim of Mountain Kim Martial Arts in Vienna, VA.

To the Taekwondo experts who gave me the front leg roundhouse and hook kicks that permitted me to come home with a couple tournament trophies in my youth, thanks!

For the basic mechanics of Krav Maga and an introduction to Shuai Jiao Kung Fu, I am in debt to Nick Masi, Kravist and Shuai Jiao Black Sash, owner of First Defense Martial Arts Center in Herndon, VA.

For an indoctrination into the world of Brazilian Jiu-Jitsu, I owe Professor Pedro Sauer, 8th Dan, and BJJ Black Belt Bill Grinnell, both of Virginia.

For what basic understanding I have of the Korean sword art of Kumdo, I owe to US Hwa Rang Kumdo of Virginia, where I took a few basic lessons so I could coherently write the sword fights into the book. Thanks, guys.

For what little I know of the amazing martial art of Taijiquan (Tai Chi Chuan), I am in debt to the following martial artists: Yang Taiji stylist Que Qijing of O-Mei Wushu, Sifu Hon Lee of Jow Ga Shaolin Institute, and Sifu Dante Gilmer, a practitioner of the Cheng Man-Ching flavor of Yang Tai Chi Chuan and owner of Still Water Tai Chi Center of Virginia.

For the tiny bit of Xingyi Kung Fu that I know, I am in debt to Virginia Mullin of O-Mei Wushu, and Clarence Burris of CMAI.

For the equally tiny bit of Baguazhang I have trained, I am in debt to Lu Xiaolin and Que Qijing of O-Mei Wushu.

For the very first Dan grade that I obtained in martial arts, I am in debt to Jim Thomas Sensei, who trained me in an eclectic form of Japanese Seieikan Karate at his dojo in Richmond, Indiana. The American Karate Association (AKA) diploma certifying that first black belt still occupies a place of honor on my living room wall, and the worn old belt is draped over a corner of our bookshelf. To this day I still belong to Thomas Sensei's martial arts organization – USA Martial Arts Alliance – in which I hold a 5th Dan ranking and serve as the 'Alliance' Virginia State Representative.

Last but not least, I am in debt to Warren Chen, Mark Kile and Raphael Chiu, friends and fellow martial artists, who have spent hours talking with me about various aspects of the fighting arts, dissecting and analyzing various techniques and concepts.

As a former police officer, SWAT member and military noncom, I possessed sufficient knowledge of firearms to portray their use in a novel. The technical nomenclature on the specific weapons depicted in this book was drawn from research, courtesy of the all-knowing Internet.

The futuristic ground combat vehicles that ravaged the town of Summitville, Indiana were purely constructs of my imagination. Summitville, however, is an actual town in north central Indiana, as is Alexandria.

The field tradecraft depicted in the book I derived from my 20 years of law enforcement experience, some of which was as an undercover narcotics task force investigator. I am in debt to my old drug task force colleagues— Drew, Mark and Rick—who taught me how not to get killed doing that job. I am also in debt to former police colleagues Bruce Dunham and Ken Hendrickson, both highly skilled SWAT professionals. Working alongside those guys in law enforcement, I managed to absorb a few things about tactics. In the real world, Sainen and JeJu Lee wouldn't stand a chance against those guys.

My hat is off to the real heroes out there—folks like Danny Ray and Mark Anderson—who put their lives on the line day in and day out protecting an oftentimes unappreciative public from the monsters that lurk in the dark, and to professionals like my pal Paul Harbourt, who inhabits a world most folks only glimpse by way of the movies or adventure novels.

Phil Humphries